FORGOTTEN THE
SHRINE

Also by Monica Tesler

Bounders, Book 1: *Earth Force Rising*
Bounders, Book 2: *The Tundra Trials*

BOUNDERS
BOOK 3

FORGOTTEN THE SHRINE

MONICA TESLER

ALADDIN
New York   London   Toronto   Sydney   New Delhi

ALADDIN

An imprint of Simon & Schuster Children's Publishing Division

1230 Avenue of the Americas, New York, New York 10020

First Aladdin hardcover edition December 2017

Text copyright © 2017 by Monica Tesler

Jacket illustration copyright © 2017 by Owen Richardson

For information about special discounts for bulk purchases, please contact Simon & Schuster Special Sales at 1-866-506-1949 or business@simonandschuster.com.

The Simon & Schuster Speakers Bureau can bring authors to your live event. For more information or to book an event, contact the Simon & Schuster Speakers Bureau at 1-866-248-3049 or visit our website at www.simonspeakers.com.

Jacket designed by Karin Paprocki

Interior designed by Mike Rosamilia

The text of this book was set in Adobe Garamond Pro.

Manufactured in the United States of America 1117 FFG

2 4 6 8 10 9 7 5 3 1

Library of Congress Cataloging-in-Publication Data

Names: Tesler, Monica, author.

Title: The forgotten shrine / by Monica Tesler.

Description: First Aladdin hardcover edition. | New York : Aladdin, 2017. | Series: Bounders ; book 3 | Summary: "Jasper and his friends are sent as ambassadors to the underwater planet of Earth Force's shady new allies, the Alkalinians"— Provided by publisher.

Identifiers: LCCN 2017018347 (print) | LCCN 2017036281 (eBook) | ISBN 9781481446013 (eBook) | ISBN 9781481445993 (hardcover)

Subjects: | CYAC: Adventure and adventurers—Fiction. | Human-alien encounters—Fiction. | Ambassadors—Fiction. | Virtual reality—Fiction. | Science fiction. | BISAC: JUVENILE FICTION / Action & Adventure / General. | JUVENILE FICTION / Science & Technology. | JUVENILE FICTION / Science Fiction.

Classification: LCC PZ7.1.T447 (eBook) | LCC PZ7.1.T447 For 2017 (print) | DDC [Fic]—dc23

LC record available at https://lccn.loc.gov/2017018347

For Jamey

I

OUR KNEES TOUCH AS ADDY AND I SIT ON crates in the dirty storage room. The place is packed with boxes and piles of papers that fall to the floor in a cloud of dust every time I shift my weight. In the corner there's a crate filled with electronics like the ones they sell at the antiques shop—old swipe screens and these odd contraptions people used to wear on their ears for sound. Near the door is a stack of dolls with plastic heads and thick, stuffed bodies. Their lips look like tiny flowers the color of blood. They stare at us with cold, perfectly circular eyes.

Whose stuff is this? Who collects dolls and old headphones?

"Are you even listening to me, Jasper?" Addy runs a hand

through her sandy hair as she rolls her eyes. From the sound of her voice, it's not the first time she's asked.

I swat away some cobwebs. "How did you find this place again?"

She shrugs. "I was bored during your last tour. Mom said I couldn't go outside after curfew, so I explored inside."

"You're not supposed to be in the basement." I lean over and pick up a pair of purple headphones. My movement launches more dust into the stale air.

"Neither are you, yet here we are." Addy grabs my knees and forces me to look at her. The way her green eyes drill into mine, I'm worried she can read my mind. She's always been intense, but since I got back from the EarthBound Academy, she seems to have taken it to a new level.

"Can we get on with it?" she continues. "I have a group chat in twenty minutes."

By "group chat" she means an online meeting of her supposed-to-be-secret Bounders' rights group, which I'm sure Earth Force is monitoring and recording. During my last tour of duty, Addy connected on the webs with some other Bounders to talk about Earth meet-ups and in-class support for potential cadets. While I think a Bounders' rights group might make sense, it's hard to care too much about help at school when you're being asked to defend your planet against the Youli, an advanced alien race.

"So skip it," I say. "This is a lot more important than your group chat. Plus, tomorrow we'll both be shipping out to the EarthBound Academy. You'll have more Bounder buddies than you can count."

A sneaky smile lifts the corners of Addy's lips. "Speaking of shipping out, am I finally going to meet your girlfriend?"

This again? "For the millionth time, Addy, Mira is not my girlfriend." I'm not exactly sure what Mira is to me, and I'm not sure how I'd ever explain Mira to Addy. I definitely don't want to tell her about the brain patches and the actual mind-reading part.

"Sure." Addy's voice is laced with sarcasm. "Either way, once we blast off, there's no more secrets, which brings us back to the whole reason we're down in this dump."

Right. I made a promise at the end of last tour that I'd stop keeping secrets from my pod mates and my sister. I'd planned to tell Addy the truth when I returned, but the news was blitzed with rumors about aliens and Earth Force lies. The Force responded swiftly, arresting a handful of protestors who tried to land their vessel at the aeroport training facility. They said anyone caught disparaging the Force would be punished.

I'm sure our apartment is bugged. It certainly didn't do much to calm my fears when an officer showed up unannounced last month to review my "confidentiality commitments" to the Force. I wonder if they suspect a Bounder of the leaks? After all, Earth Force managed to keep the Youli war a secret until they launched the EarthBound Academy. Anyway, it was just too dangerous to talk to Addy.

Still, I'm not going back into space without keeping my promise and cluing her in, and it's not like Addy would let me. She suggested we meet here in this old storage room in the lowest subfloor of our apartment building. And from the condition of the place, I'm guessing the only people to have set foot in here for the last fifty years are Addy and me.

I pluck a discarded mobile phone from beneath one of the dolls. "The person who put this stuff here has to be dead, don't you think?"

Addy shrugs. "Maybe."

I drag my finger across the dusty phone screen, drawing an *E* and an intersecting *F*, the Earth Force logo. "I can't decide whether this stuff is vintage or trash."

Addy's gaze morphs into a glare. "Jasper!"

"Huh?"

"You're avoiding the topic, the whole reason we're sitting on a stockpile of discarded electronics. What's the deal with Earth Force? You promised you'd hold nothing back if I found a safe place to talk! Look around. I held up my end of the bargain."

That's true. There is no way Earth Force bothered to bug this place. It's probably one of the most secure spots in all of Americana East. If Addy and I died in some freak accident, like say if the box of creepy dolls tumbled over and crushed us, they probably wouldn't even discover our bones for another fifty years. Still, I wish I had time to stall. As much as I want to tell Addy, as much as I've committed to tell her, it's still hard stuff to say out loud. And I'm not sure how she's going to take it.

But her eyes sear me like lasers. There's no turning back.

I take a deep breath. "So, you know how we've always been told that Earth Force needs the Bounders to expand the quantum bounding space exploration program?"

"Let me guess," Addy says in a bored voice. "There's more to it." She waves her hand in a circle for me to continue.

"Well, yeah, there is. Earth Force's agenda is not exactly what you hear about on EFAN." I pause, waiting for her reaction.

"Obviously, J!" Addy throws her hands in the air, sending a dust cloud directly at my face. "Are you going to tell me what's going on or not? It's bad enough Earth Force thinks they can make me join their ranks without disclosing the truth about my mission. Now you're acting just as cryptic as them, when you promised you'd tell me the truth!"

I don't know how to do this. I don't know how to tell Addy she's signed up to fight in an alien war. She's already angry. That might throw her over the edge.

"We've always known we're Bounders, Addy," I say in a quiet voice. "I don't understand why you're so mad. What's changed?"

"What's changed? Really? You have no idea what it was like while you were gone! Everyone knew I was a Bounder, but I didn't get to go to space! I had to face all the stares and questions on my own! Thank goodness I found the chat group. They've been a lifeline for me."

"I guess I didn't know it was so hard on you."

"Forget it. I'm fine. But where have you been since you got back from your last tour? Did you bury your head in that beanbag of yours? The rumors are rampant, and they all come back to the Bounders! What is Earth Force hiding?"

What rumors about the Bounders? The gossip I heard was about aliens. "Where'd you get this stuff? In that chat group? I thought you talked about Bounders getting help at school."

"Please, Jasper. You are so naive. That's just what I tell Mom to keep her off my back."

Naive? Hardly. If she knew how I spent my tours of duty, she wouldn't say that. The way she's talking reminds me of Barrick and the Wackies, the group of rebels we met on Gulaga. It turned out Waters was closer to them than he was to Earth Force. If what Addy's hinting about her group is true—if they're anything like the Wackies—she's lucky she hasn't been arrested. I need to tell her the truth. It may be the only way to keep her safe. I take a deep breath.

MONICA TESLER

"Fine. You want the truth? You know the Incident at Bounding Base 51? The failed bound where all the aeronauts were lost?"

Addy leans forward, her gaze latched with mine.

Here goes. "It wasn't an accident. It was an alien attack. Earth Force is at war with an alien race, Addy. And we're their soldiers."

Addy stares at me, unblinking, kind of like the creepy dolls.

I wait. Seconds pass. She doesn't talk or even move.

"Addy, do you understand? Earth has been at war since before we were born. That's why they bred the Bounders. We were born to fight!"

Addy slowly drops her eyes. I wish I knew what she was thinking.

I reach for her hand. "Look, I know this is difficult to hear, and—"

She pulls her hand away and crosses her arms against her chest. "So what they're saying is true, then? Earth Force has kept the existence of an alien war secret for years? They didn't even tell us these aliens were out there? These . . . Youli? I think that's what they called them."

She knows their name? Geez. Most cadets didn't even know the Youli existed until they attacked us on the Paleo Planet. "That about sums it up. I guess your group brought you up to speed before I did. Which, by the way, is the riskiest thing you could be chatting about." I would add *dumbest thing*, but I don't think that would spin the conversation in a positive direction.

Addy's lips quiver, and I worry I may have a sobbing sister on my hands. Not my specialty.

But then she balls her fingers into fists and clamps her front teeth over her bottom lip. She lifts her arm and waves a finger above her wrist screen. "There's still five minutes until the group chat. If I head up now, I can still make it."

"Wait . . . what? You can't just leave!"

Addy stands. "I have to talk to my friends. They need to know the rumors are true."

"No! You can't tell anyone about this, Addy!"

"I have to tell them! Some of them are Bounders! They have a right to know!"

"They'll know soon enough!"

"How can you say that? How can you act like this is no big deal?"

"That's not what I'm doing! Don't you remember the visit from the Earth Force officer? If they discover I breached confidentiality, I could go to prison! And you could be arrested for disparaging the Force!"

Addy slowly sinks back onto the box. Her face keeps contorting through different emotions, like every time she fights off the urge to cry, she decides she's going to punch someone. Hopefully not me.

MONICA TESLER

I take her hand, and this time she lets me hang on. "Do you remember what I told you before my last tour, Addy? That all of this would make more sense if you found out for yourself? Maybe I was right. Maybe you should learn the rest when you get to the Academy."

"It's not like I have a choice."

"You don't want to go to the Academy?"

"I'm not sure what I want." Addy pulls up her knees and wraps her arms around them. "Part of me is desperate to go, to experience all the things we've looked forward to since we were little, to find out for myself what's going on. Part of me wants to stand my ground here on Earth. But that's the thing, Jasper. I have to serve in Earth Force. I don't have a choice, right?"

I drop my gaze to my dusty shoes. We both know the answer to her question.

She squeezes her eyes shut and shakes her head. When she opens them, tears leak from the corners. "You're okay with this, Jasper? You don't care that Earth Force lied?"

"Of course I care, Ads. But things are complicated. And there's no ignoring the fact that Earth's at war. I want to keep our planet safe. I'm willing to fight for it."

Addy blinks another round of tears as she processes what I said. "I always thought we were special, J. We were going to be these amazing aeronauts traveling all around the galaxy, remember? Now I'm just an Earth Force pawn."

"Pawn or not, the other stuff hasn't changed. Being a Bounder is really amazing, Addy." I lean forward and wait until her eyes lift to mine. "Trust me."

I keep my eyes locked with hers, even though it's hard to watch the tears fall. I'm not used to being the strong one, at least with Addy. I know it's kind of backward, since I'm the older brother, but before I left for my first tour of duty, I always counted on her to take care of stuff. Now things have changed, and I need to step up. I'll do everything in my power to keep Addy safe.

Addy gives a small nod, then whispers, "Tell me everything, J. I swear I won't tell anyone. I won't say anything until we leave for the Academy."

I need to turn this conversation around. Because, like Addy said, she's shipping out to the EarthBound Academy whether she likes it or not. "There are these awesome gloves that let you bound through space without a ship," I start.

Addy's eyes still brim with sadness and rage, but there's a fresh sparkle at the corners. "Bound without a ship? Really?"

I spend the next hour divulging Earth Force secrets. I don't lie, but I don't emphasize the bad stuff. I spend a lot of time talking about the glove technology and the space station and my friends. I want Addy to understand that Earth Force has been keeping secrets and the battle lines are blurred, like Waters always says, but I also want her to know that there are some awesome things about being a Bounder. The more I talk, the more I realize I'm excited to head out on my third tour tomorrow. I can't wait to pal around with Cole and Marco, to hear about Lucy's dramatic adventures in Americana West, and to reconnect with Mira. I'm happy I finally get to share the EarthBound Academy with Addy.

By the time we leave the storage room and make it back to the apartment, we're laughing and joking. Although some things about Earth Force are pretty awful—especially all the secrets—it's still pretty awesome to be Bounders. I'm happy to share that with Addy. Even though I know she's still mad, I think she might be getting excited about shipping out to the space station, too.

That is, until we open our apartment door and see the Earth Force officer.

"Mom, what's going on?" I ask as soon as I walk in. Thoughts race through my head. Do they know Addy and I were talking downstairs? Has she come to arrest us? I step in front of my sister, shielding her from the officer.

Or what if she's here to take me to Waters's labs like last tour, when officers came for Cole and me the night before we were supposed to ship out? We spent a week at Waters's labs with our pod mates testing secret technology. It was definitely an unexpected change of plans.

That can't be it. Waters went missing at the end of last tour. I can't imagine he's back on Earth.

Either way, I don't want to leave Addy. I want to be with her when she ships out for the first time, when she takes the oath.

The officer tips her head. "Good afternoon, Officer Adams, Miss Adams."

Addy steps beside me. She stands tall, her chin lifted, her arms crossed against her chest.

"I've dropped off badges for your family," the officer continues. "We expect security to be extra tight at the launch, and I was sent to review the protocol."

I let out a long, quiet breath when I realize she's not here for us. Or, at least, she's not here to arrest us or shuffle us off to space ahead of schedule.

My mother invites the officer to sit and offers her a glass of water. Then she asks me to turn off the web that's streaming on a screen above our mantel.

I cross the room and stare at the screen. The EFAN ticker runs across the bottom. A colorful landscape comes into view, and the unmistakable voice of Maximilian Sheek describes the scenery. I've watched this special a dozen times, and every time it takes me back to my first battle with the Youli. Soon the hovers will glide across the screen, and Ryan, Meggi, and Annette will be in the crowd of spectators for the inaugural tour of the Paleo Planet. That was their prize for winning the Tundra Trials last tour.

Our pod was disqualified from the Tundra Trials. Our disappointment didn't last long because Earth Force sent us on a mission to plant a degradation patch on the Youli's systems. We got their ship's coordinates from our new allies, the super shady Alkalinians, a reptilian alien race that Waters called "bottom of the barrel." Gedney told us that Admiral Eames might send a Bounder delegation to Alkalinia during the next tour. I didn't mention that to Addy, probably because I'm desperately trying to block that possibility from my brain.

"Jasper?" my mom calls. "We're waiting."

Her words shake me back to Earth. I join them at the table, and the officer describes the procedures for arriving at the aeroport, including how our belongings must be stowed and packed. We're instructed not to give interviews to the press and not to engage the protestors for any reason. Next to me, Addy clenches her fists on her lap, but thankfully, she stays silent.

Shortly after the officer leaves, Dad gets home from work. He walks in expecting the usual—me playing *Evolution* on my tablet, Addy chatting with friends online—and stops cold when he sees our serious faces at the table.

"What happened here?" He glances at the blank screen above the mantel. "Did our web connection wink out?"

"We had a visitor," Addy says.

"An Earth Force officer," Mom clarifies.

"Everything still on schedule?" he asks, probably wondering whether I'll be leaving early like last tour.

"No change," I say, "just lots of rules."

Dad raises his eyebrows, but Mom shakes her head, her clue that she'll fill him in later, after we're asleep on our last night at home.

"Earth Force expects a lot from the Bounders," Addy says in a cold, dark voice.

Her words are true, but it's what she doesn't say that makes me worried. Earth Force expects us to follow orders. I'm not so sure Addy is cut out for that, especially when the orders conflict with what she feels is right. And knowing Addy, I'm sure there will be lots of those conflicts at the EarthBound Academy.

IT'S AMAZING THAT A YEAR HAS GONE
by since the start of my first tour of duty, enough life-changing events for—well—a lifetime have happened, and yet it's like I stood in this exact same spot yesterday. That's how I feel as we leave the dock for the aeroport.

My family stands against the railing of the water shuttle. I inhale the thick sea air and look below at the salty waves lashing the boat. So this is it. Back to space, this time with Addy by my side.

Dad swings his arm across my shoulders. "It's a good thing Earth Force sent you a fresh uniform. You've really shot up. Your old pants would have looked like shorts."

"I haven't grown that much, Dad." But as I turn to face him, my gaze is equal with his nose. It won't be long before we're eye to eye.

"Your mom and I don't say it enough, Jasper, but we're proud of you." He swallows hard, probably choking back a lump of emotion, since both Addy *and* I are leaving this time. "You haven't only grown in height. You've grown in maturity. I'm sure Earth Force is honored to have you in their ranks."

"Thanks, Dad." His words might be cheesy, but I store them in a safe spot in my brain in case I need to replay them later. Up ahead the aeroport grows from a spot on the horizon to the outline of a full-fledged metropolis on the water as the shuttle closes in.

As Dad turns to talk with Addy, Mom straightens the collar of my indigo uniform. She doesn't even try to hide the tears that cloud her eyes. "Your father's right, Jasper. We're very proud. Now promise me you'll look after your sister at the space station."

I stare at my shoes, the standard-issue brown lace-ups. It's a promise I've already made myself. Still, it's hard to make a promise I don't know if I can keep. "Sure, Mom," I whisper.

She plants a kiss on my forehead.

As we approach the aeroport, the new Model 770 passenger crafts gleam from the flight deck. Earth Force put them into production for the Paleo Planet tourism initiative that kicked off with Sheek's televised trip. I can't wait to see Ryan and tease him about how goofy he sounded when the EFAN production crew made him ooh and aah over all the sights. Probably the best thing about my pod getting disqualified from the Tundra Trials was not having to accept the prize and make a return trip to the Paleo Planet.

The seas near the aeroport are crowded with watercraft. Small barges packed with people float a few hundred meters from the landing zone. Armed police boats form a barrier in between. With three shuttles in front of us, we're caught in a bottleneck waiting for the docking rig.

"What's with the barges?" I ask.

"Remember the officer saying all press other than EFAN is banned from the aeroport?" Mom asks. "They must be trying to get some footage from the water."

Addy shakes her head. "It's not just press. At least half of those barges are filled with protestors." As she says this, she curls in her shoulder and lifts her arm, shielding the Earth Force logo on her uniform. I wonder whether that was subconscious or if she did it on purpose.

As we pull closer, I can see that she's right about the protestors. People on some of the barges shout and shake signs.

"What on earth are they protesting?" Dad asks.

Addy lets out an exasperated sigh. "Bounders' rights, of course. I thought about joining, but I knew there was no way Mom would let me. And I admit it would be a little weird to protest on the same day I take the oath to serve in Earth Force."

"Addy!" Mom says in that weird hiss-voice she uses when she tries to talk through gritted teeth. These days it seems like she's always aiming that voice at my sister. Mom is not into Addy's stir-the-pot politics. "Now is not the time!"

"Then, when *is* the time, Mom?" Addy says loudly. Passengers shift uncomfortably around us. "How could there be a better time than now? What they're saying is true. We don't have a choice. What would happen if I didn't want to be an aeronaut? What if I wanted to be a doctor like you? Would they say, 'Oh, no problem, go to medical school'? I doubt it. I mean—"

I kick her foot. "Addy! Shut up!" She's seconds away from getting us both thrown in the brig.

She stops her rant and stares at me. I shake my head. Her words may be fueled by her online chat group, but they're also stoked by the secrets I shared with her in the storage room. She owes it to me to hush up.

"Fine," she whispers. Her cheeks swell with air. She grips the handrail and gazes off the ship's bow. She's probably picturing herself on the protest barge, shouting at Earth Force exactly what she thinks they can do with their alien war.

As we cruise past the barges, I avert my gaze. I don't want

to know what the protestors' signs say, but I can't block out their singsong chant.

> "Just like me, just like you,
> Bounders are people, too!
> Just like you, just like me,
> Bounders have the right to be free!"

As we pass and their words fade, another chant fills my mind, one I last heard in the parliamentary chamber in Gulagaven:

> *Birthright, Bounders fight!*
> *Birthright, Bounders fight!*
> *Birthright, Bounders fight!*

I never join the chant. And I'm pretty sure Addy won't, either. We may not always see things the same way, but there's no doubt we're on the same page about one thing: Earth Force keeping the reason why Bounders were born a secret all these years is not something to cheer about.

Four guard boats pull alongside our shuttle, blocking our view of the press and the protestors, and escort us the rest of the way to the aeroport.

As we near, someone on the deck jumps up and down,

waving his arms in a wide arc. Ryan. I'd recognize his orange hair anywhere. Cole stands by his side. They must have spotted me.

"I'll catch up with you on deck," I call to my parents once the gangplank is lowered. I push through the crowded craft and hurry across. I know I should wait for Addy, but she'll be fine. She always is. Plus, I'll introduce her to my friends after we board.

I squeeze through the crowd to Cole and Ryan. When I reach them, Ryan nearly tackles me with a hug.

"Hey, guys," I say, pushing him off. "Ryan, you're a celebrity! I watched the Paleo Planet special on EFAN a dozen times."

Ryan steps back into my space. I forgot what a close talker he is. "That's right! Me and Sheek. Best buds. Hanging with the wildeboars. Lucky for us, they didn't decide to charge."

I glance around. No one's paying any attention to us. We're back in Earth Force territory. I guess it's okay to talk candidly about what happened. Because by "hanging with the wildeboars," he means the dramatic conclusion to our battle with the Youli on the Paleo Planet.

"Yeah, good thing," I say, then turn to Cole. "Nice move on the classics round. I never would've thought of that strategy to hold the front."

Cole smiles. He is always up for talking *Evolution of*

Combat. "Thanks. Where have you been? I held open your amphibious troops all week."

"Sorry. I was busy getting ready for the tour of duty. My sister's coming, remember? We had a lot to discuss." I figure Cole will know what I'm talking about. All my pod mates know I planned to talk to my sister about the real deal with Earth Force.

"You mean—" Cole starts. He is absolutely clueless when it comes to keeping things on the down low.

I cut him off. "Um, yeah, that's what I mean. Who else is here?" As soon as I ask, my cheeks warm, because as much as I want to catch up with everybody, what I really want to know is whether Mira has arrived.

"Pretty much everyone's on board," Ryan says, fortunately oblivious to my real question. "See for yourself." He nods to the back of the flight deck, where a huge group of cadets congregate.

"Let's go." I lead Cole and Ryan through the crowd of junior officers and EFAN crew to the flight deck. It's set up almost the same as it was for our first tour. There's a roped-off area for luggage, a podium set up in front of the passenger crafts, and a designated area for families.

But it's easy to spot the changes. It's not just the brand-new, ultraslick 770s (can't wait to ride on one of those!). And it's not just the absence of the press corps, other than EFAN, of course. The biggest difference is the cadets. There's a clear divide. Those here for their first tour hang back with their parents in the family area. Then there's us, the old pros. We're definitely more at ease than the new cadets, but it's more than that. We're the seasoned soldiers.

Someone slams me from behind and coils an arm around my neck. "Beg for mercy!"

"Get off, Marco!"

Marco loosens his hold, spins me around by the shoulders, and pulls me in for a hug. "Ace! I thought you'd never show! You get in here, too, Wiki!" He clamps his hand on Cole's shoulder and pulls him over. Cole stays rigid as a board. He's not a hugger.

"Hi, Marco!" Ryan says brightly.

"What's up, Red? I saw your buddy Sheek practicing his EFAN poses a few minutes ago. I hear he's cohosting the launch with Florine Statton."

Maximilian Sheek *and* Florine Statton are here? Terrific. Next to Regis and his minions, those two are probably the people I missed least from the EarthBound Academy. At least Addy will be excited. She may be all about Bounders' rights these days, but she hasn't given up her inner fangirl. She's still got the poster of Sheek hanging above her bed. She nearly died when I told her that Sheek took over for Florine as Director of Bounder Affairs last tour. I considered telling her that Sheek was a complete fake, but I didn't think she was ready for that harsh truth.

"Check out all those newbies." Marco waves a hand in the direction of the family area and the new cadets. "Should we haze them?"

"What do you mean?" Ryan asks.

"Oh, you know, have them clean our bunk room and bring us snacks, make them run laps around the mess hall in their underwear. The usual."

"That sounds like Regis's kind of thing," I say.

"Hazing is expressly forbidden under the Earth Force Code of Conduct, article five, section seventeen," Cole says.

"Kidding, Boy Scouts," Marco says. "Although having a personal manservant would be kind of great."

"Speaking of Regis . . . ," I say.

"We weren't really speaking of Regis, Mr. Cool, but to answer your question: no, I haven't seen him. I wasn't looking for him, either, so don't get your hopes up. Although, it's definitely weird to see Hakim and Randall without their fearless leader."

Ever since last tour I've had this fantasy that Regis wouldn't be here. That the powers that be would have decided not to invite him back once they discovered what a jerk he was, especially since he almost got Mira and me killed on Gulaga when he stole her glove and stranded us on the frozen tundra.

Gedney even hinted that he'd try to get Regis ejected from the Academy. It probably didn't work out. Earth Force wants to keep all the minisoldiers they can.

I shake my head, trying to dislodge all thoughts of Regis, and follow Marco through the crowd toward the sea rail where a bunch of guys from the Academy are congregating. Halfway there I get the uncomfortable vibe that someone is following me. The feeling morphs into an avalanche of sparkly energy, like I'm being tackled by a magic rainbow unicorn.

Mira.

I spin around with a smile on my face. She's right behind me, gazing at the ocean. Her lips curl at the edges, and her eyes dart in my direction.

"Hi! How are you?"

The sparkly energy rips through my brain.

Right. Brain-talk. I try again. *Hi! How are you?*

Good. The word is punctuated by a dozen images. Mira playing piano. Mira reading. Mira walking in the woods. I think she's showing me how she spent her break.

I reach my hand across the space that separates us and place my fingers against hers. It feels like ages since I've seen her; I barely know where to begin. I close my eyes and call up a picture of my family vacation to the scorch zone.

"Jasper?" Addy's voice sounds at my side.

I drop my hand and open my eyes. Addy steps next to me.

"Hi!" Addy says to Mira.

Mira clasps her hands and rocks her shoulders forward and back. Her gaze shifts between the crowd and the sea.

Addy shoots a prizewinning death stare at me. She should challenge Lucy to a death stare contest.

"My brother is so rude." She sticks out her hand. "I'm Addy."

Mira glances at Addy's hand, shudders, then walks away.

Addy turns to me. "What on earth was that?"

Terrific. How am I going to explain? "It was nothing. Look, just forget it. She's not trying to be mean, she's just . . ."

"Oh my God, Jasper," she says. "That's her! Mira! The girl you were talking about! Am I right?"

"Drop it, Addy."

"Great to know that your girlfriend is, like, the rudest person on the planet."

"Seriously, just shut up."

"Yes, do shut up and get over here!" a high-pitched voice calls from behind.

I spin around to find Lucy with her arms spread wide. I bend into her, and she plants a kiss on my cheek. Her hair is pulled to the side and secured with her signature orange and indigo ribbons. Meggi and Annette stand just behind her.

"I missed you so much, Jasper Adams!" Lucy bubbles. "How was your break? Mine was awesome, of course. I have so much to tell you!

"Who's this?" Lucy says. "Oh my God! Is this your sister, the one and only Addy Adams?"

"Hi," Addy says. "Wait a second . . . are *you* Mira?"

Lucy, Meggi, and Annette all burst out laughing.

"Good one," Annette says.

Meggi slaps Annette's arm. "That's not nice!"

"This is Lucy," I tell Addy. "And this is Meggi and Annette."

As I say hello to the other girls, Lucy throws her arms around Addy. "I'm so excited to finally meet you! We are going to have so much fun. . . ."

While Lucy talks, Meggi's eyes go wide as she stares at something over my shoulder.

Annette interrupts Lucy. "Heads up."

A second later I'm caught in another Marco headlock. Once I shake him off, he nods at the girls. "Hello, ladies!"

"'Hello, ladies'?" Lucy says. "That simply won't do!"

She waves him into a hug. Then he walks down the line, doling out hugs to Annette and Meggi (who looks like she might faint).

When Marco turns back to face me, his eyes fall on Addy. "Hi." The word cracks as it leaves Marco's mouth.

"This is my sister, Addy," I say to Marco.

Addy's cheeks color pink. She lifts her palm and places it in Marco's hand. "It's Adeline."

I cough-laugh so loudly it startles Marco. "Adeline? I

haven't heard you use that name since . . . well, maybe ever."

"Very nice to meet you, Adeline Adams," Marco says to my sister, his voice returning to a normal pitch. "I'm Marco Romero."

"Are you for real?" I ask, not even sure who I'm directing the question to. "What's with the formality?"

Marco doesn't take his eyes off Addy. "I'm just trying to show your sister a bit of our military decorum, Jasper. She probably doesn't get much of that at home from you."

I punch him in the arm. "Shut up."

"Jasper's told me about you, Marco," Addy says. "You're from Amazonas, right?"

"J-Bird's been talking about me, huh? That's right. I live right by—"

"Um, excuse me?" Lucy says. "I haven't seen you in, like, forever. Are you going to let a new cadet hog all your time?" Lucy shoots a glare at Addy. Gone is the look of *Girls just wanna have fun.*

"I wasn't hogging—" Addy starts.

"And I wasn't talking to you," Lucy says, stepping between Marco and Addy.

Geez. What's with Lucy?

Next to us, the sound system crackles and squeaks. "May I have your attention. May I have your attention, puh-*leeeze.*"

Now, that's a voice I'd never forget, despite my best efforts.

"Queen Florine is back in business," Marco says.

"Back?" I say. "It's like she never left. I can't go two hours without seeing her face plastered on EFAN, staring back at me through those dark sunglasses."

"Ex-*cuuuse* me," Florine says. She's dressed in a white suit that's the exact same color as her huge white hair. "Once again we gather for the momentous occasion of the EarthBound Academy launch." Her tone doesn't say *momentous*; it sounds put off, like she can't get over the fact that her job requires her to promote mere children. "Welcome, Bounders, new and returning. Welcome, families, officers, and esteemed members of the press corps." She speeds through these formalities like she can't wait to get to her point. "And now it is my great pleasure to introduce a man who needs no introduction . . ."

Oh, I should have guessed.

". . . the Director of Bounder Affairs, the darling of EFAN, the true Renaissance man, the face of Earth Force . . . Maximilian Sheek!" Florine lets out a disturbing squeal and flutters her fingers together in a butterfly clap.

Addy grabs my forearm. "He's here!"

"Oh please," Marco says, "don't tell me you're a Sheek Shrieker."

Addy hesitates, then stammers, "No . . . no, I'm so not. I mean . . ." Her gaze flicks between Marco and the empty podium, which, presumably, is where Sheek will be standing any second. "I just think he's a really amazing aeronaut, and a civic leader, and an arts benefactor, and—oh my goodness, there he is!"

Marco shakes his head, then clamps his hand on my shoulder. "I'll catch you on the craft, Fly Guy."

"Wait," Addy says, but there's no energy in it. Her full focus has been diverted to the podium, where Sheek now stands, the sunlight gleaming off his shellacked hair. Around us the cries and applause are deafening. I'd forgotten how much clapping was involved in this whole celebrate–Earth Force–and–the–Bounders stuff. I should have brought some earplugs.

"Save me a seat!" Lucy calls after Marco. "We need some quality pod time!"

Marco gives a thumbs-up as he fades into the crowd. Lucy turns to my sister with a strange smile, but Addy doesn't notice. She's totally engrossed in all things Sheek.

Sheek waves his hands to quiet down the audience, but his lame attempt at humility only spurs on the crowd. "Thank you. You're too kind. Thank you."

Slowly the noise dissipates as the spectators decide they want to hear what the coward has to say. I wonder what would happen if I butted my way to the microphone and told everyone how he hid during the Youli attack on the Paleo Planet. How he shoved me out of the way during the space elevator evacuation on Gulaga. If he's the face of Earth Force, it's because that's all he has to offer: a pretty face.

"Good morning and welcome to the Earth Force Aeronautical Port. We are pleased you could join us for the official launch of the third tour of the EarthBound Academy." He pauses and lifts his jaw to the row of reporters standing to the left of the podium, maximizing his angles for a photo op, and opening up to more whistles and applause. Next to me, Addy screams like a true Sheek Shrieker.

"Can you believe we have to listen to him drone on like this all tour?" Lucy says.

Addy shoots Lucy a nasty look. Even I know it means *shut up*.

"Oh, sweetie." Lucy nods her head at Sheek. "That man loses his magic fast. And so does Marco. You'll find that out soon enough at the Academy."

If there's one thing Addy hates, it's people talking down to her. Combine that with a reference to all she doesn't know about the EarthBound Academy and a cryptic comment about Marco, and she's fuming.

Addy doesn't respond to Lucy. She turns to me and says through gritted teeth, "I'm going to find Mom and Dad." She pushes through the crowd and out of sight.

"Way to scare off the young ones," Meggi says to Lucy.

"What's with her?" Annette asks.

"My sister's sensitive about all the Earth Force secrets, that's all."

"Her and everyone else," Lucy says, relaxing into her standard mode of excessive talking. "My agent must have fielded two dozen calls from reporters begging for a live interview. If that Earth Force officer hadn't shown up to remind me of my confidentiality commitments, I might have agreed. After all, you know . . ."

I half pay attention to Lucy and the updates about her acting career, and half listen to Sheek. Throughout all of it, though, I worry about Addy. I promised I'd look out for her, and I'm doing a pretty awful job so far.

"I've got to find my family," I whisper when Lucy pauses to breathe. "I'll catch you on the craft."

"Wait a second," Lucy says. "Was that really the first time Marco met your sister?"

"Yeah. Why?"

Lucy flicks her eyes to the flight deck and for a moment doesn't say anything. Then she looks up with her signature smile and shrugs. "No reason. See you on board! Remember, we're sitting as a pod!"

AS I MAKE MY WAY TO THE FAMILY AREA,
I spy Mira across the crowd. Addy can wait another minute. I haven't really gotten a chance to connect with Mira. I take off in that direction, but when I get there, she's gone. I scan the crowd. Over by the sea rail, I spot a cadet with a long blond braid. I push my way over only to discover that it's not Mira. It's a new cadet. Her hair doesn't even look that similar up close. When the cadet sees the annoyed look on my face, she runs off.

I grab the railing and stare out at the ocean. It's not the endless water to the horizon's edge like last time I was here. Fifty meters away, several protest barges float. Their signs blaze with crimson letters:

EARTH FORCE = LIARS

SAVE THE BOUNDERS!

YOULI? TRULY? WE NEED THE TRUTH!

Who broke the code of silence? Who talked about the Youli and the secret alien war? Right now most of the population think these protestors are just radical conspiracy theorists. But the thing is, they have most of it right. Someone must be feeding them information. Could it be a Bounder? Someone standing right here on the aeroport tarmac?

How long can Earth Force stay silent? And if they choose to confirm the rumors, what will happen here on Earth? No matter what, we have to keep our planet safe.

I tried not to think about this stuff too much while I was at home. But now that I'm about to head to the Academy, everything is rushing back. There's not just dissension here on Earth, there's conflict within the Force. We know Waters didn't agree with the Earth Force agenda. He was optimistic that we could make peace with the Youli. But now it's hard to see how that could be possible after I watched their ship tear the Gulagan space elevator in two.

Still, I can't help feeling that Earth Force doesn't have it all right, either, and it's not just because of the secrets and lies. That's one of the reasons it was so hard to talk up the Academy to Addy. My heart's not fully in it. And neither is hers.

The water below looks cold and menacing. My chest tightens, almost like the water is compressing me, seeping inside and slowly drowning me. I take a step back, but I can't shake the feeling that everything is about to unravel, that even the strongest bonds are threatening to break.

"Hey, kid!"

I shake myself back to the moment. An EFAN cameraman is standing next to me.

"Aren't you supposed to be on board?" He cocks his head at the new 770. "They announced last call a few minutes ago."

Oh no. I push away from the rail and run for the passenger craft.

When I pass the family area, my dad grabs my arm. "Hey, Jasper! Where have you been? We were so worried!"

Mom waves me closer to the rope and throws her arms around me. "If you weren't about to blast into space, you'd be grounded." She kisses my head, letting me know all is forgiven.

"Sorry, I kind of spaced. Where's Addy?"

"She's already on board." Dad leans in for a quick hug. "Careful with the zone-outs. We'll see you in six weeks. Now go!"

"Bye!" I take off for the craft, then stop. I turn back to my parents. "Don't worry. I'll watch out for Addy!"

All but a few of the Bounders have already boarded. Sheek

and Florine stand next to the boarding ramp and pose for photos. That must mean we're seconds from departing.

I slide by Sheek, drawing a nasty glare, and hop onto the ramp of the new 770. As soon as my feet hit the incline, it starts rolling, so that I don't even have to walk. No expense was spared in making these tourist crafts luxury rides. Inside it's like a theme park. The top third of the wall in the entrance hall is lined with screens playing video footage from the Paleo Planet. The lower part is a long mural of the planet's grasslands. A flock of fuchsia birds are painted across the mural, and every few seconds a bird flies from one screen to the next, giving the effect that the mural itself is animated.

I follow the path of faux paw prints on the carpet until I bend around the mural wall and enter a huge room with tables and a bar. The sign above the bar says THE WATERING HOLE, and there are pictures of drinks with trying-to-be-clever names like Sabre Catini, Wildeboar Brew, and the Mammoth.

"Ex-cuuuse me."

The smell of roses nearly knocks me down as I turn to face Florine Statton.

"We are filming in this area," she says. "And you most certainly are not supposed to be present."

"Sorry," I mumble. I jet for the stairs at the side of the room and head up to the passenger cabin.

The cabin is huge, but nearly every seat is taken. The EarthBound Academy has easily doubled in size. I scan the crowd for Addy. It's hard to find anyone in the sea of matching indigo uniforms.

"J-Bird!" a voice bellows. Marco stands in the back row, waving his hands in wide arcs above his head.

I take off in that direction. Halfway down the aisle I see Addy sitting next to identical twin sisters with red hair and freckles. They're all chatting excitedly.

I place a hand on Addy's shoulder and kneel beside her. "You okay?" I ask when she turns around.

"Why wouldn't I be?"

"I just thought I'd check. I didn't see you board."

Addy rolls her eyes. "That's because you weren't there. Mom and Dad were freaked when boarding started and you were MIA. Where'd you go, anyway? Never mind. Go be with your friends, Jasper. I'm fine." She doesn't say she's annoyed, but I can tell that she is. She turns away and starts talking with the twins, who now look like they're bickering.

I stand there for a second, trying to think of something else to say, but I draw a blank. So far I'm not doing so great at looking out for my sister.

I jet up the aisle and find my pod mates—even Mira—last row, dead center.

"Nice of you to show," Marco says as I squeeze into the seat between Cole and Mira.

"Yeah, yeah, yeah," I say. "Thanks for saving me a seat."

"Thought we'd get in a bit of pod bonding before we arrive at the space station," Lucy says. "I'm excited to catch up, just us."

"Actually, we need to talk tactics," Cole says. "Do you think the degradation patch we planted on the Youli vessel was successful? How do you think the Bounders fit into the current war effort? And what if Gedney's right, and they plan to send us to Alkalinia?"

That snake den? The home of our new reptilian allies? I really hope they're not planning to send our pod there. I've been ignoring that horrible possibility since we learned about it on Gulaga. Last tour we spied on the Alks' meeting with Admiral Eames in Gulagaven. The small, reptilian creatures with the cyborg arms and flying minithrones sold secrets to Earth Force that helped us launch an attack on the Youli. Waters was horrified that the admiral even agreed to talk with the Alkalinians. Everything about them shouts *deceitful scum*.

"Shut up, Wiki," Marco says. "I hate snakes. The point is, we wanted to sit as a pod, and you almost ruined it, Ace. Do you know how many junior cadets I had to stare down to save your seat?"

"I can't believe how many cadets are on this craft," I say.

Mira slips inside my brain. *An army.*

The flight to the space station goes by in a blur. It's great to connect with everyone. Meggi, Annette, and Ryan share hilarious stories about their trip to the Paleo Planet with Sheek. Apparently, all these rich people were on the trip, and they kept asking the cadets to pose in pictures with them, saying things like "I can't wait to tell my grandkids that I met a real-life Bounder," as if we're just like the alien sabre cats or amphidiles. And I guess Sheek had this colorful safari tent with climate control and tons of servants. He came out only when the EFAN cameras were rolling.

Meggi says it was fun, though, to be in space without all the pressure of you-know-what. And by *you-know-what*, she meant the Youli and the alien war.

The best part of being on board the craft is that Regis isn't. That must mean he's been expelled from the Academy. Gedney really came through for us on that score. I can't wait to see Gedney at the Academy and tell him how much I appreciate it.

There's definitely a new vibe, and I think a lot of it is because of the junior cadets on board. We're the seniors now, and we need to set a good example.

Addy buzzes around the bottom of the craft the whole trip,

getting to know the other juniors. I give her space. She doesn't need her big brother butting in. Plus, she's kind of annoyed at me, last time I checked. When the captain announces we're preparing to exit FTL, Addy looks up and smiles. That must mean everything is okay.

When we shift out of FTL, the space station is visible out the front windows. A hush falls over the juniors. I remember seeing the station for the first time—the dozens of structures connected by the curving tubes that look like metal snakes, the launchpads and hangars, the flight deck and the bounding fleet—it's overwhelming.

The perimeter of the space station is surrounded by small ships. As we close in, I see that they're gunner ships like the ones that escorted us to the Paleo Planet.

"We must be on red alert," Cole says.

"Plenty of gunners," I say.

"I don't know if that makes me feel more or less safe," Lucy says.

"Hey, juniors!" Marco shouts. "Welcome to the Earth Force Space Station!"

As the new cadets turn around to look at Marco, Addy catches my eye. Not all of the juniors know why there are so many gunner ships, but Addy does. And she's no longer smiling.

· EF ·

"Please remain in your seats and wait for further instructions," the captain says over the intercom once we've pulled into the hangar.

"Why?" Lucy whispers. "We've been on this craft for hours. Why can't they just let us off?"

"They're probably getting things prepped for the oath," Meggi says from the row in front of us. "Is your sister excited, Jasper?"

Soon Addy will be Officer Adeline Adams. I'm still not sure whether she's excited. For all the secrets I ended up spilling about Earth Force, Addy managed to keep many of her feelings to herself. I know she's mad, but I know there's more than anger beneath the surface. She's been waiting her entire life for today.

Sparks go off in my brain, courtesy of Mira. She must be telling me to pay attention, because two Earth Force officers are now standing at the bottom of the row. I recognize them from my first tour. They were part of our notoriously unfriendly wake-up crew.

"Attention!" one of them hollers. The back half of the craft, where the senior cadets sit, springs to life. Cadets hop to their feet in salute. Down below, the junior cadets are a mess. Some try to imitate us, some stay sitting, some stand and stare at the officers like they've seen a ghost.

"Salute your senior officers!" the second officer shouts.

Finally the new cadets fall in line, and even though their form is horrible, everyone stands at attention.

"At ease," the first officer says. The old cadets drop their arms. Most of the new cadets don't move.

"He said 'at ease,' B-wads!" the second officer shouts.

As the junior cadets look back to us for example and drop their arms to their sides, a voice calls out, "We didn't know what that meant!"

Addy, please don't start.

The officer approaches my sister's row. "Do you have something to say, cadet?"

I jerk in my chair. Marco puts a hand on my shoulder. "She can handle herself," he whispers.

"Yes." Addy's voice is clear and cold. "I said we didn't know what that meant. We're trying our best."

He glares down at Addy. "What's your name, cadet?"

"Adeline Adams."

"Did I ask your opinion, Adams?"

"No," Addy says.

"No, what?"

"No, sir." Her lips curl in a defiant smile.

Marco leans over and whispers, "How'd she know the 'sir' part?"

I smile. "I told her the story of how you humiliated Bad Breath."

Marco slaps me five.

"That's right, I didn't," the officer continues, "so shut up! And the rest of you, listen up! I need the following cadets to come with me: Lucy Dugan, Cole Thompson, Mira Matheson, Marco Romero, and Jasper Adams. *Adams*, huh?" He looks at me, then Addy, then back at me. Then he laughs. And let's just say there's nothing friendly about his laugh.

Lucy grumbles, "And here I thought we weren't going to be singled out this tour."

We slide out of our row and head down the aisle. I glance at Addy when we pass. She mouths, *Whatever*, suggesting that the issue with the officer was no big deal. But her arms are crossed tight against her chest, and her jaw is clenched. She's not happy. I wish Addy were excited about taking the oath and officially becoming a Bounder, but at best, I think her feelings are mixed. She raises her eyebrows, silently asking me why my pod was called out. I shrug and try to act casual so she won't be freaked. Although, knowing Addy, it would take more than that to freak her out.

We exit the cabin, descend the stairs, and cross in front of the mural wall. As we step onto the automated boarding ramp, Cole asks the officers, "Are they sending us to Alkalinia?"

"No questions," the officer on the left says.

"Are we going to miss the oath?" I ask.

The officer on the right laughs. "Why? Afraid you'll miss your sister getting sworn in?"

"Can't you just tell us where we're going?" Lucy asks.

"Shut up!" the other officer says. "Save your questions for the admiral!"

I wish I had a better feeling about this, but I don't. All signs point to another field trip for our pod, this time to the home of our sneaky, snaky allies.

MIRA'S MIND DOUSES ME WITH INQUISITIVE
energy, like she's asking me if I know what's going on. When
your superior officer tells you to shut up, it's pretty conve-
nient to brain-talk.

No clue is my response. Just because we can connect doesn't
mean I have anything awesome to add. Plus, I don't even want
to think about the possibility that the admiral is sending us
to Alkalinia.

The officers stop in front of the entrance to one of the
senior briefing rooms. The one on the left speaks quietly into
his com link, then the door buzzes open.

"Bounders," he says, holding the door for us to enter, "welcome back to space."

Lucy enters first, with Marco close on her heels. The rest of us follow them in.

The room is small, but it radiates power, mostly because Admiral Eames sits at the head of the table. She may be small, but her presence is enormous.

The table's surface is a giant screen loaded with graphs and graphics. Eight other Earth Force officers crowd around. Most of them I recognize but don't know personally. There's one notable exception: my first-tour nemesis, Chief Auxiliary Officer Wade Johnson, a.k.a. Bad Breath.

"Cadets, welcome," Admiral Eames says. "Thank you for joining us."

All of the officers stare at us. I'm not exactly sure what to do. Lucy leads us around to the end of the table so we're standing in a crescent shape facing the admiral.

"I apologize in advance for the short notice," the admiral continues. "We're sending you on a mission at zero seven hundred tomorrow morning, and you need to be briefed."

I can't read Lucy's mind, but I know what she's thinking. Any chance of us having a normal start to our third tour just went up in smoke. It also means the mystery about the potential mission to Alkalinia is solved.

We're going.

"You'll be our advance team—our first diplomatic envoy, if you will—to the home planet of our new allies, the Alkalinians."

There it is. Confirmed.

Mira's brain bristles. Distaste. Distrust. Those are her impressions of the Alkalinians, and she has a very bad feeling about the mission. My gut says the same.

Next to me, Cole shifts from side to side. Lucy must be fuming, and I'm sure Marco's not much happier. All of us are struggling to stay composed. It's important that we do. As far as the admiral knows, we've never heard of the Alks. She has no idea we spied on the meeting where Seelok, the Alkalinian leader, gave Earth Force the coordinates of the intragalactic summit in exchange for occludium. Without those coordinates, we could never have placed the worm patch on the Youli systems.

And the admiral certainly doesn't know that Gedney gave us a heads-up that she might send a delegation to our new allies' home.

"The Alkalinians have invited us to visit their planet," she says. "They asked specifically to host the pod responsible for placing the degradation patch on the Youli vessel during Operation *Vermis*."

Cole straightens. "Was the patch successful?"

"Early indications point to yes," the admiral says.

"What does that mean?" Marco asks.

"It means exactly what I said, cadet, and anything beyond that is outside of your clearance."

"Permission to ask a question, Admiral?" Lucy says.

Admiral Eames nods.

"Why would the Alkalinians request us? How do they even know the details of Operation *Vermis*?"

"Those answers are also outside your clearance. But I'll tell you this: I have other reasons why I want your pod to go. Your mission will require a bit more than diplomatic relations. We've agreed to bring the entire EarthBound Academy to Alkalinia for training. However, I won't do that until I'm sure certain safety precautions are in place."

Wait . . . what? She plans to bring *all* the cadets to Alkalinia? I do *not* want Addy going into that snake den.

The admiral nods to the officer on her right, who calls up a machine diagram on the table screen. "We believe the main settlement on Alkalinia is shielded by occludium tether technology. In other words, a certain portion of the planet is covered by a tent-like occludium shield that's anchored to the surface. This image shows specifications for the latest occludium tether on the intragalactic market. It prevents bounding in and out of the barrier and also scrambles bounds within the barrier like the block on Gulagaven. You will need to locate the tether so that we can deactivate it, if necessary. It will be outside of the main settlement and near a major power source. Once you've completed your mission, we will prepare to bring the rest of the Academy to Alkalinia to finish out their training this tour."

"You want us to deactivate their occludium tether?" Marco says. "Don't you think that will set off like a million warning bells?"

Admiral Eames stares impassively at Marco. "I didn't say I wanted you to deactivate it. I just need you to find it. You locate the tether and an access entry point, and you communicate the information to me. That is your mission. Understood?"

"And if we do that, you're going to bring the other cadets to Alkalinia?" I ask, already thinking about how I might sabotage the mission and keep Addy safe at the space station.

"We've already agreed to bring the cadets, Mr. Adams, including your sister. You completing this mission will help keep all cadets safe."

Geez. You can't get anything by Admiral Eames. It's like she has a brain patch that can read everyone's minds.

"You're sending us there on our own?" Lucy asks. "Just the five of us?"

"No. Officer Johnson will be accompanying you."

Wait . . . what? Bad Breath? I open my mouth to protest

but then shut it. What exactly can I say? That we hate the guy? Somehow I doubt Admiral Eames would appreciate our complaints. Plus, she promoted him through the ranks, so she obviously thinks he's capable of something. Maybe she doesn't want to send an aeronaut to babysit Bounders, so Chief Auxiliary Officer Wade Johnson is the next-best choice.

Bad Breath lifts his lips in a rotten grin. It was only a year ago that he shoved me into my storage bin for forgetting to call him *sir* when we first met. He's going to take every chance he can to torture us on this mission. Marco cursed us with his hazing talk. Bad Breath will teach us what it really means to be hazed.

"Now let's talk specifics. . . ." The admiral turns the meeting over to the other officers at the table, who brief us on the nuts and bolts of the mission. They talk so quickly I can hardly process what all of this means, what they're actually asking of us. Tomorrow the Alks will supply us with bounding coordinates for their planet. (Doesn't sound like too tight of an alliance if the Alks haven't even told us where they live yet.) Captain Han will pilot the bounding ship to the coordinates. Once we've arrived safely, Bad Breath will transmit additional details about the destination via advanced GPS technology back to Earth Force.

"What if they intercept the transmission?" Cole asks.

"Excellent question," one of the officers replies. "That

brings us to the tech you'll be taking." The officer shows us a small, clear disk and asks Bad Breath to hand over his tablet. The disk adheres directly to the screen and is barely visible. With a finger swipe, the officer activates it.

"This is a sound inclusion moat with paralinear encryption," he says.

"A sound inclusion what?" Lucy asks.

"We call it a SIMPLE for short," he continues. "The SIMPLE will shield and encrypt communications. This one has been custom-designed to get around any Alkalinian com blockers. Officer Johnson is under orders to provide progress reports directly to the admiral, with your pod's input, of course."

"About that," Lucy says. "How exactly do you expect us to make any progress? I kind of doubt the Alkalinians are going to let us search their planet for the occludium tether."

"I'm sure that's true," the admiral says, "but I believe we have a work-around. Seelok, the Alkalinian leader, has assured us that you'll be able to train while you're there. That means they will need to transport you outside the shield range to practice bounding. We suspect your training zone will be in close proximity to the tether."

"You *suspect*?" Marco asks.

The admiral looks at Marco and lifts an eyebrow. "Yes, Mr. Romero. Information beyond that is outside your clearance."

I guess almost everything is outside our clearance. "I'm just an Earth Force pawn." Those were Addy's words in the basement storage room of our apartment building. I tried to assure her that we were more than that, that we had an important role to play in the defense of Earth, that Bounders were special. But as I consider what Admiral Eames is asking us to do, the risks she's expecting us to take on faith, I wonder whether Addy was right. *Earth* might be worth fighting for, but maybe *Earth Force* isn't.

Admiral Eames signals to the officer at the end of the table, who stands and opens the door to the briefing room. "Now, if you'll excuse us," she says, "we have urgent matters to discuss prior to the oath ceremony. Rest up, cadets. Tomorrow is going to be a long day."

We quickly shuffle out of the room. Lucky for us, the guards who brought us here are no longer around. We can walk back to the hangar without anyone breathing down our necks. Which is good, because we definitely need to debrief from the briefing.

"I hate snakes," Marco says as soon as the door closes.

"I can't believe this is happening again," Lucy says as we set off down the hall, following the platinum stripe that marks the path of the mini spider robots. "It was bad enough last tour when we had to miss the beginning. But again? We don't even have a full twenty-four hours before we have to leave, and most of the time we'll be in bed. I barely got a chance to tell anyone about my summer."

"Or to find out about *their* summers," Marco mumbles.

"I heard that, Marco Romero," Lucy snarls. "You know what I meant. And in case you didn't, let me make it even more clear: this stinks!"

"I don't see why you're so surprised," Cole says. "Gedney practically told us last tour to expect this. I think it could be quite interesting. After all, it sounds like we'll be among the first humans to see the Alkalinian planet, if not the very first."

"And that doesn't bother you?" Lucy says. "Don't you think it sounds a bit dangerous to send kids to a planet we know almost nothing about?"

"Since when does Earth Force care about our safety?" Marco asks.

"Guys," I say. "Can we cut the arguing for a second? I have an even bigger problem. My sister. I can't just leave without talking to her, but I'm sure we'll be dismissed to our bunks immediately after the ceremony. What should I do?"

"Easy," Marco says. "Sneak out after curfew and meet up somewhere."

"That's not easy for me, let alone Addy," I say. "She just got here. She doesn't even know how to use the suction chutes."

"So have someone bring her," Lucy says.

MONICA TESLER

That's not a bad idea, but it would have to be someone from the girls' dormitory. "Are you volunteering?"

Lucy recoils. "Uh, no. Did you hear what I said a few minutes ago? We're leaving the space station first thing tomorrow morning. Sorry, Jasper, but I'm not going to spend my time chaperoning your sister."

It probably isn't fair to ask. Plus, Lucy and Addy didn't exactly hit it off at the aeroport.

"Real nice, Drama Queen," Marco says to Lucy. "Just see what happens the next time you need a favor from one of us."

Lucy plants her feet and puts her hands on her hips. "Does this involve you, Marco? No, it doesn't. But like with everything else, you think you need to insert your macho self right into the middle, especially when it has to do with some new girl . . ."

I'll do it.

Mira's words reach me, distracting me from Lucy's tirade. Is she serious?

It might be my best and only option.

I stop and turn to Mira. *Thanks. Where?*

An image of the piano behind the sensory gym fills my mind.

I interrupt Lucy, who's still shouting at Marco. "Mira will sneak my sister out after curfew. Help me catch Addy after the ceremony. I need to give her a quick heads-up."

WHEN WE ENTER THE HANGAR, I SCAN the rows of cadets for Addy. There she is, front row left. Her eyes find mine instantly. She must have been watching for me. She shifts her gaze and raises her eyebrows: What on earth is going on?

I nod and smile, trying to let her know that everything is going to be okay, which is really ridiculous because I have no idea whether everything is going to be okay.

Officers greet our pod and escort us into formation. A few minutes later the admiral and her honor guard enter the hangar. Just like on my first tour, the admiral walks along the line of cadets, carefully assessing each of us, and then takes her place at the podium.

"Welcome, Bounders," she starts, spreading her arms wide. "I am so pleased to stand before this promising new class of cadets and invite you into our ranks. You are the future of Earth Force, and we need you now more than ever."

That's the truth. Earth Force may lie about a lot, but there's no debating that their need for the Bounders—for us—is real. When we talked in the storage room, Addy said she always thought we were special. Well, the truth is we *are* special. Earth Force needs us. Earth needs us. I sneak a glance at Addy. I wish I could make her understand that the magnitude of our responsibility to our planet makes the Earth Force lies seem trivial. At least, that's how I see it.

Another truth: what makes us special also puts us right in the line of fire.

I should never have promised Mom and Dad that I'd watch out for Addy. I mean, I *want* to watch out for her, but how am I supposed to do that from another planet?

I can't even promise that I'll be okay. Who knows what we'll find on Alkalinia? With Bad Breath as our chaperone, we may be in trouble before we even make it to that snake den.

Plus, that's not the worst of it. Out there, beyond the hangar doors, the Youli are waiting for their revenge. I'm sure they've managed to trace their systems issues back to us, and they'll be looking for payback. *Ultio.*

Voices rise around me. I must have missed the admiral's

remarks. We're already at the oath. In the row ahead, the new cadets have raised their hands and are repeating back the vows.

"*. . . and to serve at all times with honor in Earth Force.*"

"Congratulations!" the admiral says. "The future of Earth Force is yours!"

With these words, applause swells, and our formation falls apart. I need to move. I have to reach Addy before they whisk us off to the dormitories.

I duck and dodge through the rows of cadets until I spot her. She's in the middle of a herd of juniors, the twins she was sitting with on the passenger craft plus a few others. My mind flashes with the memory of celebrating with Cole and Lucy after being sworn in last year. I shake my head. I don't have time to get lost in the past.

I dart forward and grab Addy's wrist.

She spins to face me. "Jasper! Hey! Everyone, this is my brother!" Addy pellets me with names. She's excited, happy even. Addy's always the center of attention, and she enjoys it.

"Hi. Congrats," I say weakly to the juniors before bending to Addy. "I need to talk to you!"

"About why those officers whisked you off the craft?"

I nod.

She steps away from her new friends and mouths, *Sorry*. As we veer away from the group, Captains Ridders and Suarez start rounding up the cadets to head to the dorms.

"I'll explain everything tonight, after curfew," I tell her. "Mira will bring you to the sensory gym. We can talk there."

Addy steps back and narrows her eyes at me. "I'm up for sneaking out, J, but I'm surprised you think it's a good idea with all your 'follow orders' and 'fall in line' advice. Plus, in case you forgot, your girlfriend wasn't exactly friendly at the aeroport."

"She's not . . . forget it, just go with Mira. It's important, Addy." I'm not sure if I'm convincing enough, so I add, "I'm leaving on a mission tomorrow."

"What? I don't understand. How can you be . . ." My sister's eyes widen, and she abruptly stops talking.

A hand clamps down on my shoulder. "Cadet, we meet again."

I glance up to face the impeccably coiffed Maximilian Sheek. Ugh.

"And who is this?" he asks, flashing an unnaturally white smile at Addy.

"Hi! I'm Adeline Adams," Addy squeaks. "So nice to make your acquaintance, Captain Sheek."

"Of course it is," Sheek says. "Hello and welcome and congratulations and all of that. Now run along." He waves his hands in a dismissive flutter like a medieval lord waving off his servants.

Even so, Addy beams.

The cadets congregate in two groups by the hangar doors— one to march to the boys' dorm, the other to the girls'. I squeeze Addy's hand and lean close. "Promise me, Addy!"

She makes an annoyed face, nods, then heads to the girls' group.

Thank goodness. Hopefully, she won't change her mind.

I jog over to where Ridders has rounded up the boys and fall in line next to Cole.

As we walk out of the hangar, Marco steps between us and places his hands on Cole's and my shoulders to slow us down.

"What's up?" I ask Marco as we let some new cadets pass.

"Notice anyone missing from the ceremony?" he whispers.

"Regis." When I say his name out loud, it's like a giant boulder I've been balancing on my back crashes to the ground and turns to dust. I can't believe he's not here. I can't believe how much I care that he's not here. I'm ashamed to admit it, but if I had to choose between seeing Regis and facing the Youli, I'm not 100 percent sure which I'd pick.

"Covered and confirmed, Fly Guy. Regis was booted. Who else?"

"Waters," Cole says.

"Obviously. He's long gone. There's no coming back for Jon Boy after the stunt he pulled on Gulaga. But where's his partner in crime?"

"You mean Gedney?" Cole asks.

"Bingo. Aren't you worried the reason Geds wasn't part of the oath ceremony is because he's not working at the EarthBound Academy anymore, either?"

I hadn't thought about that. In fact, with all the drama since we landed, I've hardly thought about Gedney at all, which is pretty stupid, since he's basically the only adult in Earth Force who has our back, even though as a civilian scientist, he's not technically in Earth Force.

"Well, what do you suggest?" I ask. "Wandering the halls aimlessly looking for him?"

"I'm open to any and all great ideas," Marco says.

"We should go to the pod room," Cole says. "He might be there. If he's not, at least we'll know whether the room looks the same, which would be pretty good evidence that Gedney's still around."

"Good thinking, Sherlock," Marco says.

"How do we ditch?" I ask.

"Leave that to the master," Marco says.

We trail after Ridders and the horde of other boys. Every few steps we hang back a bit more, opening up a gap between us and the rest, biding our time until we can turn a corner and conveniently disappear. When we're two turns from the chute that will take us to the dorms, Marco gives the signal. At the next corner we'll split.

A junior at the back of the pack keeps glancing behind him and muttering. He's skinny, with brown skin and black hair buzzed close to his scalp.

"What's with him?" I ask. "If he keeps turning around

every five seconds, he'll definitely notice when we're no longer back here."

"Let me handle this," Marco says as he waves us closer to the boy. "Hey, Buzz, what's up?"

The guy's eyes dodge all about like he's super paranoid. "Are you talking to me?"

"Who else would I be talking to?"

"You said Buzz. That's not my name."

"And my name's not Turn the Heck Around and Mind Your Own Business, but it might as well be."

The boy stops and presses a hand to his head. "That is a very unusual name."

Geez. He is totally going to blow our cover. I join Marco and try to steer things in a better direction. "Hey, I'm Jasper. This is Marco and Cole. What's your name?"

The boy keeps shifting his eyes around. "My name is Desmond. You guys are not doing what you are supposed to be doing."

"Who said it's your business what we're doing?" Marco asks.

Desmond's eyes focus on something in front of him, like he's reading an invisible screen floating in the air. "According to Earth Force regulation 407.3, when officers are walking in formation, proper spacing should be observed. You have allowed a gap to open."

"Look, Desmond," I say. "Things are a bit more laid back

around here." I place my hand on his arm. He jerks away.

"That's not the right regulation," Cole says.

"Yes, it is," Desmond says.

"No, it's not."

"Shut up, Wiki," Marco says.

"Yes, it is!" Desmond says. "Have you not read the Earth Force code? It is required."

"Of course I've read the code!" Cole shouts back.

Marco shoves Cole's shoulder. "Shut. Up."

Cole stumbles backward and—thankfully—shuts up.

"You are violating Earth Force rules," Desmond says. "I am an Earth Force officer, and I have a duty to report you."

"No, no, no, you've got it all wrong." Marco tries to throw an arm around the kid, but Desmond ducks. "Guess what? Officer Ridders is about to take us on the suction chutes. The best place to be for that is up front. Don't you want to be one of the first in line?"

That seems to excite Desmond. "The suction chutes connect the space station structures. They are constructed from an impenetrable metal composite. They operate in zero gravity."

"True." I don't know what to make of this guy, but I'm pretty sure he's going to kill our chances of ditching the group. I glance at Marco. How on earth are we going to shake him?

"Listen, Buzz—I mean, Desmond," Marco says, giving me a look that says *Follow my lead* and probably *Keep Cole in line*.

"We're allowed to hang back. In fact, we're going to take a different route to the boys' dormitory because we're here for our third tour of duty. Ridders—that's *Captain* Ridders—gave us permission when we were in the hangar."

Desmond's eyes shift to the side like he's confused.

Marco smiles. "You remember how the Earth Force code says all that stuff about how you have to follow the orders of your senior officers, right? Well, I'm a senior cadet, and you're a junior cadet. That makes me your senior officer. And I'm telling you to get to the front of the line."

Desmond's eyes open really wide, and a smile spreads across his face like everything suddenly makes perfect sense. "Yes, you are my senior officer." He spins around and heads for the front.

"Wait!" Marco calls.

What? We finally ditch the kid, and Marco calls him back?

Desmond turns. "Yes?"

"Yes, what?" Marco asks.

The confused look returns to Desmond's face.

"It's 'yes, *sir*,'" Marco says with a sinister smile.

Oh, please.

The dawn of understanding shows on Desmond's face. He snaps to attention, his right hand slapping his forehead, and shouts, "Yes, sir!"

Up ahead other cadets turn around to see what's happening. Great. Even more attention we don't need.

MONICA TESLER

Marco waves his hand at Desmond, who takes off again at a fast walk, passing all the cadets in the group.

We slow down, and when the group rounds the next corner, we bolt in the opposite direction all the way to the chute cube at the other end of the structure. The cube houses a departure grate and arrival trough for the suction chute system, the long metal tubes that connect the different space station structures.

We bow over our legs, trying to catch our breath.

"'Yes, sir'?" I say to Marco. "That was overkill."

"Nah," he says. "That Desmond kid needed to be taught a lesson."

"I need to check the Earth Force regulations," Cole says. "I didn't know about section 407.3. I wonder if they added it after our first tour."

"Seriously, Wiki?" Marco shakes his head. "You focus on the strangest things."

"Yeah, well, *I'm* focused on getting to the pod room," I say. "So let's go."

I pull open the door to the chute cube and activate the system. If there's one thing I missed about the space station, it's the chutes. And I know I'm not the only one.

"Human chain, Ace?" Marco asks.

I step onto the grate. "Need you ask?"

The whoosh of air hits my face—the only warning I get before I'm sucked into the chute.

My body races up in total blackness.

BUMP!

Marco collides with my shoes. He snakes his hands around my ankles. A second later another crash, and Cole connects with Marco. I slide my hands out front like Superman and lead us through the chute.

"Woo-hoo!" The rush of air carries my screams through the tube, picking up Marco's and Cole's along the way.

We take a corner at super speed. Cole hollers. He must have been whipped into the wall as the caboose. I scissor-kick my feet, challenging Marco to hold on.

A light shines up ahead. The arrival trough awaits. The hallway better be clear. I glide into the trough and jump out of the way to avoid a pileup.

Marco hops off and gives Cole a hand. Lucky for us, the hallway is empty.

"Let's go." I lead off down the hall.

We've been so busy since we arrived, it's hardly registered that we're really back at the space station, at least for tonight. Now that we have a moment to breathe, the claustrophobia sets in. White walls, bright lights, tofu dogs. Welcome back to the Earth Force Space Station.

"What kind of food do you think they have on Alkalinia?" I ask.

"This again?" Marco says. "Just don't think about it,

Fly Guy. Nothing can be worse than BERF."

That's true. The food on Gulaga was so disgusting I think it would be impossible to imagine how gross it was unless you were actually forced to consume it. I mean, we literally ate fungus. Every. Day.

We reach the pod hallway. So far everything looks exactly as I remember, right down to the eye sensor that secures the door.

"Do you think it's still programmed with our lens signatures?" I ask.

"We're about to find out," Marco says. "Hack Man, care to do the honors for old times' sake?"

During our first tour of duty, Cole programmed the security system to read his left lens signature so we could break into the cell block and pay a visit to the Youli prisoner. The whole escapade almost blew up in our face, but we managed to bound to the Ezone seconds before being busted. But the lens scan worked.

This time Cole leans into the scanner with his right eye. Our breath is the only sound as we wait for the scan to process. If we're not preauthorized, an alarm will go off, and then *this* escapade will come to a quick end.

CLICK.

The door disengages.

We slip inside. The pod hall is dark. The lights that flank

THE FORGOTTEN SHRINE

the platinum sensor strip are the only illumination. The door slams behind us, and a weird blend of electronic and metal noises confirms that the sensor lock has reset.

"Is it just me, or is this place super creepy in the dark?" I ask.

"Want to hold my hand, Wimpy Kid?" Marco asks.

"Shhh!" Cole says. "I think there's someone down there."

"I hope someone's here," Marco says, "and that his name is Gedney. Let's go!"

Marco dashes to the end of the hall. Cole and I race to catch up. We collide in front of the pod room.

There are voices coming from the other side of the door.

"I think I hear Gedney!" Cole whispers.

I press my ear to the door. He's right. I'm pretty sure that's Gedney, although I can't make out what he's saying. I give Cole and Marco a thumbs-up.

"Who is he talking to, Ace?"

I close my eyes and concentrate. Gedney is still talking. Then there's a pause. Then a second voice starts up.

I jump back from the door.

"Well?" Marco asks.

"I'm pretty sure he's talking to Waters."

WE CROWD TOGETHER, ME SANDWICHED

between Cole and Marco, all with our ears pressed against
the door. I can still make out only snippets of what they're
saying.

"... will take a long time to repair," Gedney says, "... years
to build . . . you can't expect things to be fixed overnight, old
friend. . . ."

Cole taps my shoulder. "Do you think he's talking about
Waters coming back to Earth Force?"

"Maybe they're talking about his relationship with the
Youli," Marco whispers.

Then Waters responds: ". . . division within their own

ranks . . . total disaster . . . I should have listened to you about the patches."

"They're talking about our brain patches," I say.

"Or it could be the degradation patch we planted on the Youli systems," Cole says.

"Either way," Marco says, "they're definitely talking about the Youli."

"The cadets just arrived." Gedney's voice rings clearer. "I hate to tell you this, Jon, but they're sending the kids to Alkalinia."

Our eyes go wide. I strain to hear Waters's response.

"That's it!" Marco says. "I'm going in!" He twists the door handle and storms into the pod room. Cole and I are right behind him.

I quickly notice three things. First, Gedney is standing in the center of the room, stooped over as always. Second, the large screen at the front of the room is filled with the image of Waters's face. And third, the room looks almost exactly as it did when we left—cushy beanbags, starry ceiling, green grass carpet, and lots of funky accessories.

Gedney turns toward us, but my gaze is glued to the screen. Waters's face is covered with a grizzly beard. His hair is long and shaggy. He's wearing a bright-colored shirt like the ones the Wackies wore on Gulaga. He looks surprised, then his face spreads into a grin. A second later the image winks out.

"That was Waters!" Cole says.

"Thanks, Captain Obvious," Marco says.

"Was that vid chat?" I ask.

"Never mind that," Gedney says. "And hello to you. Ever hear of knocking? Apparently not."

"Since when do we have to knock at our own pod room?" Marco asks. "And why were you talking to Waters?"

"You mean Jon Waters?" Gedney asks. "I haven't spoken to Waters since the day he disappeared on Gulaga." He looks at each of us with a sly smile. "Are we clear?"

I'm guessing that the admiral wouldn't be too happy that Gedney was vid-chatting with Waters.

"I guess that depends," Marco says to Gedney. "You tell us what you weren't talking about with Waters, and then we'll be clear."

"Oh, you kids." Gedney shakes his head. "I was just catching up with an old friend. That's all. Come. Sit. I want to catch up with you, too."

We exchange glances. I don't know if Marco is going to press the issue. But a second later he dives onto a tangerine beanbag. I sink into the turquoise bag in the corner and flip on a lava lamp.

Cole sits rod straight in the crimson-red bag. "We're going to Alkalinia," he tells Gedney, even though we know he knows.

"I know," Gedney says, pulling over a straight-backed chair for himself. "I warned you that was a possibility."

"Why aren't you coming with us?" I ask.

"I have responsibilities here," Gedney says. "There are several technology projects in the works, and I'll be training new cadets. Your sister is in my pod, Jasper."

"That's awesome!" I told Addy all about Gedney. She'll be happy she's in his pod. Gedney is great. Which reminds me . . . "Thanks for keeping your promise about Regis."

Gedney nods. "There's no place here for that kind of behavior. As I've told you before, my job is to keep you safe."

"Yeah, but I'm surprised Earth Force let you get rid of one of its soldiers," I say.

"It wasn't easy," Gedney says, "but when I made it clear that keeping him might mean losing one or more of you, the decision was easy. You and Mira almost died that night on the tundra."

"Any chance you can get rid of Bad Breath, too?" Marco asks. "He's our chaperone on the Alkalinia mission."

"Who?" Gedney asks.

"Chief Auxiliary Officer Wade Johnson," Cole says.

"Bad Breath, huh?" Gedney laughs. "I'm afraid there's nothing I can do about that. Try to stay out of his way. It's you the Alkalinians want, not him."

"What do you mean?" I ask.

Gedney rubs his hand across his forehead. "I'm not sure. I know the Alks specifically requested that the cadets who planted the degradation patch on the Youli vessel be part of the delegation, ostensibly to celebrate your achievements. But it's left me wary. You must stay vigilant at all times."

"That doesn't exactly fill me with comfort, Geds," Marco says.

"Nor should it. The Alkalinians have a dark past. Their planet was nearly destroyed in the last intragalactic war, largely due to their own greed and deception. They've skittered along the fringes of the galaxy for decades, getting by with technology trades and with bartering in secrets and illicit substances. Our alliance with them is risky for a number of reasons."

"Their planet was nearly destroyed?" Cole says.

"Yes. I suspect it will take generations before it's again habitable—at least, that's what our intelligence tells us. Most surmise the Alks have relocated to another system, but they've kept the exact location of their settlement a secret for as long as I can remember. Perhaps now is a time for optimism. Inviting the whole EarthBound Academy to their home is out of line with their past behavior."

"If you were trying to layer on some comfort, Geds, you have failed completely," Marco says.

"The admiral is counting on this alliance. She will do

almost anything to keep the Alks happy. For you, that means following her orders, but be cautious. I prepared a custom transmitter for the mission. Did the admiral give it to you?"

"The SIMPLE?" I ask. "Yeah, Bad Breath has it."

"Fair enough," Gedney says. "It can also shield your communications with one another from the Alkalinians. I suspect you'll be under near-constant surveillance, but with the SIMPLE you can have a private conversation without worrying that anyone else is listening in." Gedney crosses to a storage closet in the back of the pod room and reemerges a second later. "And there's something else I want you to take. I've reconfigured this voice box. It should be able to two-way translate English and Alkalinian."

Cole stands and takes the voice box. Gedney points out the controls and explains how to operate it. Then he gives us some information about the occludium tether. He saw the Alks' plans for the tether when the occludium trade was brokered. The day the Alks showed up on Gulaga for the trade was the same day Waters met with the Youli at the Wacky infirmary. Waters had no idea that Mira and I were spying on them, and we had no idea of the chain reaction that would be caused by our presence.

"What's happening with the Youli?" I ask. My stomach twists with a familiar twinge of guilt. Mira's and my brain patches allowed the Youli to follow us back to Gulaga after we placed the degradation patch on their systems at the intra-galactic summit. Even though Gedney and our pod mates assured us we weren't to blame for all the lives lost in the space elevator attack, I still feel partially at fault.

Gedney sits back down and crosses his hands in his lap. "The short answer is that the degradation patch seems to have worked. The Youli are in disarray. Earth Force has led several successful attacks against their outposts in the past few months."

"What's the not-so-short answer?" Marco asks.

"The Youli have been peacekeepers of the galaxy since long before Earth sent humans to space. Legend has it that a great war nearly destroyed their civilization, and they've rebuilt themselves according to certain principles that now govern much of the galaxy."

"Well, then they must be pretty rotten principles," Marco says.

"Quite the contrary, actually. Your former pod leader risked his career—his very life—to make others understand that." Gedney stands and walks to the door of the pod room. "But things are changing. Earth Force has managed to drive a wedge into the Youli ranks, a wedge that has cut even deeper thanks to the degradation patch. The Youli no longer see with one mind. There is division, and there are those who seek to stray from the Youli's guiding principles."

"I have a few questions," Cole says.

"I suspect you do, Mr. Thompson, but I'm all out of answers for tonight. You'd best be getting to the dormitory. Tomorrow will be a long day."

"Seriously?" Marco says. "You can't just tell us all that stuff about the Youli and then wave us out of here."

"What did the admiral say when you asked about the Youli?" Gedney asks.

"That it was above our security clearance," Cole replies.

Gedney smiles. "Then, it seems I've said too much already."

"Gedney," I ask, "if you were to talk to Mr. Waters, do you think he'd be okay?"

His smile fades. "I won't lie. It's a very dangerous time in the galaxy. Soon you kids might again be in the line of fire. But if there's one person working to prevent that, it's Jon Waters. In that respect he's very much okay. He's made mistakes, I don't deny it. If I were to talk to him, though, I know he'd say that he cares about you very much."

He lets his words sink in before adding, "Now run along! I'll see you soon on Alkalinia. You'll need to help me teach the new cadets how to use their bounding gloves."

When we arrive at the dormitory, I quickly realize we've miscalculated. While we got to have our little adventure, we completely missed out on bunk selection. Belongings are stacked on each bunk. I can't even spy a free spot.

The cadets form a line between the bunks and the center table. Ridders stands in front, while two lower-ranking officers walk the length of the line.

As soon as we enter, Ridders points at the door and marches toward us. "Hallway. Now."

We backpedal into the hall and out of earshot of the other cadets.

"Where have you been?" Ridders shouts. "We're in there counting the line, trying to determine who's unaccounted for. I should have known it was you three."

Marco lifts his hands. "We were with Gedney in our pod room, prepping for our advance mission to Alkalinia."

Ridders raises an eyebrow. "I wasn't told that a visit to your pod room was part of the prep."

Marco's such a great liar, he doesn't even blink under Ridders's cold stare. And his story is just plausible enough to make Ridders doubt himself.

"Very well," Ridders says, "grab a bunk. There should be three left. But I'll warn you, it's slim pickings."

We dart inside, calling a jumble of "Yes, sirs" over our shoulders.

I end up in a middle bunk, sandwiched between juniors—the top is occupied by a guy from Africa who has barely said a word, and the bottom was claimed by Desmond, the kid we met earlier. He won't shut up about Earth Force regulations.

He talks at me from the moment I arrive at the bunk until Ridders returns for lights-out. Good thing I'm here only one night before leaving for Alkalinia, or this bunk-selection debacle would be a major problem.

I wait until thirty minutes after lights-out and slide off my bunk. When my feet hit the floor, Desmond shifts in his bed. I'm worried he's about to start talking again or bust me for sneaking out (which definitely violates Earth Force regulations), but he flips over and starts snoring. I slip across the floor and out the door into the hallway.

The trip to the sensory gym is smooth. I have to duck into a spare room only once, when I nearly turn a corner into Captain Edgar Han and a group of officers leaving the mess hall. I make it to the gym with a few minutes to spare.

The room is dark. I can just see the outline of the ball pit and row of trampolines. I take off my shoes and let my feet sink into the cushioned floor. Then I cross to the closest trampoline and hoist myself up.

Bounce. Bounce. Bounce. I close my eyes, push off with my feet, and leap into the ball pit. In the millisecond before my body hits the beads, I feel like I'm flying. I haven't felt that way in months. I've missed it. I can't wait until I'm reunited with my blast pack, and more importantly, my gloves.

Mira presses against my brain. *Coming.*

Then seconds later, "Jasper!"

"Shhh! Over here."

Mira leads my sister across the gym to the trampolines. I climb out of the ball pit.

Addy greets me with a big hug. "That was fun in a *Let's break the rules on day one* kind of way. You know I'm always up for that."

"Did you run into anyone?" I ask Mira. Her blond hair seems to glow in the faint light of the room.

No. She follows this up with notes from a familiar song and walks toward the piano room, leaving us alone.

Thank you for bringing my sister, I tell her.

Mira lifts a hand in the air and twirls her fingers.

"Wait a second," Addy says, looking from me to Mira and back again. "Are you two communicating?"

Of course Addy would pick up on that immediately. It took my pod mates a whole tour of duty, but my sister knows me better than anyone.

"It's complicated," I say. "And confidential like everything else. But yes, we were communicating. You have to keep it between us, Addy."

"I don't understand. Is it telepathy?"

"Not really. I mean, Mira and I definitely have a connection that makes it easier to communicate—kind of like you and me, actually—"

"Eww! Gross! Don't say that! It's nothing like you and me!"

Here we go with the girlfriend talk. "I didn't mean it that way, Ads. I just mean we're pretty in tune with each other. Anyhow, Mira and I can communicate because we have Youli skin patches implanted in our brain stems."

Addy steps back. "What? You're kidding, right?"

"No. It's a long story, and we don't have much time."

She lowers her voice. "Are they going to do that to me?"

"No, Mira and I are the only ones."

Addy paces the length of the trampolines. "Look, J, I'll admit it. I'm kind of freaked. Everything you told me is sinking in now. I saw those gunner ships when we arrived at the space station. And now you're telling me you have alien cells implanted in your brain! I get it. This is real." She takes a deep breath and slowly exhales. "I'm really glad you're with me."

"Well, that's the thing." I grab Addy's hand as she paces by. "I'm leaving tomorrow morning. My pod is part of a diplomatic mission to Alkalinia."

Addy pulls away and puts her hands on her hips. "What on earth is Alkalinia? I'm starting to think there's a lot you didn't tell me."

"That's not fair. I told you the big stuff. Listen, you won't be alone. Gedney will be here. I found out tonight that you're assigned to his pod. He's the best teacher here. Plus, the admiral plans to bring the rest of the Academy to Alkalinia for training later in the tour. So we'll see each other soon. But don't tell anyone!"

"More secrets to keep? Come on, Jasper! You're the one who's not being fair!"

I shake my head. "I'm not worried about fairness, Addy. I'm trying to keep you safe."

The notes of a song drift into the sensory gym. It starts quiet and builds, like a lullaby swept up in a thunderstorm. I sink down on the edge of the ball pit and close my eyes, imagining my clarinet is in my hands.

A moment later Addy sits beside me. "Is this how you first communicated with Mira? Through music?"

I nod.

"I'm sorry I said those mean things about her earlier," she whispers. "Mira's different, but that's okay. I've lived my whole life feeling different, although I've tried pretty hard to hide it."

"Yeah, Mom made sure of that." I circle my arm around Addy's back, and she tips her head against my shoulder. Our breath rises and falls together in time to Mira's music. I remember the night before I first left for the Academy, when Addy sneaked into my room with her rosewood violin. Right now I know Addy is reliving the moment, too. In the room down the hall, Mira hovers on the edge of our shared memory—not intruding, simply observing.

"I never really give you credit as a big brother," Addy says when the song ends. "You know, the kind that's supposed to take care of you."

"We take care of each other," I say.

"Yeah," she says, "but you need to know you're pretty great."

"Thanks. You're pretty great, too, even if you don't always follow my brotherly advice."

My eyes are closed, but I know Addy is smiling. I also know that just behind her smile, anger and fear are lurking.

When I open my eyes, Mira is standing in front of us.

Time to go.

"YOU SURE YOU CONFIRMED THE MAPPING?"
Bad Breath says with a shaky voice.

"You've already asked five times," Captain Edgar Han responds. He's trying to finish the prep sequence so we can bound to our rendezvous with the Alks, and Bad Breath keeps interrupting with questions.

"Recalibrated for the extra passengers?" Bad Breath's face is glossy white. I can hear him breathing from the other side of the bounding ship.

"Triple-checked." Han's impatience is obvious.

"What about the bound coordinates?"

"Take a deep breath, Wade," Han says.

"Don't tell me what to—"

"Quiet!" Admiral Eames says. "Captain Han, proceed with the bound."

Geez. Bad Breath is freaked. No wonder he wasn't promoted to captain. If he can barely keep it together as a passenger in a bounding ship, there's no way the Force would want him piloting one.

Once the gear check is complete, Han counts down the launch. "Three . . . two . . . one . . . bound."

Slammed.

Puffed.

Double stuffed.

"And destination confirmed," Han says.

I exhale.

And Bad Breath barfs.

"Gross!" Lucy shouts as the smell of vomit fills the now extra-claustrophobic bounding ship.

"Really, Wade?" Han says. "You're cleaning this up!"

He pukes again.

"Get that hatch open," the admiral says. "Now!"

Being on a bounding ship with Admiral Eames is surreal to begin with. Being on a bounding ship with the admiral and a barfing Bad Breath is so strange I have to bite my lips to keep from laughing.

The admiral is in no mood for a laugh attack. Plans with the

Alks are already off to a rough start. From what we can gather, since the moment the oath ceremony ended last night, the admiral has been arguing with Seelok, the Alkalinian regent, about how we'll get to the planet. Despite a prior agreement, Seelok refused to provide bound coordinates. Apparently, the exact location of their settlement is still a secret.

Early this morning the admiral gave in to Seelok's demands. She agreed to meet up with the Alks at a bounding base. From there our pod will travel with Bad Breath on board an Alkalinian vessel to their planet. The admiral is along for the ride to rendezvous, because she wants to have words with Seelok.

We unload from the bounding ship and head into the base. Our pod is directed to a small dining hall to wait for the Alkalinian vessel. You'd think I wouldn't have much of an appetite after watching Bad Breath barf, but I'm starving.

"I can't believe he puked," Lucy says as we find a table. "It's going to take him ages to clean it all up."

"I can't believe Admiral Eames came with us," Cole says. "I wish I'd had a chance to talk with her about the recent mapping of quadrant 516."

"Do you think we can get something to eat?" I ask.

"Are you kidding me?" Lucy says. "I can't even think about food without feeling nauseous."

"Never seen anyone puke before, Drama Queen?" Marco asks.

"Shut up, Marco." Lucy pokes Marco in the ribs. He slaps her away.

I ignore them. This is probably our last chance to eat real food before we're in the land of reptilian nastiness. I head over to the serving line and ask the cook for a few scoops of the fried potatoes, which have probably been roasting under the heat lamp since yesterday. They look and smell a thousand times better than the slimy tofu dogs next to them that are rolling on a silver warmer like miniature logs on a river.

I pump ketchup onto my tray and return to the table. As soon as I sit down, Marco grabs a handful of my taters.

"Get your own," I say.

"Yours taste better," he says.

I don't argue. I share my taters with the table and go back for seconds. When we're on our third plate, Bad Breath walks in. His face is green, and he's got a huge wet spot on his shirt, probably from washing off the barf.

"Let's go!" he barks at us.

When we don't move instantly, he shoves my shoulder. I pitch forward, and my nose almost lands in the dollop of ketchup.

This trip is going to be delightful. Just delightful. At least I have a full belly. For now.

When we return to the flight deck, the Alkalinian craft is docked. Our duffels are stacked in a pile near the loading ramp. Captain Han informs us that the admiral is still on board talking with the Alks. Bad Breath runs back inside the base. I bet he has to puke again.

A minute later the admiral exits the craft and greets us on the flight deck.

"You'll be departing momentarily," she says. "I can't understate the importance of this alliance. I'm counting on you kids to be excellent ambassadors for Earth Force. Understood?"

"Yes, sir," we say together.

"Good. You must use the utmost caution. Be prepared for questioning. I suspect they'll interrogate you."

Lucy shoots me a glance. Interrogate us? That doesn't sound like something allies do.

"And carry your gloves with you at all times," the admiral continues. "In the event of an emergency, get yourselves outside the range of the occludium tether and bound back to the space station. Although, I must stress that's an absolute last resort. We mustn't do anything to jeopardize relations with the Alkalinians. Are we clear?"

I nod and pull the straps of my blast pack tight around my shoulders. Just this morning they distributed our gloves and packs as we stowed our belongings for the mission. My gloves are now safely zipped inside the side pockets.

"What about Officer Johnson?" Lucy asks.

Admiral Eames tips her head, signaling she didn't

consider this weakness in her emergency evacuation plan. Bad Breath can't bound. She finally says, "Officer Johnson can take care of himself. Now, if all goes as planned, I will escort the other cadets to Alkalinia later in the tour. Until then, best of luck, cadets."

We salute the admiral before turning our attention to the Alk vessel and a very scary mission. At the door of the craft, two reptilian aliens hover on flying thrones covered in crimson velvet with gold tassel trim. Their black, scaly skin shines under the lights of the flight deck, and their tapered tails wave behind them in lazy S shapes. As much as they look like snakes, their heads remind me more of the dragons that lived in the scary bedtime stories Dad read to Addy and me when we were little. They have large ebony eyes and enormous mouths that jut forward, with silver hooked teeth on the sides that hang beneath their lips even when their mouths are closed. Both of them have a metal cyborg arm like the Alks we saw on Gulaga. They wait for us at the top of the ramp to their ship, ready to escort us to whatever awaits on Alkalinia.

Boarding the Alkalinian ship was extremely anticlimactic. The two Alks led us onto the vessel, pointed at a row of seats, and disappeared with Bad Breath down a back hall. We sat down, strapped in, and waited for whatever came next. A few minutes later the ship departed, and now we're on our way to Alkalinia.

I keep thinking how weird it is that the Alkalinian ship looks just like an Earth Force passenger craft, until I realize it *is* one of our passenger crafts. The Alkalinians must have bought, stolen, or traded for one of our old crafts and then outfitted it for their own purposes. That's why most of the seats have been removed. The Alkalinians can zoom around on their little flying thrones and anchor directly into the floor. They've installed some temporary flight seats for us, but they don't look particularly stable. I hope we don't fly through the cabin when the craft shifts to FTL.

Although, it's kind of a funny image. While we're airborne, we'll look like the Alks on their flying thrones. Once we crash, not so much.

"Jasper!" Lucy leans across Marco and Cole and slaps me on the arm.

"Huh?"

"Oh, nothing, just that I've been trying to get your attention for *five minutes*."

"Try five seconds," Marco says.

She bashes Marco in the arm before asking, "Do you think the admiral knows about the . . ." She stops talking and points to her head.

"About the what?" Cole asks beside me.

Lucy rolls her eyes and points at her head again, then at me and Mira.

"I don't get it," Cole says.

I lean over and whisper in his ear. "Brain patches."

"Oh, your brain patches!" Cole says. "Why didn't you just say so?"

Lucy throws up her hands.

Marco shakes his head. "I'm changing your nickname, Wiki. From now on it's Clueless."

"Don't call me that."

"For goodness' sake," Lucy interjects. "Can you shut up and let Jasper answer!"

The admiral knows. Mira sounds confident.

I'm not sure. Probably. But why hasn't the admiral said anything about the patches? And if she knows, who else does?

"I definitely hinted at it before the Youli attacked the Gulagan space dock when I was trying to warn her. And I'm sure she gave Gedney the third degree."

"She must know," Lucy says. "That means she's free to use the patches to her advantage. So watch out."

The craft grumbles and then jerks forward. We made the shift to FTL. Fortunately, our seats are still anchored to the floor.

"It also means that Waters is on the outs for good," Marco says. "Eames would never let him come back after that breach of trust, especially since those patches led the Youli to our doorstep."

"Waters couldn't have known that would happen," I say, even as the knife of guilt twists in my gut. I'm not sure why I'm coming to his defense.

Not our fault!

Even Mira can't convince me we're not to blame.

"True," Marco says. "But facts are facts. I hope Waters stays holed up on Gulaga with his buddy Barrick and the rest of the rebels. He can do a lot more good from there than locked up in an Earth Force cell somewhere."

Is that what the admiral would do? Lock Waters up in a cell like the one that held the alien prisoner at the space station during our first tour? I wonder if that guy is still there? It didn't even occur to me when we were at the space station yesterday. I've been thinking of Barrick and the Gulagan rebels, though, ever since Addy shared stories with me about the protests on Earth. Something about them feels connected.

Lucy clears her throat in a way that can only mean there's someone behind me. I turn, expecting to be bowled over by a whiff of Bad Breath's bad breath (even worse now that it's laced with vomit). Instead I'm face-to-face with an Alk.

"Greetingsss," he hisses. "Are your sss-seatsss sss-satisss-factory?" His minithrone is purple with gold fringe. The bottom half of his body is coiled on the plump seat. His silver-black skin glistens under the lights. He hovers beside us, kicking up the air current, so there's a slight breeze.

"Totally satisfactory," Marco says. I can tell he's trying to get rid of the guy quick so we can get back to our conversation.

"Exsss-ellent," the Alk says, waving his shiny cyborg arm. His eyes are like black marbles. When he blinks, his eyelids close from the sides. "Now that we are sss-speeding along, you may sss-stand. But firssst, let me introdussse my-ssself." He crosses his metal arm in front and bows his head. "I am Sss-steve."

"Did you say 'Steve'?" Lucy asks.

The Alk nods. We exchange glances. Lucy giggles. I press a hand to my mouth to keep from laughing.

"Is there a problem?" Steve asks.

"No problem, Steve," Marco says, bringing on a new round of laughter.

"Exsss-ellent. I sss-shall be your esss-cort. Pleassse follow me."

We unbuckle from our harnesses, grab our packs, and follow Steve through the craft. Now that we're moving around, it's clear this is an old Earth Force vessel. The layout is identical to the ones we rode during our first tour.

Steve glides in front of us and navigates to the back of the craft. We pass a room filled with minithrones plugged into the wall.

"Do you always use those?" Cole asks.

Steve hisses in a way that says he has no idea what Cole is talking about.

"Those," Marco says, pointing at the thrones. "The flying air chairs, sky rides, butt lifters, whatever you want to call them."

"Not when we sss-swim."

Swim? *Eek.* I would not want to run into an Alk in the water.

We continue down the hall. We pass a room with a low table surrounded by Alks coiled on round cushions. The Alk at the center hisses and clicks. I'm pretty sure that's Seelok. I slow, and my eyes lock with his. Then he points his cyborg arm at the door, and a partition slides into place, shielding them from view.

The rest of my pod continued on. I jog to catch them.

Steve hovers in front of an open room. "Pleassse come in. Take a sss-seat."

A large, low table dominates the room. There are wires and headsets spread around its surface.

"What are we doing here?" Lucy asks as we slowly shuffle into the room.

"Time for quesss-tionsss," Steve says, closing the door behind us.

Cole glances up at me. So it begins. Just as the admiral

predicted. They're going to interrogate us and try to extract Earth Force secrets. What if we don't tell them anything? What will they do with their cyborg arms then?

"Excuse me, Steve," Lucy says. "Where is Officer Johnson?"

Good question. We need someone to get us out of this mess, and isn't that exactly what Bad Breath's job is? Although, the fact that we're looking to Bad Breath to rescue us says a lot about the safety of this whole mission.

"The offi-ssser is resss-ting. He was feeling sss-sick."

"Maybe he's feeling better now," Lucy says. "Can you check? Or send me. I'll go get him."

"There is no need. Have a sss-seat." He gestures with his metal arm to the chairs around the table. They're just like the ones in the main passenger bay, with harnesses and recline buttons. As soon as we're seated, Steve anchors his throne to the floor. With a wave of his wrist, the top of his cyborg arm morphs into a screen. He studies the image and hisses to himself.

"Jasss-per Adamsss, we'll sss-start with you. Pleassse put on the head-ssset."

I have to be the guinea pig? My breath catches in the back of my throat. Everyone's staring at me. How long can I stall before Steve gets mad? I glance at Marco. He nods. Why can't he be first?

I select a headset from the pile on the table. It's silver with lots of sensors and fits over my head like a beanie cap. Once I put it on, Steve waves his arm, and the cap buzzes. I jerk, expecting my brain to feel the buzz. But it doesn't, and when the buzzing stops, Steve clicks contentedly.

"What is your favorite food?" he asks.

"Huh?"

"Your favorite food." His slick tail waves in the air behind him as he flicks his arm and pulls up the screen again. "Our recordsss sss-say sss-some of your planet'sss favoritesss are pizza, tacosss, and meat loaf."

Why is he asking me this? And who would say their favorite food is meat loaf? I look at Lucy. She shrugs.

I may as well answer. Maybe he'll go easy on me if I cooperate. "I guess my favorites are spaghetti, garlic bread, and chocolate chip cookies." As soon as I answer, the headset buzzes. The buzz starts broad and then seems to zero in on a particular point on my skull.

"Would that be sss-spaghetti bolognessse, sss-spaghetti carbonara, or sss-spaghetti marinara?"

Why on earth is he asking me this? "You really need to know that? I think my mom makes meat sauce."

Buzz.

"Sss-so, sss-spaghetti bolognessse? Exsss-ellent."

He asks me a dozen more questions about food, then moves on to Cole. An hour later he's got a tablet full of favorite menus. And I'm starving. It definitely doesn't help to think about all these awesome Earth foods right before landing on an alien planet where they'll probably serve you barely edible awfulness. I didn't think anything could be worse than Gulaga, but I bet the Alkalinians will try.

Next he asks us about favorite activities, then places, then sports teams, then hobbies. Every time I respond to Steve's questions, the helmet buzzes. It feels like it's digging deeper into my brain, using my answers as guideposts to mine for more details. The questions never end. It's like he's preparing a special dossier on each of us for the dating show Mom and Addy sometimes watch on the webs during their monthly girl-bonding nights.

When it's Mira's turn, Lucy tells Steve that she doesn't talk. He asks her to put the headset on anyway, and the rest of us tell him what we know about Mira's favorites. When we answer, the headset Mira's wearing buzzes. Luckily, no one is stupid enough to suggest I translate for Mira brain-to-brain. We definitely want to keep our brain patches secret from the Alkalinians. I just hope they don't already know.

Finally, after we've been at it for hours, Steve deactivates his screen, and it disappears inside his arm. He disengages his anchor, and his throne lifts off, hovering just above our low table.

"You may return to your sss-seatsss. We sss-should be at the planet sss-shortly."

We all practically leap from the table and run from the

room. When we get back to the passenger bay, Lucy huddles us up. "What was *that* about? I was sure we were about to be questioned about all our Earth Force secrets."

"No joke," Marco says. "Favorite foods? Sports teams? I don't get it. You got any ideas, Wiki?"

"Not really, but I'm fascinated by their cyborg limbs. As far as I know, Earth has nothing like that morphing metal technology."

"All I know is I'm starving," I say. "I've been thinking about my mom's spaghetti since his first question."

"You're always starving," Lucy says as we buckle into our harnesses.

Mira reaches into her blast pack, withdraws a cup with a napkin stuffed inside, and hands the cup to me.

Plucking off the napkin, I see that the cup is filled with taters from the mess hall at the base. She brought these for me? My cheeks grow warm.

"Thanks," I say to Mira as I toss a cold, mushy tater into my mouth. It's delicious.

You're welcome. She darts her eyes up at mine, then quickly looks away.

Twenty minutes later a buzzer sounds in the bay, alerting us to the shift out of FTL.

"Well, Bounders, this is it," Marco says. "Prepare to descend to the snake den."

"Can we try to have a tad more optimism?" Lucy says.

"Go for it, DQ. I'm just trying to be realistic."

Seconds later Bad Breath appears. He staggers down the aisle, grabbing hold of the chairs for balance, and slides into an empty seat. His face is still green, and he reeks of vomit. Once he's strapped in, he fixes his eyes on me.

"What are you looking at, B-wad?"

My brain tingles, and I'm filled with a feeling of restraint, like a cowboy just looped me with a lasso. I know it's Mira's way of telling me to stay quiet. I bite my lip.

"I'm talking to you, plebe," Bad Breath grumbles.

Lucy leans over me and asks in a sunshine voice, "Are you feeling better, Officer Johnson?"

He makes a face. "Shut up." He shifts in his seat and turns away from us. I guess he's not feeling well enough to go into attack mode. Although that's good for now, it doesn't bode well for the mission. As soon as Bad Breath is on firm footing, his mean streak will kick in full force.

Marco is right. It's best to be realistic about our trip to Alkalinia. Bad Breath couldn't care less about us, and our reptilian allies are probably up to something sinister. Like Admiral Eames said, now is the time for utmost caution. Sorry, Lucy, but optimism isn't going to keep us safe.

WHEN WE SLAM OUT OF FTL, I SNEAK A
glance at Bad Breath, sure he'll be reaching for a barf bag, but
it looks like he survived the shift with his stomach intact.

Cole jabs me in the ribs. "Are you seeing this?"

A gray planet is visible out the front window. That must
be Alkalinia. Unlike Earth, the Paleo Planet, or even Gulaga,
there are few contrasts in color. It looks like one of the dull
coins my grandmother had in her collection.

"Not the prettiest," Lucy says.

"But home sweet home for now," Marco says.

The craft descends into the atmosphere through a thick,
turbulent layer of high clouds. When we emerge on the other

side, the surface of the planet spreads beneath us, still just as gray and monotonous as before.

"Where are the cities?" I ask. "I don't even see any buildings."

"I think . . . ," Cole starts, pushing up in his chair for a better view. "Yes, definitely. That's water."

I loosen my harness and climb onto my knees for a better view. So that's why it looks so gray. The surface is entirely covered by water.

The craft continues its descent.

"Where are they taking us?" Lucy asks as we angle for the water.

"Look!" Cole points ahead. "Over there! And there!"

Narrow sensor towers jut from the water. They have rotating blades and shiny disks on top. Near the towers, long stretches of panels float like giant life rafts. "What are those?" I ask. "Is that where we're going to land?"

"I don't think so," Cole says. "Those must be some kind of solar panels."

The craft glides even lower, so low that the Alks must be setting up for a water landing, even though that makes zero sense. There's nothing in sight other than the sensors and panels.

Then there's a disturbance on the surface. A large funnel twists out of the depths, spilling waves away in a whirlpool as it rises. The craft flies past the funnel, curves up in an arc, then tips and dives directly into the funnel's mouth.

"Whoa!" I grab hold of the armrests and quickly tighten my harness. Mira places her palm on top of mine. She digs her nails into my skin. Across the aisle, Bad Breath mutters a string of swear words all smashed together.

Pink air streams from vents and fills the funnel. Once the craft is completely inside, we start to slow and eventually come to a complete stop. It's like we're hanging halfway upside down in a pink cloud.

"Fascinating." Cole's voice is filled with intrigue but holds no trace of the panic that courses through me. Somehow this situation must be in the range of possible variables that Cole equated when he found out we were traveling to Alkalinia.

"What's so flippin' fascinating, Wiki?" Marco asks. Even he sounds stressed.

"Using air to halt and cushion an airborne object for a vertical landing in a siphon port. I've read about it but never seen it done in practice."

Although I can't see anything but pink smoke outside the windows, I can tell that we're moving again. The craft shifts so that we're no longer vertical. When we're level with the surface, the pink smoke fades and the world outside the craft comes into focus.

The ship is inside some sort of huge, clear bubble deep

under the ocean. Outside the bubble, hundreds of meters below, the Alkalinian settlement spreads before us. Dozens of structures stretch across the ocean floor, interconnected by clear tubes. Most of the structures are dome shaped and windowless. A long tube extends away from the settlement. It's hard to see much detail from this far away, but it looks like it dead-ends at a huge silver disk anchored to the seabed.

"What's that?" Lucy asks, pointing at the disk.

"It looks like a spaceship," Cole says, "but it must be part of their settlement, the new Alkalinia."

My stomach seizes, and the taters from earlier threaten to make a reappearance. I sink back in my chair and bow my head between my legs. I can't pull a Bad Breath.

Okay? Mira places her hand on my shoulder.

"I don't get it," I whisper, slowly pushing myself up as the nausea passes. "Gedney tells us all that stuff about the Alks leaving their planet, and he doesn't think to mention that their new home is underwater?"

"Maybe he didn't know, Ace," Marco says. "Just pretend you're a fish and you'll be fine."

The craft rocks, nearly sending my pod mates to the floor. They sit down as the craft starts to lower. Soon we're no longer in the clear bubble. We pass into a walled zone and then descend into a domed chamber with bright lights.

Once we touch down, the craft is surrounded by an army

of machines. They must use the same technology as the Alks' flying thrones, because they hover around the craft like annoying metal insects. Some of them whip out enormous windshield wiper blades. One of them zooms in front of the window, squirts purple liquid onto the glass, and swipes it clean with the blade. Other slaps echo on all sides. The whole craft must be getting a wipe-down.

"What's going on?" Lucy asks.

"I believe it's a decontamination protocol," Cole replies.

Decontamination from what? I wonder, even though I'm not sure I want to know.

Once the machines complete their work, they fly to the edge of the chamber and plug themselves into the wall. Doors unfold on the far side of the room, and a group of Alkalinians coast in. They don't look exactly like the Alks we've met so far. Where Seelok, Steve, and the other officers have a single cyborg arm, these Alks have three small lizardlike arms on each side of their bodies, close to their heads. And instead of using ornate flying thrones, they ride on souped-up scooters loaded with mechanical contraptions. They cross the chamber floor and form a line in front of our craft.

"Did I mention how much I hate snakes?" Marco asks.

"More than once," Lucy says. She stands on her tiptoes and hisses in Marco's ear.

He slaps her away.

Steve zooms in on his throne. "Greetingsss, Offi-ssser John-ssson!" he says to Bad Breath. "I trussst you are feeling better."

Bad Breath grumbles something in Steve's direction.

"Exsss-ellent! Welcome, all of you, to the Alkalinian Sss-seat!"

"The Alkalinian what?" Lucy asks.

"Sss-seat. The sss-senter of our government and sss-sivilization." Steve steers his chair to the front of the passenger area. "Pleassse sss-stay in your sss-seatsss. We will be exiting the sss-ship into the sss-siphon port sss-shortly. The esss-teemed Regent Sss-seelok and hisss guardsss will disss-embark firssst."

There's a commotion in the front of the craft as Seelok and his entourage descend. As soon as his throne clears the ramp, all of the Alks in the siphon port bow their heads and wave their scaly tails. Seelok keeps them in this deferential pose for a solid minute before waving them up with his cyborg arm. Seconds later two scooters glide to his side and escort him from the port.

When the other Alks have left the craft, Steve instructs us to follow him. We grab our blast packs and follow Steve through the passenger cabin.

Bad Breath shoves Cole out of the way so that he's first in line. He turns on us once Steve disappears around the corner. "Listen up, B-wads! Don't forget who's in charge here. I'm running this mission, and you losers fall in line. Got it?"

I brace for Marco's predictable comeback, but none comes.

Once Bad Breath spins back around and heads for the exit, Marco whispers, "I don't have the energy to battle him every time he opens his mouth. Hopefully, we can manage to ditch him soon."

We head down the ramp and onto the floor of the siphon port, where Steve is waiting for us. "Thisss way, pleassse."

We follow him across the port, a few steps behind Bad Breath. When we're almost at the corridor where the other Alks exited, two scooter dudes race in to meet us.

Steve and the two Alks hiss and click. Then Steve turns to Bad Breath. "Offi-ssser John-ssson, my compatriotsss have arrived to esss-cort you."

Bad Breath shifts, and a confused look crosses his face. "I'm chaperoning this group. We should stay together."

Steve circles him with his throne. "But that doesss-n't sss-suit an offi-ssser of your sss-stature. You de-ssserve sss-special quar-tersss. *Offi-ssser* quartersss. You will be reunited with your chargesss for working hoursss."

Bad Breath considers this. "Of course, you're absolutely right." He turns to us. "No misbehavior. I'll know. I always know." And with that, the scooter Alks rush him out of the siphon port.

It turns out ditching Bad Breath was far easier than expected. He essentially ditched himself with the help of Steve stroking his ego. Maybe we should be worried about that, but for now I'm just happy not to have Bad Breath around.

Steve leads us into one of the long, clear connecting tubes we saw from the craft. The floor, walls, and ceiling join in a perfect circle. It makes walking a bit of a challenge. I suppose it doesn't matter for the Alks, since they don't walk.

The ocean is everywhere I look. Above, beside, below. My head throbs. I keep my eyes on my shoes. I don't want to trip on the curved floor, and I can't bear to look out at all that water. I can't believe we're staying in an underwater city.

Why do we have to be in the ocean? First Gulaga with its subterranean metropolis and now this? Can't we just be stationed on a planet with a nice surface city for once?

Outside the tube, some of the sea structures bob in the current, and others are anchored to the ocean floor. Large domes and cylinders are connected by tubes like the one we're in. The whole complex looks to be a bit larger than the space station. So while it's not small, it doesn't look like much of an alien civilization, either.

"Is all of Alkalinia underwater?" Lucy asks.

"It is now," Steve replies.

What does he mean, "it is now"? What was it like before?

"I'm sss-sure you'll find the Alkalinian Sss-seat to be very comfortable," he continues.

We wind from one clear tube, through a domed structure,

into another clear tube, seeing no one. The place is basically the opposite of the bustling metropolis of Gulagaven. It kind of gives me the creeps.

Eventually we enter a huge domed structure and make our way to a long interior hall with rows of doors on either side. We follow Steve to the last door on the left.

"Thessse are your quartersss," Steve says, inserting his cyborg arm into a slot on the frame. The door slides open. "I am sss-sure you will be quite comfortable. Sss-see you in the morning."

Steve waves us in. The door slides closed and clicks.

Marco tries the handle and shakes his head.

"Did Steve just leave us here?" Lucy asks. "What's going on?"

"We're locked in, that's what," I say.

"Check this out," Cole says.

Mira touches my arm.

I turn around and take in my surroundings. We're standing in an empty room with squishy orange floors, orange walls, and an orange ceiling. The air has the faint smell of canta-loupe.

"This place reminds me of—" Lucy starts.

"The Youli ship!" I shout. "It was made of this squishy orange stuff, too!"

"I don't get it," she says. "Nothing else on Alkalinia looks like this."

"Nor does it meet the minimum requirements for guest quarters," Cole says.

A buzzer sounds, followed by hisses and clicks, then there's a translation: "Presss organic material againssst the wall to activate."

Lucy lifts her eyebrows in a quizzical fashion. I shrug.

"Organic material?" Marco asks. He raises his hand, looking at it for a second before saying, "Here goes nothing," and pressing his palm against the wall.

Instantly the room transforms. We're no longer standing in a room filled with orange mush; we're in a lounge filled with recliners and big screens blaring reruns of classic futbol matches from across Earth.

"What just happened?" I ask.

"This is awesome!" Marco shouts.

"Yeah, it's like we bounded directly to Marco's man cave," Lucy says.

"You betcha, sister."

"Don't you 'sister' me," she says, slamming her hand against the wall.

The room shifts. Not all the Marco macho evaporates, but it definitely tones down. Half the screens are playing classic films. And it's hard to miss the fancy pink pouf chair in the corner.

"That has my name on it!" Lucy says.

Mira places her hand on the wall, and a gorgeous Steinway piano materializes in a corner of the room. Once Cole and I add our bio signatures, there's a whole corner dedicated to *Evolution of Combat* with special gaming chairs and an extra-large sync-up module.

"This is awesome!" I wave Cole over and initiate a joust match.

"I am never leaving," Marco says, leaning back in his recliner and flipping through channels.

Mira plays a familiar chord on the piano, and then her fingers are running across the keys. She plays at just the right volume to entertain but not overpower the *Evolution* sound system.

"If only I had some good game grub, this would be perfect," Marco says.

As if on cue, a small tub rises up from the ground next to Marco's recliner. It's filled with sodas and juices. Beneath the row of mounted screens, a counter extends from the wall, topped with serving dishes. The familiar smell of freshly baked chocolate chip cookies reaches my nose and lures me over.

I chase the smell to the counter and discover the oddest assortment of amazing foods. There's a huge bowl of spaghetti and a basket of garlic bread. Next to those are a platter of buffalo wings and a tall glass cylinder filled with gummy bears. A bowl of strawberries sits next to a large ham-and-pineapple pizza. A tray of tacos rests behind a carving board topped with a thick steak. At the end of the counter is an enormous chocolate cake and a plate of fresh-from-the-oven cookies.

Marco grabs one of the wings and takes a bite. "It's good. Different. Something tastes a tiny bit off, but it sure beats anything they serve at the mess hall." He tosses a handful of gummy bears into his mouth before grabbing another wing.

I snag a cookie. It's still warm. I break it in half, watching the chocolate chips slink apart in their meltiness. I take a giant bite, and my whole body tingles.

If this isn't heaven, it's close. Maybe Alkalinia won't be half as bad as I imagined.

Cole carves a piece of steak and slips it onto his plate next to a slice of pizza.

"Hold on just a minute," Lucy says, with her hands on her hips. "Doesn't anyone notice anything weird about this?"

Mira gestures to the plate of cookies, then to my mouth.

"Go ahead, have one!" I say to her in between bites.

It's what you wanted!

"Of course it's what I wanted!"

"I hate it when you two use your brain patches," Lucy says, "but that's exactly it! These are the foods we told Steve about! Every last one of them!"

Cole, Marco, and I take a step back and assess the spread. There's no way around it. Lucy is right.

"So?" Marco asks. "They want us to feel at home. Guess what? I do! At least, this is the closest to home I've felt since leaving Earth." He fills a plate with wings, gummy bears, a taco, and one of my cookies, then returns to his recliner. As soon as he gets settled, he takes a big, crunchy bite of the taco. "I forget who said they like these, but excellent choice."

Lucy looks at me.

"What's the harm, Lucy? We need to eat, right?"

I pile a plate with spaghetti and garlic bread. At the other end of the counter, Mira slices a piece of chocolate cake. She licks some extra frosting from her finger.

Good? I ask.

Amazing.

I think I'll leave room for a piece myself.

I DON'T KNOW HOW LONG WE SPEND EATING (all of us, but especially me and Marco), playing *Evolution* (me and Cole), painting our nails (Lucy and then Mira, although I think Lucy kind of strong-armed her into it), watching web shows (all of us), and playing piano (Mira), but I'm in a half-food, half-video-game coma when the lights darken.

"Ummm . . . why are the lights going out?" Lucy asks. "Wait a second, were those doors always there?"

I pause the aerial-combat obstacle course, happy to have an excuse not to lose to Cole for the thirteenth consecutive time. The perimeter of the room now has five doors, each with one of our names on it.

"Cool!" Marco shouts, running to his door. "Private bedrooms? I thought we were going to be couching it."

As the rest of us get up to check out our rooms, the lights continue to fade.

"Something tells me it's bedtime for Bounders," Lucy says.

"Come to think of it," I say, swallowing a yawn, "I'm exhausted."

Mira touches my arm as we step to our side-by-side doors. *Good night.*

The lights in my bedroom are dim, almost as dim as the lights in the common room, so it's hard for me to see much of my surroundings. I stumble to the bed in the corner and pull back the covers. Almost asleep on my feet, I shrug off my shirt, step out of my uniform, and slide beneath the sheets in my underclothes.

I honestly don't know if I've ever been in a bed quite as comfortable as this. These sheets are so soft. This pillow cradles my head like it was made for me. This . . .

Something clicks in the wall, and my eyes blink open. The room is dark. I'm fading. Hisses. I swear I hear Steve. Steve? I try to say his name out loud, but I can't. Clicks. That's a robot arm. Or is it? It's too dark. It's too bright. Something's not right. No, it's only a dream.

It must be a dream.

· *EF* ·

Sunlight drifts in from the window and tickles the backs of my eyelids.

Sunlight? I thought we were underwater.

I shoot up in bed. My head spins. I must have moved too fast.

This whole place has got to be virtual. The bed, the video games, the food. The sun is definitely virtual. Even if we weren't underwater, there's no way the star in this system gets that kind of light through the cloud layer. Sure enough, out the window a fake sun shines over a fake ocean in a fake sky without a cloud in sight.

I pull back the blanket and grab my clothes from the pile on the floor. They smell like they need to be washed—which they obviously do, since I wore them for the trip from Earth to space and then from the space station to Alkalinia. I wish I'd asked Steve about our duffels. I could really use some clean clothes. Our blast packs were the only things we carried off the craft yesterday.

As I pull on my pants, I look around the room. They really spared no details in creating this virtual haven. On the shelf beside my bed, all my favorite books are neatly stacked, including some I didn't mention to Steve. Pennants from my favorite sports teams cover the walls. There are even some action figures from *Stellar Rangers*, a show I sometimes watch on the webs. I pick up Galaxo, my favorite Ranger, and

MONICA TESLER

swipe his cosmic sword through the air, taking out the other Rangers at the knees.

Right beside my door is my duffel bag. How did that get here? Did the Alks drop them off? How did I forget that?

I'm not sure what to expect when I pull the door handle, but the common room is the same as we left it last night. The only thing missing is the counter piled with food.

Except that it's not. Almost as soon as I have the thought, the counter reappears from the wall. This time it's piled high with breakfast favorites: waffles and syrup, scrambled eggs and a plate of extra-crispy bacon, a mountain of pastries oozing with sweet fruit centers or warm sugar or chocolate. The smell alone nearly sends me into sensory overload.

"What's cooking?" Marco yawns as he stumbles out of his room. He drags himself over to the table and claps his hands. "Ace! We've hit the jackpot! I don't know why we ever doubted our slithering friends. This isn't training. It's vacation! Dig in!"

Why not? I grab a plate of waffles and bacon and one of those flaky pastries topped with icing and cherries. Marco and I plop down in the twin recliners and turn on the screens. One of the best futbol games of all time—Amazonas versus Real Europa for the Clasico Cup—is on.

I go back for seconds, then thirds. At some point I realize

Cole is awake, too. He's sitting in the gaming corner playing *Evolution* and eating pancakes.

Then Mira is next to me, napping on a beanbag on the floor, an empty plate by her side. She looks so peaceful, but she must be exhausted. Dark circles rim the bottoms of her eyes. Lucy is reading a magazine on the pink pouf with a half-eaten pastry on a plate in her lap. Did they just wake up? Or have they been here for a while? The game's still on. Maybe if I close my eyes for a minute . . .

A noise jerks me awake. The counter retracts into the wall. I close my eyes and drift back off. When I open my eyes next, the counter is back, piled with food, and Cole is filling a plate.

Next to me, Marco shifts in his seat. "Chow time already?" He pushes himself up with a groan and drags himself to the table.

I force myself out of the recliner and grab a plate. This spread rivals last night's. There are deep dishes of chicken Parmesan, platters of mozzarella sticks, mashed potatoes, onion rings, pork lo mein, cupcakes, and pumpkin pie.

This place really is a dream come true, especially for space, which has been nothing but one bad food event after another. Okay, so I have this gnawing feeling in the back of my brain that something's not quite right, but things could be much worse. I mean, we could be sitting on the frozen tundra eating BERF.

I fill my plate and climb into the recliner. I eat. We watch futbol. Maybe I take a nap. I eat some more. I think. I'm not sure. Yeah, I definitely went back for another cupcake.

The lights dim.

"Time for bed," Lucy says.

"Already?" I ask. "But we just got up." Didn't we?

"I wonder where Bad Breath is?" Cole says.

Marco yawns. "Off somewhere being a jerk. I'm going to sleep." He hauls himself out of his recliner and lumbers across the common room to his door.

I follow him. My feet feel like lead, and I can barely make it. Geez. This is the worst sugar crash ever.

As I twist the door handle, Mira touches my brain. *Something isn't right.*

For the tiniest of seconds, her words jar me, and I almost stop. But then the curtain falls, and I fear I'll fall asleep standing up if I don't lie down.

Tomorrow, Mira.

The next morning the sunlight streams in. I wake with a major headache, like I fell off the bed in the middle of the night, crashed my skull against the wall, and somehow managed to crawl back into bed. I rub my hand across the base of my neck to check for signs of a bruise.

Nothing.

Well, nothing except the slight bump on my skin where the Youli patch is implanted. I used to run my fingers against it every day, especially when Waters shaved my skin and placed it there, and then every day after, I could feel my hair grow back a little more, just as I learned how to reach Mira more and more.

Mira. One thing I haven't tried since arriving on Alkalinia is brain-talk from a distance. I close my eyes and reach out with my mind.

Mira?

Can you hear me? Mira?

Nothing.

Then my skin prickles at the back of my neck, and from far away I hear a call.

Mira!

Her calls grow louder, more urgent. She needs help.

I squeeze my eyes shut and focus all my energy on our brain connection. My headache shifts and crystallizes as a sharp pain around my patch. I break the connection and press my palm against the back of my head, half convinced my hand will come away covered in blood.

That's not going to work.

We'll have to do this the old-fashioned way. I push myself out of bed, squinting through the fake sunlight, which makes my headache ten times worse, and pull on my pants. I stumble to the door, tumble out, and ignore calls of "Chow time, Ace!" and "Good morning, sleepyhead" as I stagger to Mira's room.

I try the door handle. It's locked. I start pounding. "Mira! Get up!"

"Let her sleep, Jasper!" Lucy shouts.

I ignore her and keep knocking.

I try the door again, worried I'll have to force it open. Shows of brute strength are not my specialty.

But this time the door opens so easily I pour into the room and fall to my knees on her floor. Mira is lying in bed. When I hit the ground, she sits up, alarmed. As soon as she moves, her face twists in pain. She reaches a hand to the back of her neck.

"Are you all right?" I ask.

Mira squeezes her eyes shut and rubs her head. *I think so?*

Her words reach me without setting off a wave of pain like before.

"You were calling for me in your sleep! At least, I think so." I sit down on the edge of her bed, very aware that she's wearing only a T-shirt and shorts, which is basically what I wear every day at home, but I'm used to seeing Mira in uniform. I scoot to the very edge, as far from her as I can get while still sitting on her bed. "I'm not sure what to believe anymore. This place is getting to me. I mean, the food is great, but I kind of think they're messing with us."

Mira still has her hand on her head.

"Yeah, there's that, too. My head is killing me."

Mira takes a deep breath and drops her hand to her lap. When she opens her eyes, I know she's pulled upon her inner strength to push the pain aside.

"What do you think we should do?"

Leave this room.

"I know. Marco said that breakfast is here."

No. Leave this room. The orange room.

And then it really hits me. No matter what we see or taste or feel, none of it is real. We are standing in a mushy orange room in the middle of an ocean on Alkalinia. And we haven't left in almost two days.

"We need to talk to the others," I say.

Mira presses a finger to her lips, then circles it around the room.

Quiet. They're listening.

So it turns out that trying to talk to your pod mates about your suspicions about the Alks is a challenge when you're 99 percent sure the Alks are listening. It's even harder when you're competing for attention with futbol games, fashion magazines, and *Evolution*. With the smell of fresh Belgian waffles and real maple syrup threatening to take me on the fast track to a food coma, I'm almost too distracted to do anything other than sit and eat all day. Just like I've done since we got here.

Mira shakes her head at my failed attempt to get everyone's attention, and takes matters into her own hands. She turns off all the screens and video game consoles and snatches the magazine from Lucy's hands.

"Hey!" Lucy shouts. She holds her hands out to her sides like a chicken so she doesn't smear her wet nail polish. Her hair is piled on top of her head in an elaborate braid secured with hot-pink ribbons.

Marco and Cole also grumble about the interruption, but they reluctantly gather around the center recliners when Mira waves them over.

I clap my hands. "Mira and I were thinking we should explore Alkalinia today."

"Why?" Marco says. "We've got everything we need right here."

"Marco's right," Lucy says. "If they need us for something, they'll come and get us."

"That's just it," I say, lowering my voice. "We've been here for almost two days."

"Has it been that long?" Cole asks. "I didn't notice."

"Doesn't that strike you as odd?" I wave my hand in a circle, trying to get the rest of them to fill in the blanks on their own.

"If you've got something to say, Ace, say it," Marco says.

I shake my head in frustration. The Alks must be listening, and I'd rather not let them know that we're onto them.

Mira reaches for a tablet and jots down some letters. She turns it to our pod mates: *LISTENING*.

"What's that supposed to mean?" Cole asks. "Who's listening?"

"Oh, for earth's sake!" I say.

Mira throws up her arms and spins around the room.

"Ahh!" Lucy says. I can tell from her face that she finally understands. "You're so right. I am starting to feel a bit cooped up in this place. Let's take a stroll."

"Can I play one more level first?" Cole asks. "Another victory and I'll earn triple points in Crusades free-play mode."

"No," Lucy and I say at the same time.

Lucy grabs the tablet from Mira and scribbles something. "Remember, we told the admiral we'd be good guests, and that means asking the Alkalinians to show us around their planet."

She turns the tablet around to reveal what she's written: *MUST FIND OCCLUDIUM TETHER*.

And below those words: *SHHHHH!!!*

As soon as everyone's read what she wrote, she erases the screen.

Marco nods grimly. "Got it."

Fortunately, Cole seems to get the message, too, and doesn't say so out loud.

"Change into uniforms and meet at the door in five minutes," I say. "And Cole, bring that voice box Gedney gave us. You never know when we might need it."

While I wait for my pod mates, I try the door handle. It doesn't budge. We're still locked in.

"So we're trapped?" Lucy asks when she comes out of her bedroom.

"Patience! Patience!" Marco says. "Coming through!" He swapped his futbol jersey for his Earth Force dailies.

"And what exactly do you plan to do to fix this, Mr. Macho?" Lucy asks.

"Step aside, DQ, and let me demonstrate how it's done." Marco grabs the handle and yanks. Nothing. He braces his feet in a lunge position and yanks again. "It's locked."

I throw up my hands as the five of us gather around the door with our blast packs and gloves.

"As if we didn't know that," Lucy says. "Cole? Try your luck at the keypad?"

"I suppose I could."

As soon as Cole starts jabbing at the panel, the door swings open.

Steve stands at the threshold. "Greetingsss!" he hisses. "I hope you had a good sss-sleep."

"A good sleep?" Lucy says. "Try two."

"Exsss-ellent! Nothing like a little exsss-tra ressst to

make you feel sss-sharp for your training sss-schedule."

"Training schedule?" Cole asks.

Was he really about to come get us for training? What are the odds? They must have heard us talking about wanting to leave our quarters. That's reason enough to get out of here. We need to find a place to talk in private.

"Yesss! Right thisss way!"

As we follow Steve out of our room and into the hall, my claustrophobia roars back. The cozy quarters we've been hanging out in for the past two days are fake. We've been holed up in a carbon copy of the mushy orange Youli ship in the middle of a cold gray ocean. What a reality slap to the face!

I wonder if the VR tech came from the Youli? After all, the Alks are using our passenger crafts. What if they acquire all their tech from other species in exchange for secret information or—what else did Gedney say?—illicit substances?

Marco puts out a hand, slowing our pod and letting a gap open between us and Steve. "Jasper and Mira are right, poddies," he whispers. "Things are off. We need to talk."

"How?" I ask. "We can't exactly chat in front of Steve."

"Leave it to me," Lucy says.

I actually have a bit of confidence in Lucy until I hear the words that come out of her mouth. "Hey, Steve! Please take us to see Officer Johnson."

APPARENTLY, STEVE ISN'T TOO CONCERNED about us seeing Bad Breath, because he simply shrugs (or what looks like a shrug where his robot arm attaches to his serpent body) and turns right at the next hallway. A few turns later we find ourselves in front of a door that looks identical to the one for our quarters.

Steve punches in a code and cracks it open. "Greetingsss," he hisses before pushing the door open the rest of the way.

The room looks absolutely nothing like our quarters. In the center is the largest bed I've ever seen. It's crafted of dark mahogany and has crimson satin sheets and drapes hanging from a canopy. Flames roar in a fireplace across from the bed. The mantel above holds a gold-framed portrait of Bad Breath himself. The window opens to a garden with naked stone cherubs spitting water and a hedge in the shape of Bad Breath's profile.

Bad Breath reclines on the bed. He's dressed in shorts and a pink silk robe. A woman stands next to him wearing a tuxedo. She plucks grapes from a bunch and places them one by one in Bad Breath's mouth. Next to her is a sideboard stacked with bottles of wine, platters of cheese, bowls of fruit, and a giant hunk of meat on a carving board.

This place is . . . a little much.

As we make our way into the room, we steal glances at one another. Marco bites his finger to keep from laughing. Mira's sparkly giggles tickle my brain.

Bad Breath slowly processes our arrival. He pushes up in bed. "What on earth are you B-wads doing here?"

"Who's she?" Marco asks, pointing at the grape girl.

Bad Breath looks at the woman as if it's the first time he's seen her. "No idea. Go away!"

I'm not sure if his last words are meant for us or his tuxedoed guest. Either way, she sets the bunch of grapes next to the meat and leaves the room through a door by the fireplace.

"Very nice treatment of women," Lucy says.

"I don't think she's a woman," Cole says. "She's virtual."

Lucy rolls her eyes. "You know what I mean."

Bad Breath grabs a shirt from a pile next to his bed and puts it on. His face is red and getting redder. There's no doubt he's about to freak out on us.

Steve seems to sense that the interaction is not going particularly well. He steers his throne in front of us. "Offi-ssser John-ssson. It is time to sss-start the training. The cadetsss are sss-set. Sss-shall we depart?"

"What training?" Bad Breath asks. "What time is it?"

"Time to go," Marco says. "We've been in here for days!"

Bad Breath tips his head and considers what Marco said. He must think we're trying to trick him. "Speak when spoken to, Romero," he finally says. Then he tells Steve he'll meet him in the corridor in five minutes.

We retreat into the hall to wait. Steve excuses himself, saying he has to check in with the regent and ready the training facilities. We're to wait in the hall until his return.

We're finally alone. I wave over my pod mates, and we huddle near the wall. "What do you think is going on? Why'd they want to keep us in our quarters?"

"I'm not sure," Lucy says, "but they've obviously been spying on us. I'd say we should ask Steve, but we have to assume he's in on it. I really miss Neeka. She was the best junior ambassador ever. And Steve is . . . not."

"Few could really compare to our furry friend," Marco says.

"You loved Neeka, and you know it!" Lucy says.

"It's true! I do miss Neeks! No sarcasm here."

I think about this morning—the pain in my head where the patch is implanted, and the sensation that Mira was screaming for help. What if spying means more than listening in? What if the Alks are actually doing something to us? I don't want to freak anyone out without proof, but I have to stay alert. Like the admiral said, we need to exercise extreme caution.

"What if they're listening to us now?" Cole says, looking up and down the hallway. He pulls his tablet out of his pack and starts paging through screens.

"I guess that's a chance we'll have to take," Lucy says. "Don't forget we have a mission."

"I almost *did* forget," Marco says. "I swear there's something in the food here, even though it won't stop me from eating it."

"We haven't been in our quarters for two days," Cole says, still staring at his tablet.

"Yes, we have," Lucy says. "I distinctly remember going to bed twice."

"I double-checked my time and calendar apps," Cole says. "We've been in our quarters for an entire week."

"What?" Marco and I say at the same time.

Cole flips around his tablet. The screen shows a calendar that highlights the current date, exactly one week since we left the space station.

Mira's mind bristles with confusion and fright.

"How is that possible?" Lucy asks.

"Think about it," Cole says. "It wouldn't be that hard—everything in our quarters is virtual. The Alks completely control our perspective of time: the meals tell us the time of day, the fading light tells us it's time to sleep, the morning sun says it's time to wake up."

"And what seemed to us like two days was really a week?" I ask.

Cole nods.

"Oh my God," Lucy says.

We stare at one another, not sure how to process what we just learned. Something is definitely wrong about this place, but what are we supposed to do about it? Plus, when we wanted out of our room, they let us out, so we're not technically held hostage against our will.

"Well, we made it out of our quarters," I say. "We need to get on with the mission. Who knows how long we have before the Alks start pressuring the admiral to come with the other cadets?" The last thing I want is Addy caught up in this Alkalinian mess.

"Our mission, right," Lucy says. "Any thoughts on how we find the occludium tether?"

"Nope," Marco says.

I shake my head.

None, Mira weighs in.

"Cole?" Lucy asks. "What do you think?"

"I don't have any ideas. From the short look I got at the keypad this morning, it's not something I could hack without setting off alarms."

"That means we need to explore," Marco says. "We have to find the tether as soon as possible. Something fishy is definitely going on here. And I want to know we have a getaway plan."

Seconds later Steve returns, and Bad Breath emerges from his quarters dressed in uniform.

"Thank goodness he put some clothes on," Lucy whispers as Bad Breath talks with Steve. "Although, I'll never be able to unsee that horrible pink robe. Who does he think he is? The star of a cheesy romance novel?"

"I guess we know Bad Breath's secret fantasy," I say.

Steve waves us over with his cyborg arm. "Exsss-ellent. Now that you've sss-settled in, it'sss time for a tour of Alkalinia. Follow me."

Just in case we didn't understand Steve's perfectly under-standable words, Bad Breath snorts, "Fall in line and don't try anything stupid!"

Steve turns his chair and zooms up the hallway with Bad Breath at his side.

Settled in? Is he for real? We've been here a week! What is really going on?

We fall in line behind them and wind through interior halls, one after the next. After the first few corners, I'm completely turned around. It helps my claustrophobia not to be staring at all that water, but it's horrible for my sense of direction, and I still can't shake the feeling that the walls are closing in around us. It reminds me of the space station, except that instead of the vastness of space, it's the Alkalinian sea waiting to crush me under its weight.

"Where are all the . . . uh . . . people?" Lucy whispers.

"You call these snakes people?" Marco asks.

"For lack of a better word."

"No clue," I say.

We follow Steve through the halls until he comes to a stop in front of a door with silver markings branded on the front.

"Boundersss," Steve says, "we have reached the round table of the Alkalinian Sss-seat. Regent Sss-seelok will sss-see you now."

Steve raps on the door with his cyborg arm. The door buzzes open, and he glides through.

We funnel in behind him.

The room is perfectly round and filled with thick smoke that smells like cedar. The walls are lined with heavy, multicolored tapestries, and torches are mounted around the perimeter, casting enormous shadows on the floor and ceiling. In the middle of the chamber is a large, circular table, and a bowl in the center is filled with brilliant gemstones. Around the table are at least twenty Alks hovering in tiny thrones. Flying a meter higher than the rest is Seelok.

"Ahh, cadetsss!" Seelok shouts. His throne thrusts forward, and he flies over the table. "Allow me to formally introdussse my-ssself. I am Sss-seelok, regent of the Alkalinian Sss-seat, repre-sssentative to the Intragalactic Coun-sssil, and friend to your Admiral Eamesss and all of Earth and itsss peoplesss. On behalf of Alkalinia, I welcome you."

Friend? I'm thinking foe.

Beside us, Bad Breath clears his throat.

"Yesss, forgive me," Seelok utters. "Welcome, Offi-ssser Wade John-ssson. I am sss-so very pleasssed that sss-such an esss-teemed and trusssted sss-servant of Admiral Eamesss's would blesss usss with hisss company."

All the Alks in the room, including Steve, raise their robotic arms and hiss. It's terribly scary, but there's no doubt it's a show of respect.

Bad Breath bows his head. "It is my honor, Regent Seelok."

"Offi-ssser John-ssson," Seelok continues, "my comradesss would like to give you the grand tour while the cadetsss conduct their training drillsss."

Bad Breath looks from Seelok to us, then back to Seelok. "Y-y-you want me to go with your men while the Bounders train?" he stutters, like he can't quite process what Seelok is asking. Maybe because he knows the admiral would definitely not approve.

"Exactly," Seelok says. "Caring for children doesss not sss-suit a man of your sss-stature. Don't you agree?"

Bad Breath scrunches up his face like he's trying really hard to think through Seelok's question. His eyes dart from side to side. Then he stands straight, tips up his chin, and puffs out his chest. "Absolutely."

"Exsss-ellent. After, you may wish to retire early to your chambersss."

"Yes, that would be grand," Bad Breath says.

Grand? Really? Seelok is totally manipulating him. I'm sure Bad Breath would *love* to retire to his chambers with the rare roast, grapes, and virtual butler. But isn't chaperoning us the whole reason he's here?

Within moments five of the Alks hurry off with Bad Breath, leaving us behind. The remaining Alks click and hiss and wave their cyborg arms at the same time, which is greatly disturbing and also leads me to question how they can begin to understand one another.

"Cadetsss," Seelok says, "you may return to your quar-tersss."

What? I thought we were supposed to start training. How are we going to find the occludium tether if we're locked up in our room?

"Excuse me, Regent Seelok, sir," Lucy says, "but we need to practice. If we don't get our training in, we'll fall behind the other cadets. It's ever so important."

"It's also what the admiral negotiated," Marco says coldly. "Daily training outside of your occludium tether."

Leave it to Marco to lay it all out there.

Seelok flies his throne across the table until he hovers half a meter before us. He flicks his tail in front of Marco's face. Marco doesn't flinch, even though I know how much he hates snakes.

"Very well, cadetsss," Seelok says. "Sss-steve will esss-cort you to your training area. But do not sss-stray, for your own sss-safety, of courssse. We wouldn't want you to be harmed—lossst forever like your beloved aeronautsss of Bounding Basssse 51." Seelok stares at Marco as he says this. "I need not mention that Admiral Eamesss is counting on you. Relationsss between Earth and Alkalinia are of the utmossst importanssse." Then he hisses something at Steve, turns his throne around, and flies out of the room. The other Alks hurry after him.

Marco looks at me with wide, hard eyes. We both heard Seelok's warning: if we don't do as directed outside of the occludium tether, we'll be putting our planet at risk. The admiral told us as much the day we left for Alkalinia. I guess we won't be bounding back to the space station anytime soon.

We follow Steve to the siphon port where we arrived a few

days ago. There's no sign of the passenger craft we arrived on. Steve leads us through the empty port and into another bay filled with small ships, each stranger and more alien looking than the last. He steers us to a vessel that looks like a fat green frog. The top of the vessel flips open when he presses a button on the side. A second button lowers stairs to the ground. He waves us in.

We fill the back compartment as Steve checks some controls on the exterior of the vessel.

"What's with all the weird ships?" Marco asks.

"This one looks like a frog," I say.

"Do you think they traded with other aliens for these vessels?" Cole asks.

Traded or stole, Mira thinks.

"Mira believes some of these crafts might not have come from a fair trade, if you know what I mean," I say.

"I'm with you, Mira," Lucy whispers. "These Alks are bad news."

"I'm with Jasper," Marco says, "and we're calling this thing the Frog."

Steve scoots into the pilot seat and closes up the craft. He hits some switches, and the Frog springs to life. And I mean it literally springs. The Frog hops over to a grate on the far side of the room. The grate opens, revealing a narrow tube. The Frog squeezes in, so that there's no air between the vessel and the walls.

"Compre-sssion commensss-ing," Steve says.

Wind builds to a loud whistle, and then . . .

Pop!

We fly out of the tube like a spitball from a straw. Next thing we know, we're cruising through the water.

"Awesome!" Cole says. He asks Steve about the compression technology. Steve mostly dodges his questions.

My stomach turns. The farther we travel from the Alkalinian Seat, the more dizzy I get. I'm thinking I may need a barf bag like Bad Breath.

Mira places her hand on the back of my neck. *Look back at the Seat. That might help.*

I turn to the window and press my forehead against the glass. The Alkalinian Seat starts to fade in the distance, but there's a structure that runs along the seafloor leading back. It's some sort of tube with a sickly yellowish glow. I keep my gaze fixed on it as we glide along.

I count my breath. Five counts to inhale, five counts to exhale. Finally the nausea starts to pass.

But . . . am I seeing things? Something long and black is headed for the Frog.

I blink, but the thing is still there. It's some sort of creature. It has huge onyx eyes and sharp silver teeth. It's headed straight for the Frog.

Slam!

THE SEA CREATURE BASHES THE WINDOW
and circles around.

"Whoa! What was that?" Lucy asks.

Slam!

It collides with the Frog again. The dark shape moves along my side of the vessel. Silver teeth jut like serrated knives from its open mouth. It glides across the bow and circles around to the back.

"If we travel quickly, it won't bother usss," Steve says.

"Yeah, but what is it?" I ask with a shaky voice.

"You never told us there were sea monsters here," Marco says. "You've been holding out on us, Stevie."

"Nothing to caussse con-sssern. The creaturesss rissse from the depthsss when they sss-senssse currentsss like the onesss causssed by our sss-ship."

Sure. I won't be concerned at all about a giant sea monster with razor-sharp teeth that keeps bashing our boat.

"Shouldn't there be more fish?" Cole asks. "That's the only one I've seen."

"There isn't much that can sss-survive here. The water is contaminated."

"What do you mean the water's contaminated?" Marco asks.

Steve hisses and flicks his tail. I have the sense he wasn't supposed to say anything about the contaminated water. Marco presses him for more information, but he refuses, saying only that we'll be at the training facility in a few minutes.

Soon another structure is visible up ahead. It's an enormous silver disk that is tied to the ocean floor with thick cables along its perimeter. The tube that stretches all the way back to the Alkalinian Seat connects with it. Near the tube, a second shaft leads from the structure down to the seabed at an angle. There's a clear dome at the bottom that glows silver.

"Bingo!" Marco says.

That must be the occludium tether giving off that silver light.

Mira squeezes my hand. *Confirm.*

"So . . . umm . . . Steve," I start. My voice sounds as queasy as I feel. "Is that the occludium tether?"

"Yesss, that'sss it. Can't wait to be free of it, huh? Try to bound in-ssside it and bye-bye!"

"Comforting," Lucy says.

Mission accomplished. We found the tether. *Can we leave now?* I ask Mira.

I wish. She sends me a wave of images and emotions that amount to one thing: she doesn't trust the Alks at all.

Soon we squish through a tube that looks just like the one we left from, except we're sucked inside the second structure, not blown out.

Once we're inside, though, the differences are obvious. Only half of the lights work, and some of the ones that do blink on and off. Along one wall, big pieces of paneling are peeling off. And there's junk everywhere.

"Ever think of calling a handyman, Stevie?" Marco asks.

"What is a handyman?"

"Why is it everything gets lost in translation with you aliens?" Marco says. "Most of my jokes go up in smoke. My audience barely knows the half of my humor."

"They're not missing much," Lucy says.

"I think what Marco was trying to say . . ."

Cole as translator? We're doomed.

". . . is that this facility is not as well maintained as the Alkalinian Seat."

"True," Steve says. "The sss-sau-ssser is no longer inhabited.

It hasssn't been for many yearsss. My people lived here while the Alkalinian Sss-seat was con-ssstructed, but now our re-sssettlement is complete. We maintain the occludium tether from here, and we ussse the sss-sau-ssser for sss-storage and misss-ellaneousss other thingsss, but not much of sss-significanssse. Lotsss of room for you to practissse uninterrupted."

He brings the Frog to a stop, pops open the roof, and folds out the ladder. "I'll be back to get you at sss-sixsss-teen hundred hoursss."

"You're just leaving us here?" Lucy asks.

"The hangar is sss-secure. You will not be able to leave thisss sss-section of the sss-sau-ssser. It wouldn't be sss-safe to wander around. Have an exsss-ellent time."

As soon as we've climbed out of the Frog and unloaded our packs, Steve bounces back to the launch duct and disappears. At first it feels great. Anything would be better than being cooped up in the Frog with an enormous sea creature banging against the glass. But as I take in the broken-down hangar, a new kind of discomfort sets in. After all, we're underwater in a contaminated sea on an alien planet.

"Do you think this place is safe?" I ask.

"Honestly?" Lucy says, looking around. "Not really."

"It's safer than the Alkalinian Seat," Marco says. "At least we don't have snakes slithering around us at every turn."

"Do you think we're locked in like Steve said?" Cole asks.

"Probably," I say. "I don't know why he'd lie about that."

"Maybe because they're nothing but sneaky, deceitful reptilian scum?" Lucy says. "Something's wrong about this whole planet. It's like my mind knows what's wrong, but I'm too tired and foggy to figure it out. Know what I mean?"

"That's exactly how I feel," I say.

Me, too, Mira calls from the other side of the hangar, where she's checking out some of the abandoned junk.

"We know they were listening to us this morning," Lucy says. "Gedney said they'd probably have surveillance, and it's the only explanation for why Steve would show up exactly when we tried to leave for the first time in a week!"

"No kidding." I almost tell them I heard Mira calling for me this morning, but I stop myself. My pod mates are still pretty creeped out about how we communicate. Plus, maybe I imagined it. Mira ended up being fine, minus our mutual headaches. Stupid brain patches.

"You know what would make us feel better?" Marco asks. "Some exercise. Let's get some bounding and blast pack practice in and then do some exploring. There's got to be a way out of this hangar."

"You heard what Steve said," Cole says. "We can't go wandering around this place."

"How else do you think we're going to locate the occludium tether?" Marco asks. "Sure, we saw it from the water, but since we don't know how to get to it from the inside, that doesn't do us much good, unless you want to go for a swim in the contaminated sea."

"So practice first, then snoop around?" Lucy asks.

We slap palms in a round of high fives.

I throw down my blast pack and pull out my gloves.

Even though we're thousands of kilometers from the space station and stuck in the middle of a contaminated sea with a bunch of snakes, I truly feel like I'm back at the Academy the moment I slip my hands into my gloves. Nothing beats the feeling.

As I reach out with my mind and practice building a bounding port, pictures pop into my head: training in the Ezone, bounding across Waters's laboratory on Earth, zooming across the frozen tundra in Gulaga. Across the hangar, Mira is smiling. She's sending me shared memories.

I close my eyes and focus on the memory of us winning the pod competition at the end of our first tour.

Seconds later an image forms in my mind of Mira playing piano in the sensory gym at the space station and me standing beside her with my clarinet.

My turn. I send Mira a memory of the night we were caught out on the tundra, the two of us gazing up at the star-filled sky, my arms wrapped around her waist.

Mira severs our connection.

My brain feels cold, empty.

I try to catch Mira's eye, but she turns away.

What happened? Was that memory too personal? Is she mad because that's the night she lost her glove and almost died? I reach back out to her but then break it off. Maybe she's trying to give me the message that the night I remembered wasn't special, no matter how close we were in the moment. We're friends, sure, but I'm just another member of the pod.

I am such a loser.

Something collides with my shoulder.

Ouch!

Marco's fist.

"Hey! Why'd you do that?"

"I've just been calling your name for a solid minute, Zone-Out."

Lucy laughs. "Leave him alone."

Mira's sparkly laughter reaches my mind. She's laughing, too? I don't get it.

"Wiki found some empty crates in the corner," Marco says. "Want to play catch?"

I shake out my arms to get some energy flowing. "Definitely. I have to wake up."

We spread across the hangar. Mira and Lucy pair off. Marco, Cole, and I form a triangle. Marco trains his gloves on one of the empty purple packing crates stacked against a wall.

He seizes control of the atoms and hurls the crate at Cole. A little rusty, but his skills are still there.

Cole lifts his hands to block the crate. He stops it half a meter before it hits him, but then the crate drops to the floor. He couldn't make the catch.

I'm out of practice, too, but I totally tune in when Cole lobs the crate at me. I reach out with my gloves and feel the atoms hurling in my direction. Rather than focus on stopping the crate, I work to shift the atoms to my control. The crate lands softly in my hands. I backpedal, but only because it's heavier than I expected.

"Nice catch, Ace," Marco says.

"Thanks." I place the crate on the ground and focus my attention. Then, just like Gedney taught us in the Ezone, I tap into the source and shoot from my brain out my fingertips like I'm pulling the rod of a pinball machine. The crate rockets into the air. I stop its progression when it's nearly at the ceiling and let it hang suspended, then I zip it down at a forty-five-degree angle at Marco.

"Take it easy," he shouts as he barely makes the catch.

Soon we're launching trick shots from across the hangar, trying to top one another with each toss.

I wonder if Addy has started bounding training with Gedney at the space station. I can't wait for her to experience the gloves for herself!

Mira and Lucy lift crates with their gloves to build a tower all the way to the ceiling. As soon as their last block is in place, Marco whips a crate into the center of the tower, and they all crash down.

"Hey!" Lucy shouts. "That wasn't nice! We're going to have to teach you a lesson. Girls versus boys!"

Marco looks back at me and Cole.

"You're on!" I holler. "In the hangar. Anything goes."

Wait! Over here! Mira's standing on the far side of the hangar near the stack of crates, which is considerably shorter than when we started our practice.

"Hold up!" I say. "I think Mira's found something."

We zoom over to where she's standing. Sure enough, we've pulled down enough crates to reveal that they were blocking a door.

"Clear the rest of these out!" Marco says. "Let's see if our serpentine friends forgot to lock this beauty!"

When the crates are moved aside, Marco tries the handle. We're in luck. The door swings back to reveal a dark hallway. "Bingo!" he says, stepping through the door.

Lucy grabs the back of his shirt. "Not so fast. Practice first, snoop later, right? And if I remember correctly, you accepted my girls-versus-boys challenge. What? Are you scared?"

Marco turns around. "Me? Scared? Are you kidding? Let's go!"

Lucy grins and clasps Mira's hand. They duck around the corner to talk strategy (which really means Lucy jabbers away at Mira with instructions, and Mira does exactly what she wants to do, although they both stay focused on the main objective of clobbering us).

"As if they stand a chance," Marco says as we fly to the center of the hangar and get ready for battle.

"We do have the numbers," Cole says.

Before we can plan our attack, crates crash down on us from above, and Lucy and Mira soar by in their blast packs.

"No fair! We weren't ready!" Cole shouts.

Lucy turns to face us in midair and smiles. "Who said anything about playing fair?"

"You asked for it," Marco yells. "Game on!" He chucks a crate, narrowly missing Lucy. She giggles and chucks a crate back. He dodges and kicks off, heading straight for Lucy.

"Oh, no you don't, Marco Romero!" She lets Marco come in close, then kicks off and under him. She spins around and taunts him with a gigantic grin.

I loosen the control straps from my blast pack and lift off. I was so excited about my gloves, I forgot how awesome it feels to fly. Swooping low to the ground, I pick up speed. Wind blows against my face, sealing my hair flat on my forehead. I stretch long, almost like I'm riding through one of the chutes at the space station, pushing faster as I go.

I'll catch you!

I sneak a glance over my shoulder. Mira is gaining on me.

Racing to the end of the hangar, I swing low and left. Mira cuts me off. She flies straight for the ceiling, drops her grips, and grabs my atoms.

She holds me for only a second, but it's enough to throw me off. As soon as she lets go, I fall to the floor, luckily only a meter or so. She lowers herself slowly with her gloves and smiles in my direction.

You okay? she asks.

Never better.

Then, catch me if you can. She pushes off and flies for the other side of the hangar by the launch duct.

I brush off my pants and pick up my grips, then I'm flying. I stop and hover in the center of the hangar. *Try to pass me*, I dare her.

My brain hums with sparkly energy. She's laughing at me.

She takes off, speeding straight for me. This is too easy. I use her own tactics against her. I fly straight for the ceiling, drop my straps, and grab crates on either side of the hangar. I fling them toward each other, aiming them to collide at their midpoint: Mira's trajectory.

At the last second Mira flips. She crosses just above the crates as they collide and pushes off them with her feet. She zips past me, across the hangar, and out the door we uncovered.

"Hey!" Cole calls. "The game's in here!"

I ignore him and chase Mira out of the hangar.

The hallway is dark, narrow, and curved like the ones at the Alkalinian Seat. This place was definitely not built for humans. There is no way I could stand up without hitting my head. It's like I'm back in Gulaga.

Mira slows as she takes the corner, so I make up some ground.

I close in, ready to grab her shoes. As I drop my hands and lunge for her ankles, she drops her feet to the ground. My body keeps going. I slow myself with my gloves just before I crash into the next corner wall.

Graceful. Mira glides past me with a smile. Then she stops. *Whoa.*

What is it?

Mira's mind is a question. Whatever she's seeing, she doesn't have a word for it.

I pick myself up off the ground, stoop low, and drag myself to her side.

She's standing at the threshold of a door that looks just like every other door we've passed. But it's what's on the other side that is perplexing.

We're looking out at a rocky landscape. Light from a star bears down on the stone, casting glimmers of reflection in the silver rock formations. In the distance a turquoise-blue sea stretches to the horizon.

MONICA TESLER

"What is this place?" I ask. "It must be virtual, right?"

Mira shrugs and takes a tentative step into the room.

I grab her arm. "Maybe that's not the best idea."

She smirks at me, shakes her arm free, then slowly walks across the rocks. When she's fully in the room, she tips her face to the sun. *Warm.*

A few seconds later Marco, Cole, and Lucy show up.

"Amazing!" Cole shouts, walking right into the room. "This is incredible VR tech! So lifelike!"

"What do you think this place is?" Lucy says.

"No clue," Marco says, "but it beats the rest of this dump."

He runs across the rocks and lifts off in his blast pack. "Hey, J! Let's race!"

Why not? I enter the room, grab my blast pack straps, and take off after Marco. Within seconds I almost forget that I'm in a virtual simulation. The rocks below are covered with moss that smells like the gardeners' trucks that maintain the green blocks near my apartment in Americana East. I touch down on the rocks and press my hands against the cool stone. Then I breathe deep and let the rays of the powerful star warm my skin.

"Fly Guy, what gives?" Marco shouts. He stands at the edge of a cliff.

I zoom to where he is. When I'm almost there, he grins, then turns around and dives off the cliff. I zip after him and tip my pack into a near-ninety-degree dive, headed straight for the water.

Marco rights himself a meter from the surface and skims the water. He slows to let me come up beside him. The spray from the waves spritzes my face. I lick my lips and taste the salt.

"Awesome, right?" he asks.

As soon as the words leave his mouth, we hit the ground.

The ground? I thought we were flying above the ocean.

The world has shifted around us. We're lying in a dense thicket of decaying leaves. A hundred meters above us, a tree canopy shields the star. There's stirring in the brush and a loud shriek that definitely came from some sort of creature.

"What was that?" I ask.

"Not sticking around to find out!" Marco says, taking off in his blast pack, heading roughly in the direction we came from. Hopefully, that will take us to the door.

It seems like we've been flying too long, like we must have taken a wrong turn, when I hear Lucy calling. "Over here!"

Finally I spot Lucy, Mira, and Cole through the dense brush. They're gathered around a large metal box roughly the size of the chute cubes at the space station, about three meters square. It looks incredibly out of place in the middle of the jungle.

I drop to my feet in front of the box. Cole is examining a panel right in the center. This must be the door to the VR room.

"Let me guess, we owe the abrupt change of scenery to you, Wiki?" Marco asks when we touch down. He walks his hands against the wall of the cube right to the edge, then keeps walking them right off. What looks like the continuation of the jungle is actually a solid surface—the boundary of the VR room—the metal box is actually a two-dimensional square.

"Yeah, thanks for scaring us half to death," I say, pressing against what looks like open air but is actually the wall. I blink, trying to reorient myself, and step back from the edge.

"Sorry about that," Cole says. "I wasn't sure how to work the panel. I decided to wait until you returned to try another shift."

He presses a button, and the room changes again. This time it's a mountaintop covered in snow, looking out across a hundred more snowy peaks. The next shift takes us to a marsh. Our feet sink into the ground.

Lucy squeals. "Yuck! Change it! My socks are all wet!"

The next few settings call up landscapes so foreign I hardly have the words to describe what I see. They must be vistas from alien planets.

Finally Cole twists the knob and the room resets. Beyond the metal entrance, the walls, floor, and ceiling are all orange mush. The room is huge, but not limitless. No matter what we experience in VR, the physical boundaries of the space must be the same.

"Their VR tech is truly amazing," he says.

"Go back to one of those super strange planets," Marco says. "I want to explore."

"Hold on," Cole says. "I want to get a closer look at the room in its dormant state. I'm pretty sure this is the same material used in the Youli ship, the same material I believe they're using in our quarters."

"Do you think they traded the Youli for it?" I ask.

"Or stole it?" Marco asks.

"I hate to break up the party," Lucy says, "but we only have an hour before Steve returns, and we need to be back in the hangar when he arrives. Right now we should look for the occludium tether access point."

"Lucy's right," I say. "We can mess around in here the next time we come for training. We need to get going. We told Admiral Eames we'd search for the tether immediately, and instead we vegged in our quarters for a week, not that it was our fault."

"Since you mentioned that," Lucy says. "Even though the glove practice wiped me out, I don't feel half as tired as when I woke up this morning."

"Same," Marco says, "which makes zero sense."

"It's almost like they want us to be tired," Cole says.

Maybe they do.

"Mira thinks that might be their plan," I tell the others.

"You and your brain-talk," Lucy says. "It's creepy."

"Probably not as creepy as whatever Seelok and his crew are up to," I say.

"I'm not sure," Marco says. "This morning I was convinced the Alks were up to no good, but now they're meeting their end of the bargain. They're letting us train."

"True," I say, "but we need to stay alert. And we need to execute our plan. The sooner we locate the access point for the occludium tether, the sooner we have a bona fide escape route once Admiral Eames arrives."

We fly back to the hangar and set out down an adjacent hall that has illuminated floor runners. Since we know the Alks need to maintain the tether, we figure the hallway that's in the best shape must mark the route. And since this is the only hall with lights, it's our best guess.

The lights lead us all the way across the abandoned saucer. Given how long we've been flying in our packs, we must be nearly there.

At our next turn Mira pulls up short. *Look!*

I stop at her side and glance down the short, branching hall. It ends at a purple marble door no higher than my waist. Thick silver handles shaped like serpents are affixed in the center.

"Hey, guys!" I call to my pod mates. "I think we need to check this out."

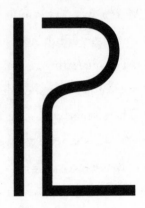

"WHOA, WHAT IS THIS PLACE?" I ASK AS
we crawl through the tiny door into the room. The floor is
made of smooth, dark stone that is polished so finely I can
see the reflection of my face. The ceiling is domed and covered in white cloth that drapes all the way to the floor. The
thick smell of musk and cinnamon fills the air. The scent is so
heavy it makes my head spin.

I drag myself to the center of the room and collapse on a
pile of velvet cushions fringed with gold thread.

"This place is a tad fancy," Lucy says. "Do you really think
the occludium tether is in here?"

"Definitely not," Cole says. "Do you even know what an occludium tether looks like?"

"Do you?" she asks.

"Obviously."

Mira waves her hands, then draws a finger to her mouth to signal silence. A low hum fills the room, kind of like the pull of a minor note on Addy's violin, then the hum blends with a second note, and another, until the room sings with a lulling, eerie melody. The dome above flickers to life, and a picture emerges across the white-cloth ceiling: an image of a planet.

It's not like any planet I've ever seen. There are hues of purple and silver and a brilliant blue, striped with the whites of clouds. We recline on the cushions and gaze at the planet as the vantage point of the camera lens rotates through different angles. Then it zooms in like we're traveling by ship, crossing through the atmosphere, heading straight for the planet's surface.

Lucy gasps. "Where is this?"

"*What* is this?" Marco asks.

We cut through the clouds, and the screens reveal the planet beneath. The music swells as we glide across the surface. It's breathtaking. Purple-gray rock with veins of white ore covers the surface. Crevices show where water has cut its way through the stone to reach the shining turquoise sea.

Patches of silver stretch from the rocks and arc over the water.

"Are those buildings?" Cole asks.

"They must be," I say. "But they're so beautiful. They blend perfectly with the planet's landscape."

As we're brought in even closer, we can see that dense lichen covers much of the rock, and more silver structures rise up from the crevices. As we pass above the cliffs and look down at the banks of the river delta, there is movement. It isn't possible to tell what's down there from this distance, but it's clear this planet is inhabited and is home to an advanced civilization.

Amidst the music a strange scraping noise fills the room, like someone dragging a bag of sand across the floor. I squint at the screen, wondering what that noise is supposed to be.

Something brushes my leg. Twice. Three times.

"Cut it out!" I say to my pod mates.

"Cut what out?" Cole asks.

"Someone keeps kicking my leg."

"Mine, too!" Lucy snaps.

Marco bolts up with a squeal. "Snake!"

I pull in my knees. Sure enough, a long reptilian creature circles the room. It keeps right on circling until it can nearly close its mouth on its own tail. It stops when it's a perfect circle in the center of the room with us in its middle (hopefully not about to be literally in its middle).

MONICA TESLER

"Uhhh . . ." Marco makes a shaky noise like he's trying to talk. Finally he whispers, "Did I mention I hate snakes?"

"Yep," Lucy whispers back. "And if you didn't, the squeal would have given it away."

Now all of us are sitting up. I'd stand if I could, but I'd bonk my head on the ceiling. This room was definitely not built for humans.

We sit with our backs pressed together, crammed in the center of the room, in the middle of the creature's extraordinarily long, unbelievably snakelike body. It sort of looks like an Alk, but not the ones we've met so far. The creature is easily five times as long as the other Alks. And it doesn't have a cyborg arm. Instead it has three sets of tiny arms and webbed hands near its head, kind of like the Alks riding scooters we saw when we first arrived at the siphon port. As we stare, the creature lifts its chest off the stone floor, jerks its head in our direction, and juts its forked tongue in the air between us.

"Ummm . . . guys . . . bright ideas welcome right about now," Lucy says.

"I got nothing," Marco says. "Except I hate snakes."

"You've mentioned that," Lucy says. "But let's try to shift the focus, shall we?"

"Hey," I say to the snake. "Do you speak English? We're the Bounders here for training. Maybe you've heard of us?"

The snake's tongue whips out of its mouth, and it bobs

its head from side to side. It slides its thick body around the circle and stops in front of me. At first I think maybe it understood me and is about to deliver a lecture about busting into its private movie theater. Instead it rises up, flaps its tiny arms, and hisses right in my face.

I scoot back against my pod mates.

The snake hisses again, then clicks, then hisses. It lifts its head even higher and glides forward. Its tongue juts out and almost touches my nose.

"Some . . . help . . . here . . . ," I manage to squeak.

"Hold on, hold on," Cole says. "I think it's trying to say something."

"Yeah, something like 'Get the heck out of my snake den,'" I sputter.

Cole pulls the voice box Gedney gave us from his pack and sets it on the ground in front of him. "This should only take a second. I just have to figure out how to make it two-way translation."

The snake waves its head in front of my face and hisses again. Its eyes are black marbles. I can see my own reflection staring back at me, just like when I looked at the stone floor. And I look freaked.

"A little faster," I whisper. "We have a situation here."

"Almost got it," Cole says, monkeying with the box. "Okay . . . I'm close . . . there." He lifts the box to his mouth and says, "Hello! We are from Earth. We're here for training on Alkalinia." Out of the box comes a strange assortment of swish noises and clicks that sound vaguely similar to the noises that have been coming from our snaky friend.

The snake swings its head away from me—thank goodness—and slides around to where Cole sits. It starts up with the hissing and clicking again.

Cole raises a finger, then calmly lifts the box and speaks his introduction in English again. After the box translates, Cole presents the box to the snake.

It dips its head to the box and senses it with its tongue. Then it lifts its onyx eyes to Cole again, who nods. The snake positions its mouth near the box and hisses.

"Welcome to the Shrine of Remembrance, the Temple of End of Days," the box translates.

"Welcome? Really?" Marco says. "This isn't my idea of welcoming."

"I hope that doesn't mean it's our end of days," I say.

"Yeah, let's stick with Shrine of Remembrance," Lucy says.

Cole glares at us. "Thank you," he says into the box. "Who are you?"

Again the snake hisses and clicks into the translator. "I am Serena, the Great Mother, Guardian of the Shrine, the One Who Remembers."

"That's quite a title for a snake," Marco says.

Serena tips her eyes at Marco, as if to ask for a translation.

Cole lifts the voice box, but I grab it from him. "He says it's nice to meet you."

After it translates, Serena hisses at me. "And who are you?"

"I'm Jasper Adams, and these are my friends: Cole, Mira, Lucy, and Marco."

Serena nods her head. "Yes. But who *are* you?"

Lucy kicks me in the side. "Tell her about us! Tell her what we're doing here!"

That's tricky. Who exactly are we in the bigger picture of the galaxy? Who are we to an Alkalinian? Or, in particular, who are we to Serena, Guardian of the Shrine, and other miscellaneous titles, who apparently has no idea about Earth Force and our diplomatic delegation, or she wouldn't be asking.

I lift the voice box. "We're Bounders from planet Earth. We're like this special group of space travelers. Our planet has a kind of partnership with yours. That's why we're visiting."

After the translation Serena circles us, taking us in one at a time. "But you seem young, yes?"

"Right. We're pretty young, or at least, we're not old."

"Ask her about this place," Lucy says. "What is the planet in the pictures?"

"Can you tell us about the shrine?"

Serena lifts her head to the top of the dome. The image has zoomed out to the first still frame—a picture of the planet from space. "This is where we come to remember, although no one comes anymore. You are the first visitors to the shrine in many years."

Lucy grabs the voice box. "And you've been waiting here all this time?"

"Yes. I am the guardian. The One Who Remembers. That is my calling."

"What is that planet?" I ask, tipping my eyes to the ceiling.

"That is our home," Serena says.

"This planet looks nothing like those pictures," Marco says.

"Our true home," she hisses. "Alkalinia."

"Oh!" Lucy says to us. "Remember what Gedney said?"

That's right. Gedney told us that the Alks had nearly destroyed their planet and had been forced to relocate to another system. Seelok and Steve and the rest of the Alks may call this Alkalinia, but it's really not.

"What happened to your planet?" Cole asks.

Serena pulls her heavy body around and around until she's tightly coiled. In the image above, the star slides near the edge of the horizon, casting deep shadows across the planet. The surface glows with a deep-purple light.

She flicks her tail, and the image above changes. The camera zooms out, and there are a dozen planets on the screen, then it pulls back again to show multiple solar systems. She hisses and clicks into the voice box. "There was a great war. Many battled. Many died. I wish I could say we were mere victims, but alas, that is far from the truth. Alkalinian greed, dishonesty, and betrayal fueled the conflicts that were already raging across the galaxy. The strong preyed on the weak. The advanced races exploited those that were just making their way into the world. My kind stoked the flames and pulled riches from the ashes."

"Wow," Lucy whispers. "What drama!"

"What war?" Cole asks.

"The only war that matters," Serena says. "The war that preceded the peace and the rules and the universal light that prevailed. The Alkalinians were not on the side of victory, and our planet was destroyed through our own misdeeds. We were forced to leave aboard our saucer and live in space for more than a generation, taking refuge on planets that would have us, refueling when we had the currency. This planet was also brutalized during the war. Its civilizations were destroyed. Only the barest of life remained in the oceans. But there was enough that we could rebuild. Just like the dawn of Alkalinia, we could lay down our cities in the seas. So we landed our saucer and began again. Someday, perhaps, this planet will be healthy enough—and we will be wise enough—to rise from the seas and truly start again."

Marco grabs the voice box. "Look, Serena. I hate to break

MONICA TESLER

it to you, but your people aren't all underwater. We flew here on your spaceship. And your buddies in the other building don't seem to be pining for their old planet."

Serena sighs wearily and lays her head on the cold stone. "We must remember. If we do not remember, we will forget. If we forget, we will repeat."

So that's why it's called the Shrine of Remembrance.

For a solid minute no one speaks. Then Cole grabs the voice box. "Serena, do you know where the occludium tether is?"

Marco slaps Cole's back. "Good thinking, Wiki. Hit the snake up for info."

As Cole's voice translates through the box, Serena recoils. She rears up as if she might strike, then lowers her head to the box and hisses. "That foulness is the root of our evils!"

Lucy takes the box. "We don't want any occludium, Serena. We just want to know where the tether connects to the saucer. We saw it from the water. It's probably near a major power source." She recounts what the admiral told us back at the space station.

"I do not know, child," Serena says. "I do not leave. I rise from the depths to attend the shrine, then I descend. I don't abandon my children. Where are the others? You must bring them! We must remember!" Serena coils in circles, flicking her tongue at the images above.

Marco knocks me on the shoulder. "Let's go, Ace. If we want to find the tether before Steve shows up to cart us back, we need to get looking."

I grab the voice box. "Nice talking to you, Serena. We've got to go."

Serena still twists her muscular body and thrashes her head. Our visit seems to have really disturbed her. "Come back!" she hisses into the box. "Tell the others! They must come! They must remember!"

Lucy pulls the box back and promises Serena that we'll remind the Alkalinians about the shrine. I'm not sure that we will, and I'm not sure it would do much good if we did, but it's definitely what Serena wants to hear. She settles down and rests her head on her thick black scales.

I glance back as I crawl through the velvet curtains. Her onyx eyes are fixed on the ceiling and the image of her former home. I don't know if snakes cry, but her eyes glisten like they're filled with tears.

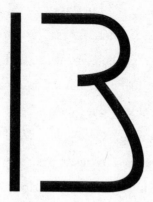

WE WIND OUR WAY THROUGH THE HALLWAYS
of the saucer. Since we met Serena, the place has taken on new
meaning. This structure—the saucer—must be the spaceship
the Alkalinians lived on when their planet was destroyed.
They stayed in space for a generation, until they landed here.
This planet is where the Alkalinians plan to rebuild their civilization. As Serena said, they vowed not to repeat the mistakes
of their past. But have they really changed? The Alks still seem
pretty greedy and dishonest.

"How long do you think that snake has been there?" Marco
says.

"Her name's Serena," Lucy says.

"Don't mind Marco," I say. "He's just afraid of snakes, remember?"

"How could I forget?" Lucy asks.

"It's not fear, Ace," Marco says. "It's hatred. I *hate* snakes. But as far as snakes go, Serena's not so bad."

"Thank you for using her name," Lucy says.

"I didn't do it for you, Pretty Face."

"Don't start arguing," Cole says. "We only have five more minutes before we need to head back. Stay focused."

We keep following the lit power strip until the hall we're in dead-ends into a wall of windows. We must be on the edge of the saucer. Some of the black sea creatures we saw from the Frog swim just beyond the windows. When they spot us, they spin back and wave their long, scaly bodies to propel themselves toward the saucer, opening their cavernous mouths and baring their silver fangs. When they reach us, they lash at the windows with their tails and circle around for another pass.

"Are we sure this place is safe?" I ask. "What if those things break the glass? Millions of liters of contaminated water would pour in. We'd be crushed from the pressure before we drowned. Marco may be afraid of snakes, but I'm afraid of that." I point at the window. It's not just the water. It's everything. The water, the sense of being trapped, the low ceilings, the narrow halls, the air that feels like it hasn't circulated in a decade.

"I'm not *afraid* of snakes," Marco says. "I *hate*—"

"Shut up, Marco," Lucy says. "I think Mira's found something."

Mira stands at the next corridor, waving us on. My pod mates kick off in that direction. I try to shake off my claustrophobia and trail after them.

Mira guides us through a few turns, until we reach another hallway. She twists the handle on the first door and leads us in. The room is filled with machinery, and much of it is working.

"Bingo," Marco says. "This stuff is definitely not as abandoned as the rest of this place."

"But how do we tell which one of these machines is the occludium tether?" Lucy asks. "I have no idea what we're looking for."

"Wiki? Any thoughts?" Marco asks.

Cole is fast at work surveying the various machines. "These are generators. It looks like most of them are redundant power sources. The Alkalinians have gone to great lengths to make sure whatever they're powering doesn't go offline."

"Breathe deep, Poddies," Marco says. "Smell anything?"

Aside from the must that infects the whole saucer, the air here has a faint metallic scent. That's the giveaway: we're definitely near occludium.

Here. Come. Mira calls to me from across the room, somewhere behind the generators.

Following my mind's direction, I find her in front of a wall of windows. Her hands are pressed against the glass. Next to her is a firmly secured hatch.

When I reach her, I see that the hatch connects to a narrow shaft barely big enough to fit one person. Wires and cables and pipes are mounted inside the shaft and trace back to this room. Looking up, I see that one of the pipes is mounted to the ceiling and stretches across to a thick metal door near the generators. I bet that's where they store the occludium.

The shaft extends down to the ocean floor. At the bottom, a small bubble of a building is anchored. There's not much inside, but one of the machines looks almost exactly like the diagram of the occludium tether Admiral Eames showed us. The bubble glows silver in the water. I can just make out the shimmer of the shield radiating from the tether back toward the Alkalinian Seat and beyond.

Fifty meters from the anchored bubble is a long tube running across the seafloor. I recognize it as the one I saw from the Frog. It also reaches back to the Alkalinian Seat. It connects here at the abandoned habitat, probably a few floors below where we stand. The water around the tube is crowded with the black sea creatures. A chill runs through me. I am not a fan of those things.

"That's it!" Cole says as he comes to stand by my side. He points down at the silver bubble. "That's the tether. It makes sense that they'd anchor it. All the ones I've read about are on land, but they're all anchored to the ground for additional stability. Also, water is a conductor, but the ocean floor grounds the energy. I don't know what would happen if a bound tried to come through an unanchored underwater shield. In theory, it could produce an electrical current that would annihilate anything in a several-hundred-meter radius."

"Okay, Junior Einstein," Marco says, "you said some really disturbing stuff just then. I don't want to get a step closer to that tether."

"Hopefully, we won't need to," I say. "But just hypothetically, what would we need to do to deactivate it?"

"I'm not entirely sure," Cole says. "There's probably a way to power it down remotely, but I don't know how we'd figure that out. The best bet is to descend that shaft and kill the power."

"And exactly how does one 'kill the power'?" Lucy asks.

"Flip the switch?" Cole says. "That's how it works with most things."

"So you have no idea," I say. "We go all the way down there and hope we find the big red button that turns it off?"

"We're not going down there," Marco says. "The admiral told us to find the tether. We did. Mission accomplished."

"I hate to break up the party," Lucy says, "but we need to get back. And we need to hurry. Steve could be here in ten minutes."

"But what if something happens," I say, "and it's up to us to deactivate the shield?"

Marco slaps my back. "Then I nominate you to crawl down there and search for the red button. I know how much you love confined spaces."

My pod mates laugh, but I squirm inside. I can't think of a place I'd like to be less than inside that shaft, except maybe in that tube with all the black sea creatures circling, or out there adrift in the contaminated water.

When we get back to the hangar, we stack the crates to block the exit, leaving a small gap between the crates and the wall, enough room for us to slide through the next time we come. Then we toss some of the remaining crates around with our gloves, killing time until Steve arrives. While we wait, Lucy asks whether we should give the admiral the green light to bring the other Bounders to Alkalinia for the rest of their tour.

An image of Addy fills my mind. I really don't want her coming here. Even though we've located the tether, I don't feel safe. The Alks are definitely up to something. We still don't know why they kept us in our quarters for a week. *So you could enjoy our virtual hospitality* is not a good enough explanation from our serpentine hosts.

"No," I say. "There's something wrong here."

"We completed our mission," Cole says. "Our orders are to report the information to Admiral Eames. She'll decide whether to bring the other cadets."

"Maybe we should investigate some more before reporting to the admiral," I say. "We all know there's something fishy about them keeping us in our quarters for a week."

"Don't get too hung up on that, Ace," Marco says. "The Alks might just measure time differently than us. Ever think of that?"

"That could be it," Cole says. "After all, they have almost complete control over our body clocks, since we're inside their manufactured VR environment."

"That's creepy," Lucy says.

"Creepy," Marco says, "but not necessarily fishy, right, J?"

"I don't know." I think back to this morning and how I could have sworn I heard Mira calling out to me in the moments before she woke. I want to tell my pod mates, but I don't know how to describe what I experienced. Maybe I imagined it, or maybe I was still half-asleep and dreaming. Still, I definitely don't feel comfortable with Addy coming, at least not until we have more sense of what's really going on here. "We know they bugged our quarters."

"So?" Marco claps me on the shoulder. "I would've been surprised if they hadn't bugged our quarters. I mean, they're sneaky snakes. But ignoring that, I figured you of all people would be psyched about the culinary improvements this tour."

"Of course I'm pumped about the food. But there's something not right, something I can't put my finger on, and it's not just the eavesdropping." I shake my head. "Let's give it another day—and by *day* I mean twenty-four hours. If everything seems okay tomorrow, we can ask Bad Breath to contact the admiral."

Just then the Frog hops into the hangar, and Steve waves us on.

"Greetingsss!" he says as we board and settle into our seats. "Sss-so, did you accomplisssh what you wisssshed with your training?" He bounces the Frog over to the launch duct.

Cole shoots me a guilty glance. Hopefully, he keeps his mouth shut about our occludium tether discovery mission and side trip to the forgotten shrine.

Lucy rolls her eyes at Cole. "Oh, yes!" she says to Steve. "We were very rusty in the skills department after our time off since the last tour. We really needed the practice. In fact, we'll need to come back every day for more practice. Practice makes perfect! That's what I always say!"

"Since when?" Marco mumbles.

Lucy punches him in the arm.

"Yowch!" he says. "I take that back. You've obviously been practicing your combat skills."

"And you've obviously been practicing your clueless skills," she snaps, throwing a side-eye at the front of the Frog, where Steve sits. "Has Cole been giving you lessons?"

"Lessons on what?" Cole asks.

"Please stop yelling," I say. "I'm not feeling well." I close my eyes, but I can't keep my insides from rolling all around. I'm glad I didn't eat much this morning, or I'd probably pull a Bad Breath and puke everywhere.

Okay? Mira asks.

I shake my head and bend over my belly.

She places her hand on my neck. My brain patch is implanted just beneath her fingertips. The warmth from her palm spreads down my back. Even though I feel awful, I can't stop a smile from spreading across my lips.

"Oh, you two," Lucy says. "You're talking about us, aren't you?"

"Quiet, Chatterbox," Marco whispers. "Inquiring minds."

The Frog falls silent. Lucy must know Marco's referring to Steve. I open my eyes and turn my gaze to the Frog's rearview mirror. Steve stares back at me. It's only for a second, because he quickly turns away. But it's enough for me to understand.

Steve knows exactly what Lucy was talking about. He knows about me and Mira.

Now I'm certain the Alkalinians are up to something.

· E_F ·

"You're sure you've got this?" I ask Marco. We're trying to talk in code, since the one thing we definitely agree on is that our quarters are bugged. We knew they would be before we even left the space station.

When we got back to the Alkalinian Seat and followed Steve to our quarters, Marco whispered that he had a way to rig our door so we could slip out without anyone noticing. He wants to pay a visit to Bad Breath.

Nothing in me thinks talking to Bad Breath sounds like a good idea, but it's necessary. We need to tell him about our suspicions and find out what he knows. Even more importantly, we need to get the SIMPLE from him so that we can talk without the Alkalinians eavesdropping. Gedney told us we can activate the SIMPLE even if we're not making a transmission. And Cole swears he knows how to do it.

The plan is that Mira, Marco, and I will sneak out of our quarters and trek to Bad Breath's room. Mira claims she remembers how to get there. Lucy and Cole will stay behind in case Steve or any of his buddies show up. If they ask, Lucy will say we're taking a nap.

Marco grasps the door handle. "Don't you trust me, Ace?"

I shrug. "Sort of."

"You of little faith, watch and be impressed." He slowly twists the handle and pulls. The door edges open. No lock. No alarm. He lifts a finger to his lips and points to where the lock engages. It's stuffed with some crumpled paper he lifted from the saucer earlier today.

Clever, Mira thinks.

Old-school. I like it. I give him a thumbs-up, and we set out with Mira in the lead, Marco and me close on her heels.

"You sure you know the way?" I ask. This whole place is like a maze to me.

Mira shoots me an annoyed glance and keeps on.

"Assuming we get into his room," I whisper, "don't tell him we found the tether. We need to make sure the admiral holds off bringing the other cadets to Alkalinia until we're sure it's safe. Stick to the script. Don't make him mad."

"Who, me?" Marco asks. "Why do you think I would make him mad?"

Mira gives a second annoyed glance over her shoulder, this time at Marco.

"Okay, fine, so I'm not always the best at kissing butt," Marco says, "but back up a second. Did we actually agree that the admiral delaying her trip was a good idea, Ace?"

Not exactly, but I need to find a way to keep Addy as far away from Alkalinia as possible, at least until we know what's going on. "You know it's the right call," I say. "Just let me do the talking."

Mira pulls up short in front of a door that looks exactly the same as every other door we've passed.

"You're sure this is it?" I ask.

This time Mira gives a full-on eye roll and gestures at the door. *See for yourself.*

Marco nods. I rap on the door.

Nothing happens. Why isn't he responding? What if he's not even here?

Marco shoves me aside and pounds on the door.

Seconds later there's a grumbling noise from the other side. Then: "I'm coming, I'm coming."

The door flies open, and there stands Bad Breath. He has red stuff smeared on his face, and his robe is half-open on top, revealing a gross, hairy chest. He sticks his head out into the hall, looks both ways, then slams the door.

"Jerk," Marco mumbles, then pounds on the door. He keeps on pounding, right up until the moment Bad Breath swings the door open again.

"What do you want?" he grunts.

Marco shoves his arm into the room to block the door from closing. "Nice to see you, too, Officer Johnson. We need to talk. Now."

"I'm busy. We'll talk tomorrow."

"This won't wait until tomorrow." Marco pushes by Bad Breath, and we slide in behind him. "Oh, I see you have company again."

This time there are two VR females and one VR male in the

room. One of the females is dressed in a cat costume, the male is dressed like one of the superheroes from *Stellar Rangers*, and then there's the tuxedoed butler from this morning. On Bad Breath's sideboard, right next to his elaborate spread of meat and cheeses, I spy his tablet with the SIMPLE attached.

My brain sparkles with Mira's laughter.

"*Stellar Rangers?*" Marco asks, barely holding back his own laughter. "Really?"

"Shut up, Romero." Bad Breath turns to the VRs. "Get lost!"

Once they exit, he spins on us, backing Marco right up against the wall. "What on earth do you want, B-wads?"

"We need to activate the SIMPLE." I head for the sideboard.

"Don't you dare touch that!" he shouts at me. "It's not like I'll let you use it."

"Relax," Marco says. "We just came to talk."

"So talk." Bad Breath cinches his robe and slices a chunk of rare meat. He takes it to his bed, reclines on his satin sheets, and tears off a bite with his teeth. Bloody juice drips from the corner of his mouth as he chews.

"It would be better if we could activate the SIMPLE." I gesture toward the ceiling, hoping that he'll catch on about the room being bugged.

"If you've got something to say, say it. Then leave before I decide to teach you a lesson for invading my privacy."

Mira's words take shape in my brain. *Distract him. I'll grab the SIMPLE.*

Steal it?

Borrow it.

I position myself between Bad Breath's bed and the door, so he has to turn to face me. Now that I have his attention, I'm not sure what to say. It's clear Bad Breath isn't going to be any help. I suppose we have no choice but to report our suspicions directly to Admiral Eames. "We want to contact the admiral."

"Already done," Bad Breath says. "She's escorting the rest of the cadets here tomorrow."

Wait . . . what? Did he just say the other cadets are coming tomorrow?

"What do you mean you already contacted her?" Marco asks. "You were supposed to talk with us first. You don't even know whether we found . . ." He throws up his hands. The last thing we want the Alkalinians to know is that we were searching for the occludium tether. "Whether we found the you-know-what."

"Well, did you, B-wad?"

"That's beside the point!" Marco shouts.

"So you did," Bad Breath says. "Then, there's no issue. The admiral will be here tomorrow with the other cadets. Now get out of my room!"

"I don't think that's such a great idea," I say. "We need

more time. There's stuff going on here that we need to figure out first. We really don't want the other cadets arriving on Alkalinia until we have a full understanding of—"

"Stop your paranoid ramblings, cadet. My friend Seelok and I spoke with the admiral together this afternoon. It was his suggestion as an act of cooperation and diplomacy."

"Your *friend* Seelok?" Marco asks, barely holding back his laughter.

"You mean the Alkalinians already know the other cadets are coming tomorrow?" I can't believe this. Bad Breath is so stupid. Seelok totally played him. This basically kills any chance of delaying their trip without raising a huge red flag for Seelok and the other Alks.

"That's right, B-wads. So do me a favor. Turn your pathetic little selves around and go back to your pathetic quarters and play some pathetic video games for the rest of the night. In other words, leave me alone!"

Mira breezes by me out the door.

Marco looks at her, then raises his eyebrows at me. "Are we just going to—"

"Yes!" I say. We should have known Bad Breath would screw everything up. We have to take matters into our own hands now. I grab Marco by the sleeve and pull him from the room. "Thank you, Officer Johnson. Have a great night with your . . . uh . . . friends."

ONCE THE DOOR SHUTS BEHIND US, I TURN
to Mira. "Did you get it?"

She reaches into her pocket and withdraws a clear disk: the SIMPLE.

"Miss Mira, you rock," Marco says. "Let's head back."

The first thing we do when we reach our quarters is hand the SIMPLE to Cole. I ball my hands into fists and squeeze, barely able to contain my frustration with Bad Breath. As soon as Cole affixes the SIMPLE to his tablet screen and gives the thumbs-up, I spill the story of what happened.

"How long before Bad Breath realizes the SIMPLE is gone?" Lucy asks.

"He may never notice," Marco says. "He's got a lot of distractions in his quarters."

"Not that VR again." Lucy rolls her eyes.

"Three of them," Marco says. "One dressed up as a Stellar Ranger."

"Original or second series?" Cole asks.

"Only you would ask that, Wiki," Marco says.

"Did you hear what I said?" I ask. "The admiral is bringing the other cadets here tomorrow!"

"We have the SIMPLE," Lucy says. "Let's just call the admiral back and tell her not to come."

"It's not that easy," I say. "Bad Breath said he contacted the admiral with Seelok, so the Alkalinians would know if there was a change in plans. That means they'd be onto us."

"Onto us that we're onto them?" Lucy asks. "Is that really such a big deal?"

"It is if we want to figure out what's actually going on," I say.

"*If* there's anything going on," Marco says, "other than the Alks being a bunch of sketchy dudes who like to eavesdrop. If there is, the admiral bringing the other cadets is not such a bad thing. We'll have a much bigger army to defend ourselves if anything goes wrong. And anyway, we found the occludium tether like the admiral asked. She knew there might be issues, and this is what she wanted accomplished before she came."

No, no, no. This is all moving too fast. I wish there were something we could do to delay the other cadets. To delay Addy.

"Okay, so let's review," Lucy says. "We know where the occludium tether is. The other cadets are coming tomorrow. And we're still somewhat convinced that there's more going on."

"Somewhat convinced?" I say. "Did you see the way Steve looked at me in the Frog when you were dumb enough to mention the brain patches? He knew about them! It proves something else is going on!"

"I didn't mention the brain patches, Jasper," Lucy huffs. "I just hinted at them. So what's the plan?"

"Wait until the admiral comes," Cole says. "We'll report to her what we know, and she can decide what to do. We completed our mission."

"That's not enough!" I say. "They're spying on us, they know about the brain patches, and they kept us in here for a week!" What I don't say is that I think Mira cried out for help in her sleep, because I only heard it in my mind. I could have been dreaming. Everything that happened in our quarters is kind of foggy.

"How about this, Ace?" Marco says. "We kick off our own spying mission and get to the bottom of what's really going on. We can do it while the admiral and the other cadets are here."

MONICA TESLER

I think about what Marco is proposing. It may be our only option. I don't see how we stop what Bad Breath already put in motion with his *friend* Seelok. "At least that's something. We can't just pretend like nothing's happening."

While we talk, the banquet table emerges from the wall, piled high with delicious foods. The smells alone threaten to derail my thoughts. We all drift closer to the table, like we wouldn't be able to stay away even if we tried.

"Maybe the Alks are just really big on hospitality," Lucy says. "That could explain why they kept us comfortable in our quarters for so long, and it definitely explains the food. Speaking of which, I'm starving."

"I'm down for a pod investigation," Marco says, plucking a mozzarella stick off the buffet table and stuffing it in his mouth, "but right now I'm down for a pod eating contest. And let's just say I'm the top contender."

"After dinner we can play a gladiator round in *Evolution*," Cole says as he loads his plate with chicken fried rice. "I'm basically a shoo-in for the title, but you can fight for second place."

I turn my eyes to Mira. *What do you think?*

She takes a plate piled with chips and salsa to the piano bench. *I need some time alone.*

No one wants to talk to me except the fresh-from-the-oven pizza that's beckoning me to the buffet. I guess that settles it. Time to dig in.

· 𝐸𝑓 ·

Once I've devoured an entire pepperoni pizza and a sleeve of chocolate vanilla-cream cookies, I claim the beanbag next to Cole and power up my avatar. Cole's playing an aerial combat level. I join in but crash almost immediately. My avatar is incinerated in a giant fireball. I'm just too tired to play.

"I'm headed to bed," I tell my pod mates. No one responds. Marco and Lucy look like they're already asleep.

I drag myself into my room and stumble for the bed. My eyes are closing as I kick my feet under the covers. I slap the light switch by my pillow, and the room goes black.

Why am I so exhausted? What is happening? . . .

Jasper! Jasper!

The lights are blinding. My eyes are open and I can see, but I can't move a muscle. Three Alks hover over me.

Jasper! Jasper!

Mira?

One of the Alks checks a monitor next to my bed that's blinking and buzzing. He clicks and hisses. Another Alk comes to my side with a syringe and injects something into my arm.

As I fade, I hear Mira calling . . . Jasper! Jasper!

I jerk up in bed. The fake sunlight streams through the window.

The memories rush in. The bright room. The Alks. The syringe. Mira calling my name.

MONICA TESLER

Was that a dream? It felt so real. I run my fingers along my upper arm. The skin is tender. Or am I imagining things?

There's pounding at my door. "Wake up!"

The room spins when I try to stand. I'm so exhausted. I feel like I didn't sleep at all.

More pounding. "Jasper, wake up!"

I stumble to the door. When I open it, Lucy rushes in. "Do you have any idea what time it is? The rest of the cadets will be here soon."

The other cadets? I shake my head and press my eyes closed, trying to focus my brain.

Oh my God, that's right! Addy is coming today!

Lucy is saying something. I know I should pay more attention to whatever it is. And I should probably try to figure out what the deal is with my Alk dream. But all I can focus on is the fact that my sister is coming.

I shoo Lucy out the door, warning her that I'm seconds away from changing my clothes (which sends her fleeing on her own). Then I grab my dailies and rush to get dressed.

When I emerge from my room, all my pod mates except Mira are gathered around Cole's tablet and the SIMPLE we swiped from Bad Breath yesterday. The webs are turned up full volume outside the SIMPLE range, probably so the Alks don't get suspicious about why they can't hear us talking.

"Where's breakfast?" I ask.

"Not here yet," Marco answers. "And breakfast might not be the best name for it."

I look at my pod mates. Something isn't right. "What do you mean? What's going on?"

"We're in your camp now, Jasper," Lucy says. "There is definitely something strange happening."

"We slept in again," Marco says, "and I mean *way* in. It's nearly three o'clock in the afternoon."

"I thought someone was going to set an alarm," I say.

"I did," Cole says, hanging his head. "But I slept through it."

"We're lucky the admiral arrives today," Lucy says. "We need to talk to her."

The dream from last night comes rushing back into my mind. The Alks. The syringe. Mira calling my name. "Where's Mira?"

"I knocked on her door, but she hasn't come out yet," Lucy says. "I tried the handle, but it's locked."

My heart jumps in my chest. I dash for Mira's room and pound on the door. "Mira! Wake up! Mira!"

Marco hollers across the room, "Cool it, Ace! I'm sure she'll be out in a minute."

"You don't understand! The Alks were doing something to us last night! I saw them!" I can almost hear the echoes of Mira's calls in my mind. She must be in trouble!

184

Lucy lifts a finger to her mouth and waves me back to the SIMPLE. "What are you talking about? All of us were here last night. I found you in your bed this morning."

"I don't know how to explain it," I say once I'm within blocking range. "We were in a really bright room. They had me hooked up to machines. They were running some sort of tests. I could see them, but I couldn't move. Mira was there. She was screaming for me. Not out loud, because we were paralyzed, but in my brain."

"That's one crazy nightmare," Marco says.

"It wasn't a nightmare! I swear I—"

The door opens, and Mira peeks her head out. She looks awful. There are dark circles under her eyes, and her blond hair has pulled free of its braid.

Time?

"It's almost three o'clock," I tell her. "Are you okay? Do you remember anything from last night?"

My mind swells with a sense of questioning. She doesn't know what I'm talking about. *Last night*, I tell her. *The Alks had us. You were calling for me.*

A look of confusion passes across her face, and then she lifts a hand to her brain patch. Her eyes shift, like she's about to access the memory. Just as quickly it passes, and she shakes her head.

I start to describe what I saw, but when I get to the part

about her calling for me, the door flies open, and Steve glides in.

Cole quickly flips over his tablet, deactivating the SIMPLE.

"Greetingsss!" Steve says, circling the room on his flying throne. "It'sss time to go. The other cadetsss have crosssed into our atmo-sssphere."

My story will have to wait. It's time to see my sister.

When we arrive at the siphon port, the passenger craft has just touched down, and the robots wipe off the residue from the pink smoke.

Apparently, a lot more formality is in store than when we arrived. Seelok and his honor guard are lined up in front of the craft. Most of them are draped in velvet robes and jeweled crowns. Even Steve has a crimson velvet stole around his shoulders.

Seelok sits atop a double-wide flying throne upholstered in blue velvet with silver thread. He reclines against one side and swishes his tail. The slippery skin around the tip is studded with emerald-green jewels. He wears a crown with matching adornments.

Behind Seelok and his entourage, fifty Alks on low scooters stand at the ready. They're like the ones we saw the first day. Instead of cyborg arms, they each have three little lizard limbs on each side of their snaky bodies. Steve waves us in and instructs us to stand to the side.

"I'm feeling a bit underdressed," Lucy says. "I should have at least switched up my ribbons for something a bit fancier."

"Can you say 'over the top'?" Marco says.

Next Bad Breath enters. He's covered head to toe in flowing gold lamé fabric. Over his shoulders is a purple velvet robe with gold embroidered trim. He wears heavy strands of rubies and sapphires around his neck.

"Oh my God," Lucy whispers.

Marco bursts out laughing. Lucy jabs him with her hip. I cover my mouth with my hands to keep from cracking up. It doesn't help that Mira is practically radiating with sparkly laughter.

"What on earth is he wearing?" Cole asks.

That sets Marco and me off again. Lucy gives Cole the evil eye. Then she glares at the rest of us.

Bad Breath strides past us without a greeting and marches to Seelok's side. I can't hear what they're saying, but it's clear that Seelok is humoring Bad Breath—making him feel important, valued, special, regal, basically everything he's not. It's easy to see how Seelok manipulated him. I wonder how much Earth Force intelligence Seelok managed to extract from Bad Breath thanks to his fake admiration and flattery.

The ramp to the passenger craft lowers, and a dozen Earth

Force officers descend. I recognize most of them from our prior tours, but none of them are aeronauts. They're combat soldiers. They don't look like they're carrying weapons, but I'm sure they have something concealed. They're probably ready to spring into action the second there's a hint of a conflict.

Next the admiral's honor guard exits. The last four guards stand at the top of the ramp and descend as a group. Their formation hides a fifth person—the admiral herself. Once they've reached the floor of the landing port, their ranks split and the admiral emerges. She walks straight through her ranks of officers to stand alone in front of Seelok.

"Greetingsss, Admiral Eamesss, Earth Forssse offi-sssersss," Seelok hisses. "Welcome to the Alkalinian Sss-seat. We are mossst honored by your presss-enssse."

The admiral nods. "Thank you for your hospitality and stately welcome, Seelok. We look forward to a productive visit that will solidify the partnership between our races."

"Of courssse. But you mussst be weary from your travelsss. We will sss-show you to your quartersss for ressst and nour-issshment."

"Thank you," the admiral says. "That is gracious, and I will accept your invitation on behalf of the cadets who have traveled with me. However, I would like to proceed directly to our chamber session. We have much to discuss."

Bad Breath steps forward. He glances at Seelok, who nods. "Admiral, if I may suggest that you visit your quarters first—they are most comfortable. The Alkalinians have prepared refreshments for you and your crew."

The admiral looks at Bad Breath as if she's seeing him for the first time. She takes in his ridiculous clothes and gaudy jewels. Her gaze slowly travels from Bad Breath to Seelok and back again. "Thank you, Officer Johnson, but we decline. You, however, are free to return your quarters."

"Uh . . . no . . . I mean, I will accompany you to your meeting with Seelok, sir."

"That won't be necessary," Admiral Eames says to Bad Breath. "Thank you for your service, Officer Johnson, but you are the one who looks weary. I believe rest is in order."

She turns her back on Bad Breath and nods to her guards. The one closest to the ramp signals the craft, and seconds later a group of aeronauts emerges, including the one and only Maximilian Sheek.

Sheek is here? When are the cadets going to get off the craft? I can't wait to see Addy.

The admiral waves Sheek to her side.

"Seelok, allow me to introduce Captain Maximilian Sheek. Perhaps you are familiar with him."

"Of courssse," Seelok says, sitting up a bit straighter on his throne. "Everyone in the sss-starsss knowsss the face of Earth

Forssse. We are beyond honored to hossst you here at the Alkalinian Sss-seat, Captain Sss-sheek."

Sheek tips his head and smiles, his signature pose. "The pleasure is all mine, Regent Seelok."

"Sheek will be joining us in chambers," Admiral Eames says.

"Admiral," Bad Breath sputters. "I must object! I should be the one to accompany you. I've been at the Alkalinian Seat for more than a week working on relations between our planets. I've prepared a detailed briefing."

Admiral Eames turns to Bad Breath and eyes him coolly. "Consider yourself on leave, Officer Johnson, effective immediately."

Bad Breath opens his mouth, probably to object again, but then closes it. He takes a step away from Seelok and stares at his shoes.

Marco leans over. "I bet he feels pretty silly in that gold getup now."

Lucy shakes her head. "Rubies will never look the same again."

"We need to catch the admiral before she heads to chambers," I say to my pod mates.

The admiral exchanges quiet words with her guards, and Seelok hisses at his entourage. Seconds later Steve glides to Bad Breath's side and escorts him from the room. Seelok flies his throne toward the exit, flanked by two of his men. The admiral and Sheek follow close behind.

The admiral stops when she reaches our pod. She smiles and thanks us for our service.

"Admiral, could we speak to you in private?" Lucy asks. "It's important."

The admiral pauses, and a flash of concern washes over her face. I cross my fingers it's enough to make her stop.

"Later, cadet," she says. "I have business I must attend to first."

And with that, she briskly walks from the port.

AS SOON AS SEELOK AND THE ADMIRAL
exit the bay, the general unloading of the passenger craft gets
under way. The Alks on the low scooters rig a second ramp
to the craft for the luggage. The rest of the pod leaders disembark first. At the end of their ranks, Gedney hobbles off.
When he sees us, he heads in our direction.

"How are you, kids?" he asks. "Officer Johnson didn't provide a very detailed report."

"That's because Officer Johnson has no clue how we're
doing," Lucy says. "Did you see him in that blinged-out gold
jumpsuit? That tells you all you need to know."

"He's been occupied with food, wine, and friends of the virtual variety," Marco says.

"They're using VR here?" Gedney asks.

Cole fills him in on the VR tech, but I don't listen. I scan the cadets as they disembark from the craft. First the Bounders in my class head off. Ryan, Meggi, and Annette descend the ramp and join their pod leader, Captain Ridders, in the corner. Then the new wave of cadets spills out. Ryan flags a group of them over to the corner. Those must be the juniors in their pod. Still there's no sign of Addy.

Gedney touches my forearm, and I jerk.

He smiles. "I didn't mean to scare you. I asked how you've been, Jasper."

"Oh, I . . ." I keep my eyes on the exit ramp.

"Don't worry. Your sister will be along soon. She's in my pod, you know, so you'll be training together. I suspect you'll be back to sibling bickering in a matter of hours. Not that I'm looking forward to that. I have about all I can handle in the sibling bickering department."

What's that supposed to mean?

The new cadets keep coming, and finally I spy my sister.

Addy steps out the craft door flanked on both sides by other cadets, who appear to be hanging on every word she says. She stops at the top of the ramp and scans the port.

When she finally spots me, she takes off running.

"Hi, J!" She crashes into me with a giant hug. When we break apart, she waves to Cole, Marco, Lucy, and Mira. "Hi, senior pod mates."

"Hey!" I say, giving her another hug. "You okay?"

She pulls away and gives me an odd look. "Yeah, why wouldn't I be?"

I shrug. "Just asking." I check out the other cadets and recognize the two girls as the twins Addy was sitting with on the trip to the space station. They both have curly red hair, green eyes, and freckles, and I doubt I'll ever be able to tell them apart. One of the guys I've never met, but he has jet-black hair and is almost as tall as Marco. The other boy is Desmond, the annoying kid we met on the first night. Addy is standing between me and Marco.

"How goes it, Adeline?" Marco asks.

"It's Addy," she says, correcting her odd formality on launch day. "Let me introduce everyone else."

"Isn't that Gedney's job, *Adeline*?" Lucy asks, squeezing into the small space between Marco and my sister.

Addy looks quizzically at Lucy. "I said, *it's Addy*."

Lucy tips her head and grins. It's not a friendly smile.

Gedney nods at my sister. "Go ahead."

Addy gestures at the twins. "This is Orla and Aela. They're from Eurasia—northwest in the Scandinavian archipelago."

MONICA TESLER

She moves on to the tall kid. "Minjae is also from Eurasia, but the opposite side." Then she nods at Desmond. "He says he already knows you."

"I've never met him," Lucy says.

"You don't know Desi?" Marco says, swinging his arm around the kid.

Desmond sidesteps him. "I am Desmond from Australia. Pleased to make your acquaintance."

"Well, Desmond from Australia, I'm Lucy from Americana West, and these are my sometimes-awesome, sometimes-annoying pod mates, Jasper, Cole, and Mira."

"What about me?" Marco asks.

"Ah yes, I forgot. That's the always-annoying Marco from Amazonas."

As the others keep chatting, I pull Addy to the side. "How are you really?"

"Seriously, I'm good," she says. "You were right, Jasper. It feels great to connect with other Bounders in real life. What about you? How are things here? There are so many rumors about the Alkalinians, I don't know what to believe!"

I don't get a chance to answer because Steve and other members of Seelok's entourage return to the port and wave us all to the center. The nerves I've had about Addy being here come rushing back, replacing the excitement of seeing my sister.

"Greetingsss, offi-sssersss and cadetsss," Steve says. "Welcome to Alkalinia. We are sss-so very happy for your arrival. You will now be sss-shown your quartersss. Cadetsss in one wing; offi-sssersss in another. All of your mealsss will be sss-served in quartersss. We will retrieve you for training in the morning. Esss-cortsss, pleassse pro-ssseed."

"Wait," I whisper to Gedney as the cadets and officers start to break up. "We need to talk. There's something going on here."

Lucy nods. "We're hoping to speak with the admiral tonight."

"I'm afraid that's unlikely," Gedney says. "Admiral Eames has a full agenda. I wasn't even able to get on her briefing schedule before . . ." Gedney abruptly stops talking, his face shifting into a stern gaze.

I glance over my shoulder. Steve hovers on his flying throne.

"Time to sss-scoot along," Steve says.

"Hello," Gedney says to Steve. "These cadets were just telling me about your hospitality during their time here."

Steve circles around and stops directly in front of Gedney. "Do you train thessse exsss-eptional children? They are mossst interesssting."

"Yes, I'm Gedney, their pod leader," Gedney says, placing a protective hand on Lucy's and my shoulders. "And you are?"

"Sss-Steve, offi-sssser in sss-service to hisss exsss-ellen-sssy Sss-Seelok, regent of the Alkalinian Sss-seat."

"Steve, if I may ask . . . ," Gedney says, smiling in an unusual way. His lips turn up, but his eyes stay cold. "I'm a bit of an anthropologist, and I'd like to speak with some of your people while I'm here, particularly the Alkalinian youth. I'd like to understand how you're adjusting to your new home."

Gedney obviously knows the Alks relocated here. He must know some of the secrets from the shrine, like how the Alks destroyed their planet. But why is he asking about the youth? Why would he want to spend a second more than he has to with these snakes, young or old?

"Perhapsss," Steve says, "but you have a very busss-y sss-schedule."

Gedney inclines his head. "I'll revisit the request at a later time."

"Children," Steve says to us. "It is time for you to retire to your quartersss. The arriving cadetsss need time to get sss-settled."

He circles around the junior cadets and swishes his scaly tail in a hypnotic wave above his head. The twins watch his every move with a look of panic on their faces.

Gedney turns his back on Steve and pulls me and Lucy to the side. "Don't worry. We'll talk tomorrow. And I'll try my best to get you an audience with the admiral."

He gives our shoulders a squeeze, then heads over to Steve and lets our snake ambassador usher him to the other side of the port, where the remaining Earth Force officers are gathered.

Lucy shoots me a worried glance. I guess we have to go another night before we can report our suspicions about the true Alkalinian agenda. And who knows how long it will really be until morning?

As we walk with the other cadets to our quarters, there's lots of chatter about what to expect here on Alkalinia. I don't know how Lucy manages to get the gossip mill churning so quickly, but we're still a few turns away when Ryan grabs me from behind and gets right in my face.

"Is it true?" he asks. "They have gaming consoles and swimming pools and a never-ending supply of your favorite foods?"

"The games and the food are basically right," I say. "But swimming pools? Where'd you hear that? The last thing I want to do around here is swim. Not with all that contaminated water out there."

"The water is contaminated?" Ryan stands so close I can see the remains of the fluffed tofu he must have had for breakfast stuck in his gums. He'll be psyched about the VR menu.

"Yep. It's, like, radioactive or something. Ask Cole."

Ryan finds Cole and starts pounding him with questions.

Meggi bounces along beside me and links her arm with mine. "We missed you guys!"

I smile. The truth is I missed her, too, and many of the other returning cadets. "What did you do at the space station this week?"

"Lots of refresher training. And we helped the new cadets adjust to the routine. Since your pod wasn't around, Captain Ridders asked me to be your sister's mentor. Addy's really sweet, Jasper."

"She can be."

Meggi lowers her voice. "She told me about the protests in Americana East. In fact, she told a lot of kids about them." Meggi stops and pulls me to the side. "You may want to talk to her, Jasper. Earth Force really frowns upon those kinds of stories. If the admiral found out, Addy could get in some serious trouble."

It's not like I'm surprised that Addy talked about the protests. Addy follows her own beat when it comes to justice and doing what's right. But I *am* surprised that I feel an urge to come to my sister's defense.

"She's not lying," I tell Meggi. "Those protests are real."

Meggi tips her head. "Still . . ."

"Understood. I'll talk to her. How did the new cadets react when they found out about the Youli war? Did the admiral tell them they're training to be soldiers?"

She bites her lip. "No one said too much about that, to be honest, but all the cadets seem to know. Did you tell your sister about the Youli, Jasper?"

I'm not sure how to answer. Addy probably shared everything she knows about the Youli with the other juniors, but how could Earth Force justify *not* telling them? Meggi looks at me expectantly. I open my mouth to stumble through an answer, but I'm saved by Steve.

"Cadetsss, we have arrived at the quartersss hall. Line up by a door with your pod matesss."

I squeeze Meggi's wrist. "We'll talk more later, okay?" Before she has a chance to answer, I sprint down the hall to our door.

Desmond is standing there.

"Take that room," I say to him, pointing to the next one in the row. "This is ours."

"That's not what Steve said. He said to line up by a door." He jabs at our door with his pointed finger. "I pick this one."

"We've been here all week, Desmond. This is our room."

Desmond shakes his head. "That's not what Steve said. He said to line up by a door. I pick this one."

"I heard you the first time, dude. Just move."

Marco walks up behind Desmond. "Is there a problem?"

I shrug. "Just tell him to pick another door."

Marco shoves his shoulder between Desmond and the door to our quarters. "Listen up, Desi, when we tell you to do something, you do it. When my man Jasper says to move, you move." He puffs up his chest and leans over Desmond. "Move!"

Desmond backpedals and crashes into the other junior cadets in Gedney's pod, who just so happen to be standing right behind us. I'm pretty sure Addy and the others watched the whole exchange.

"Nice," she says to Marco.

He grins. "*Effective* is the word I'd use."

"I was being sarcastic," she said. "Don't treat my pod mates like that."

"Or what?"

She puts her hands on her hips and steps within centimeters of Marco. "Do you really want to find out the answer?"

Marco grins. "Actually, yes. I'm incredibly curious."

Addy smiles in a way I haven't seen before. It's like she's daring Marco to back down through sheer force of will—that's a look I'd recognize—but this is something more.

Marco holds her gaze for several seconds. Then he bursts out laughing. He places his hand against the door to our quarters, pushes it open, and heads inside.

Addy has a smug look on her face. I'm not sure what to make of that exchange, but I'm pretty sure she came out ahead.

"We'll catch up more tomorrow, okay?" I say to her.

"Can't we talk now?" she asks. "I haven't seen you in over a week. I want to spend time with you, Jasper. I want to talk about Bounder stuff."

Down the hall all the doors are closed. Addy and I are the last two cadets out of our rooms. "I want to talk, Ads, but we're supposed to be with our pods in our quarters."

Addy shrugs. "Who would know?"

"That's not the point," I say, thinking about what Meggi mentioned earlier. "It's against the rules."

She laughs. "Fine. I want to get a look at our custom pod room anyway. See you tomorrow, Jasper." She gives me a quick hug and disappears behind the door.

As soon as I step inside our quarters, I realize I'm super hungry. What's for dinner? I head over to the buffet table. It's piled high with pizza boxes, a pasta station, and a sundae bar for dessert. It seems like the food just keeps getting better. Maybe it does. Maybe the simulation is adjusting based on our food choices this week.

Marco already has a plate and is slipping pizza slices on. "Dig in!"

As soon as the pizza hits his plate, Lucy shouts, "Wait!"

Marco slings on another slice. "Why?"

"That's it!" she whisper-yells. "Don't eat! Get the thingy!" She waves her arm at the SIMPLE. Somehow she manages to convey her meaning to Cole without actually using the word (a challenge). He rigs it up, and we gather in the gaming corner, spread out on the beanbags.

"Speak fast, DQ, 'cause I'm starving," Marco says.

"That's just it!" Lucy says. "I'm famished, too. And every time the dinner food shows up, we stuff our faces and pass out for a really long time, like a week. There must be something funny about the food—or at least the dinner food. I think it's what's been knocking us out."

"Please don't say that," I beg. "The food is about the only thing going for this place." I try not to think about what Lucy said, but I can feel the idea she planted wriggling beneath the surface.

"Just don't overdo it tonight," she says.

"I'm not happy, Twisted Sister." Marco shakes his head. "I am not loving everyone telling me what to do."

Lucy glares at Marco. "You're an Earth Force cadet. Everyone tells you what to do."

"Officers, maybe. But not other cadets."

I laugh. Addy really managed to get under his skin.

"Shut up, Ace!"

"Shut up, both of you, and listen to me!" Lucy says. "I think one of us should stay awake tonight."

"Huh?" I'm not sure where she's going with this.

"You said yourself, Jasper, that there was something funny going on at night," she says. "We need to figure out what it is. I'm staying up."

"All night?" I ask.

Lucy shrugs. "We'll see. If I get tired, I'll crash on the couch."

"That's not a bad plan," Cole says. "Observe, hypothesize, report. We'll be prepared when we talk to the admiral tomorrow."

"Right." Lucy gives Cole a thumbs-up. "Whatever you said. Show me how to work the SIMPLE. I may need to use it. And I'm counting on it actually being simple to use, because technology is not my specialty."

"No, your specialty is obviously nail polish," Marco says. "You must have painted your nails a dozen times since we got here!"

"Shut *up*!" Lucy says again.

"Can I eat now?" Marco asks. "Because I'm going to start raging any second if I have to keep smelling that pizza without getting it into my belly."

"You're disgusting," Lucy says. "Go ahead, ignore me, eat. But don't be surprised if you're asleep in twenty minutes. I'm almost sure the reason we're tired all the time has something to do with the food. It's the only thing that makes sense! And I, for one, plan to test my hypothesis like Cole said so I'm prepared to back up our suspicions when we're finally able to talk to the admiral."

After showing Lucy how to work the SIMPLE, Cole fires up *Evolution*. Marco goes back to his plate of pizza. Mira drifts to the piano. Lucy joins me on the sofa and talks at me about what we missed at the space station this week. As much as she spreads gossip, she's able to gather it quickly, too, because she gives me a play-by-play of basically everything that happened while we were away. I only half pay attention. I don't really need to know much of this stuff. And also I'm hungry. Like, really hungry. The sundae bar is calling my name. But what if Lucy's right? What if part of the problem is the food?

Eventually I cave in and grab a small slice of pizza and a single scoop of Rocky Road ice cream drizzled with hot fudge.

After I eat, I stretch out on the recliner to watch some futbol reruns with Marco, but I can't really focus on the game. I keep thinking about what Meggi said. Did Addy clue the juniors in on all the Earth Force secrets I shared with her? I'm not mad if she did. The juniors are about to put their lives on the line for Earth Force. They have a right to know the truth. The really awful thing is that Earth Force wasn't the one to tell them.

My eyes grow heavy, and after a while I'm slipping in and out of sleep, seeing images of Addy and Meggi protesting, and one of a Youli eating a giant sundae with strawberry sauce. That's not real. I need to get to bed.

I stumble to my bedroom door. Something tickles at my memory. Right. Lucy. I glance over my shoulder. She's watching me from the sofa with a concerned look on her face.

"You staying up?" I ask.

She nods. "Good night, Jasper."

"Good night."

I'M ON A TABLE. MY EYES ARE OPEN. I
can't move. I can't even blink.

Where am I?

Hisses and clicks sound behind me, and then an Alk comes
into view.

What's going on?

Words press against my throat, but I can't get them out. What
are you doing? I want to scream. What's going on?

The Alk wheels a cart filled with strange metal tools next to my
bed. He lifts a silver paddle from the cart. It looks like a hammer
with a wide, flat disk on top.

What is he going to do with that?

He waves it across my body from head to toe. Then he reaches for another device. It kind of looks like a glow stick.

My body feels different. I wriggle a finger. It actually wriggles! That paddle must have unfrozen me. Or maybe Lucy was right, and I can move because I barely had any dinner.

I can't let the Alk know I'm awake.

I stay as still as possible as he scans my body with the glow stick. He steers his hover over to a screen against the wall. He plugs in the stick and inputs data.

His back is to me. Here's my chance.

I take a deep, silent breath and hoist myself off the table. My plan is to take off running, but I'm so groggy I nearly fall flat on my face.

The Alk must have heard me get up, because a riot of clicks and hisses erupts behind me.

I quickly take in my surroundings. I'm in an orange room that looks like a medical facility. There are five beds, spaced far apart, three of them filled, but I can't make out faces. At the end of the room is a door. I run for it.

An alarm sounds. I keep running. I grab the door handle and stumble into the hall. I've never been in this part of the Alkalinian Seat. I propel myself down the hall until I reach the corner. Up ahead is a tube that leads to another structure. I rush in that direction.

When I step into the tube, the ocean bears down on me, and

I fall to my knees. Water is everywhere. I crawl. The alarm is sounding. Someone's coming.

Four Alks rush me. One is the guy with the glow stick. He inserts the stick in his pocket and withdraws a vial filled with yellow liquid. In his other hand he holds a syringe. He plunges it into the vial, then steers it toward my neck as the other Alks hold me down.

The needle pierces my skin.

I'm fading.

"Jasper!"

Someone's calling for me.

"Jasper!"

Mira?

No, it's not in my brain, it's . . .

"Jasper, wake up!"

I shoot up in bed. What's happening?

BAM! BAM! BAM!

Someone's pounding at my door. I need to get up.

I pull back my covers and flip on my light. My quarters are exactly as I left them before I went to sleep.

I rub my hand against my neck. Was I dreaming?

"Jasper!"

BAM! BAM! BAM!

That's no dream. Someone's pounding on my door.

"Coming!" I haul myself out of bed and almost collapse

on weak knees. I stagger for the door and manage to grab the handle. I pull back, supporting my weight against the doorframe.

"Oh, thank goodness!" Lucy throws her arms around me, which almost sends both of us tumbling to the ground.

"Lucy? What's going on?"

The orange room and the Alks fade into my dream memory.

No! I have to hold on to those images. Something tells me they're very important.

"Are you okay?" she asks. "You look awful." She helps me out into the common room and settles me on the sofa.

"What's happening?" My words are slow and slurred. I'm so tired. Why did I get out of bed?

"Hold on!" she says. She grabs her tablet from the side table and activates the SIMPLE, just as Cole showed her last night. Then she starts talking a mile a minute. "I knew there was something wrong! I just knew those slimy snakes were up to no good! After all of you went to bed, I waited, and I was about to fall asleep myself when I heard this noise, kind of like an alarm, and when I got up, there was bright light under all of your doors, like you were up and had turned your lights on, and then I tried to get in and see what was going on, but all of your doors were locked. So I tried to wake you up, and next thing—"

"Wait! Stop talking! Did you say you heard an alarm?"

"Yes! And the lights were on in your rooms! They just went out moments before I managed to wake you up."

"Whoa," I say. "Maybe it wasn't a dream."

"What wasn't a dream?" Lucy asks.

I tell her what happened, or at least what I can remember of it—my brain is super fuzzy. The orange room, the examining table, the Alks, my escape attempt.

Lucy's eyes go wide as I describe what happened. "Oh my God. What do you think they're doing?"

"I'm not sure. Running some sort of tests, maybe?" I wish I could remember more. I'm just so tired. "They injected a vial filled with yellow liquid into my neck. I think they're drugging us." I rest my head against the arm of the sofa. If I could just close my eyes for a minute . . .

Lucy jumps to her feet. "That's it! That must be what the food is all about! It works as a drug to get you groggy, and then once you're asleep, they give you even more drugs so you're knocked out for all those tests."

I lift my head. "Maybe. I'm not sure." I grip the armrest and try to stand. "We'd better wake the others."

"Not so fast," Lucy says, pushing me back down.

"Why? Whatever happened to me is probably happening to them. You said so yourself."

"I know," Lucy says, "but if we wake everyone up, the Alks

will know we're onto them. This has been going on every night, right? And we're still okay in the morning. One more night of testing won't kill anyone. Plus, they're probably done with the testing for tonight. The lights are off."

I sure hope she's right, because I'm feeling way too out of it to argue.

"What should we do?" I ask.

"Take a nap? I'm pretty sure whatever happens in the rooms doesn't happen out here. Hopefully, the Alks will just think we fell asleep in the common room."

I'm not sure that's the best idea, but I'm in no shape to protest. I'm already slipping back into sleep. "Lucy? Help me remember, okay?"

"I will, Jasper. Good night. And this time I really hope it *is* a good night."

I drift to sleep. There aren't any light or needles or Alks chasing me, but there are nightmares.

When I wake up the next morning, Steve is hovering in the common room.

Lucy is already on her feet. "Good morning, Steve! How are you this lovely day?"

"Is everything sss-satisss-factory?" He flies around the room, eyeing things up and down. "Is there a rea-ssson you are sss-sleeping on the sss-sofa and not in your bed, Jasss-per?"

I shake my head, still trying to wake up. "Ummm . . ."

"He had a nightmare!" Lucy interjects. "I fell asleep reading a magazine on the sofa, and he stumbled out in the middle of the night. He woke me up because he wasn't feeling well and he wanted to tell me about this terrible dream he had about the battle at the intragalactic summit. You know all about that, right? Anyway, he had this dream that we were caught and taken hostage on the Youli ship, and his sister was there, too, and they shot her out the air lock and she died instantly and it was absolutely horrible. Jasper didn't want to be alone, so I sat with him, and we both must have nodded off for the rest of the night." She punctuates this awesome lie with a huge smile and a bat of her eyelashes.

As the person who supposedly had the nightmare, I try to look distraught, which isn't too hard, since Lucy just painted a dramatic picture of Addy's death, even though it was totally made up.

Still, thank goodness for Lucy. Her monologue seems to have successfully sidetracked Steve.

"Wake the othersss," he says. "We are sss-shuttling groupsss of cadetsss to the sss-sau-ssser in twenty minutesss."

He presses a button on the wall panel, and our pod mates' doors swing open. Seconds later a breakfast buffet pushes out from the wall. Steve gives the room one last look, then leaves.

"Good morning, Super Friends!" Marco says. He stretches

his arms above his head as he walks into the common room. "Time for breakfast?"

"Do you think he was onto us?" Lucy asks me about Steve.

I shrug. "Maybe. He was acting pretty suspicious."

"Onto us about what?" Marco asks as Mira and Cole emerge from their rooms.

"Nothing." Lucy lifts her thumb and pointer finger to her lips and makes a zipping motion.

I raise my eyebrows. Nothing? Really? That's very unlike Lucy not to want to run her mouth, especially because she was right last night about the food. Although she's also right that we shouldn't talk about any of this stuff without the SIMPLE activated.

"There's not enough time to get into it," she continues.

Marco stops in his tracks and looks at me. "No time to get into what?"

"How did your spying mission go last night?" Cole asks.

Lucy slaps her forehead and glares at Cole. She climbs over me, grabs her tablet with the SIMPLE, and waves everyone over.

Marco sets down his plate of Belgian waffles and huddles with the rest of us next to Lucy on the couch.

She fills everyone in on our night—the lights in the rooms, the alarm, Lucy waking me up, my report about the Alks and the testing, and our decision to wait until the morning to tell the others.

"If they're testing all of us, how come Fly Guy is the only one who remembers?" Marco asks.

I shrug. "I'm not sure. I've always had trouble sleeping. Maybe I just wake up easier than the rest of you. Or maybe it has something to do with my brain patch. Do you remember anything, Mira?"

Mira's thoughts are jumbled. *Not memories, but memories of memories.* She closes her eyes and shares that she has a colossal headache.

Cole looks particularly disturbed. He rubs his hand against his neck. "Why on earth didn't you wake me?"

"It was too risky," I say. "We can't let the Alks know we're onto them. Until we understand what they're up to and how to stop them, we need to go along with it."

"Let them keep testing us?" Cole says. "No way. I'm not doing it."

"No one said that," Lucy says. "We're talking with the admiral today, remember? She'll know what to do."

"Does that mean we can't eat?" Marco stares longingly at his Belgian waffles, heavy with butter and maple syrup.

"I've been thinking about that," Lucy says. "Breakfast must be okay. Or at least not as bad. It doesn't make us sleepy like dinner. And I think that's because the Alks do the testing at night. I hope I'm right, because I didn't eat anything last night, and I'm starving."

"Me, too," I say. "And I definitely don't have the willpower to stay away from those waffles."

After breakfast I quickly change into my training uniform. The Alks aren't the only thing on my mind this morning. I have to talk to Addy. I rush from our room and knock at her quarters.

The door swings back. Desmond stands there staring at me.

"Can I come in?" I ask.

He keeps staring. "I'm not sure. Is that against the rules?"

I shake my head. "Just move, Desmond. I need to talk to my sister."

He doesn't budge, so I squeeze around him into their quarters. Desmond could teach Addy a thing or two about following rules.

Their common room is roughly the same size as ours, but it looks entirely different. It has four distinct corners, with an awesome circular couch in the center. In one corner there are detailed drawings of dragons, wizards, and elfin warriors hanging on the walls. There's a stand-up drafting table, where Minjae stands drawing a new picture with oil pastels.

Another corner is decked out with Earth Force signs and slogans. A metal table and chair are pushed against the wall. My guess is that's Desmond's space.

In the back, part of the wall is covered in rainbow posters

with unicorns and winged ponies. There are matching pink poufs on the floor, kind of like the one Lucy has. There's no sign of the twins, but it's clear that's their corner.

The twins' space kind of bleeds into the far corner of the room, which looks like a carbon copy of Addy's bedroom at home. She's perched on her bed writing in a journal. A bookshelf lines the wall behind her. She smiles and waves me over.

"You guys heading out on an early shuttle, too?" she asks as I plop onto her bed.

"Yeah, we'll be on one of the first Frogs."

"Frogs?"

"That's what they look like," I tell her. "You'll see. By the way, your quarters are pretty great."

"Aren't they amazing? I'll have to visit yours later."

I glance at the bookshelf behind her bed and at the violin on the desk. "You could have anything in the galaxy, and you choose your room in Americana East?"

Addy shrugs. "There's not much I need. My journal, my books, my computer. It's not like I can connect to the webs from here, but I like the symbolism of it."

There's no longer a poster of Maximilian Sheek above her desk. Instead Captain Malaina Suarez stares back from the inside of a quantum ship.

"New poster," I say.

Addy laughs. "Yeah, you were right, Sheek got old fast."

"I think Lucy was the one who said that."

Addy rolls her eyes. "I'll give you the credit."

I'm not sure what the issue is between Addy and Lucy, but I don't have time for it now. "We haven't had a chance to talk. How were things at the space station?"

"The food sucks," she says, sliding her journal into a bedside drawer.

I laugh. "How many times did they serve tofu dogs?"

"Too many." Addy tucks her legs beneath her on the bed. "Most of the other cadets are pretty great, and I love Gedney. We went back to the sensory gym a few times. That place is awesome!"

"Have you tried the gloves?" I ask.

Addy nods. "You were right, Jasper. They're amazing. The way they bind with my brain—I've never felt that kind of connection before."

"Have you practiced bounding or building ports?"

"Not yet," she says. "Gedney showed us, and he said we'd start working up to it once we got here, but we weren't ready yet. He collected our gloves before we left the space station. I think we're supposed to get them back this morning."

Addy sounds really good. She seems like she's enjoying the EarthBound Academy, just like I'd hoped she would once she connected with other Bounders.

We don't have much time before the Frog leaves. I have to get to the main reason I came to talk with her this morning. I need to bring up what Meggi told me yesterday. "Addy, I heard that Earth Force didn't say much to the new cadets about the Youli, but that you filled in a lot of the blanks."

Addy looks at me with an air of defiance I've seen a million times at home. "So? You said I couldn't tell my friends back home. I didn't. You also said no more secrets—that you were loyal to me, to your pod mates, to the other Bounders. Well, guess what? So am I."

It's not that I disagree with her—I think the juniors have a right to know now that they're part of the Force, too—but how do I make Addy understand that her actions have consequences? The admiral would not be pleased that Addy was sharing information with other cadets that the Force wants under wraps.

And since Addy isn't supposed to know that stuff herself, the admiral would definitely not be pleased with me.

There's a knock at the door, and Desmond opens it. He starts to give the same speech about how it might be against the rules to admit guests. Marco just shoves past him.

"Good morning, Adeline." Marco crosses to their breakfast buffet and snags a cinnamon roll.

Addy's face brightens. "Good morning yourself." She slides off her bed and hops onto the circular couch in the center of

MONICA TESLER

the room next to Marco, grabbing her own cinnamon roll on the way.

There's something funny about the two of them. I should pay attention, but I can't focus. I cross the room and look at Minjae's awesome art. While he tells me about the character sketches, I keep thinking about what Addy said, how she's loyal to the Bounders, how she's loyal to me.

Something else is bothering me. I know cluing Addy in on our suspicions about the Alks would be a mistake. That makes me uncomfortable, because that means I'm back to keeping secrets.

Marco claps a hand on my shoulder. "Time to go, Ace." He turns back to my sister. "See you on the Frog, Adeline!"

"Not if I see you first!" she says.

"Hey, Addy," I call from the door. "You know what we talked about? I think you're right. Just be careful, that's all."

Addy nods at me and grins at Marco. "Always."

GEDNEY'S PODS, BOTH JUNIOR AND SENIOR, are assigned to one of the first Frogs over to the saucer. I'm crammed in the back at a window seat with Mira at my side. Steve hops us over to the launch duct and—*POP!*—out we shoot into the water.

I close my eyes and tip my head against the glass. At least when we're in our quarters or in the siphon port or over at the hangar in the saucer, I can trick my brain into forgetting that we're stuck hundreds of meters underwater in the middle of a contaminated sea. Now, as we bob in the current, not so much.

I wrap my arms around my chest and try to stay calm,

even though the waffles and bacon I gorged on this morning are threatening to make a repeat appearance. Every time I'm out here, I feel like it will be my last, like maybe those nasty black sea creatures will manage to rip the Frog apart with their tiny arms and powerful tails and cast me out into the ocean. Who knows what will kill me first? The contaminated water? Or the sea creatures' razor teeth? I fix my gaze on the tube on the seabed that stretches from the Alkalinian Seat all the way to the saucer, hoping that will keep me grounded. The sea creatures swarm around the tube, maybe attracted to its yellow glare.

You okay? Mira asks.

Not feeling the best.

She places her hand on mine. I close my eyes and let her energy wash over me.

Her energy is mixed with something else. Or . . . maybe . . . *someone* else?

I open my eyes. From the front of the Frog, Addy stares back at me. Her eyebrows lift, and she tilts her head. She wants to know if I'm okay, too.

I nod. I'm fine.

She smiles, but the questioning look on her face doesn't fade. Before she turns around, her eyes dart to Mira.

I'm not sure what that's about. And right now I don't care.

I turn my head back to the window. One of the sea creatures

is headed our way. It's almost like the thing wants my attention, too. It opens its mouth and shows me its sharp silver fangs.

I close my eyes, but that's no better. My mind fills with the image of a bright room and a dozen Alks poking me with needles and prodding me with sharp silver sticks. Tubes connect to my body, pumping thick yellow liquid into my veins.

"Ace!" Marco whispers. "Look!"

Out the window, all the way down inside the tube, I can just make out movement.

"Are there Alks in there?" I ask.

Marco nods. "I think so. They must be headed for the saucer. What do you think they're doing?"

I shrug. Trying to puzzle that out is way too much for me right now.

Tube. Connection. Mira paints a picture of the tube in my mind, showing the route from the Seat to the saucer.

Yeah. Got it. I might be sick, but I'm not stupid.

"Might call for a bit of investigation later," Marco says. "You in?"

"Quiet," whispers Lucy. "Can't you see he's about to pull a Bad Breath?"

"What does that mean?" Cole asks.

"Yak, hurl, toss his cookies," Marco says.

"You guys had cookies for breakfast?" Desmond asks from the row ahead.

I press my hands against my ears and curl up on the bench. I wish I were anywhere but here.

Soon. Mira presses her hand against my back. *Soon.*

I sit up just in time to watch Steve pilot the Frog into the launch duct and squeeze our way through. We pop out the other end into the broken-down hangar.

"This is where we train?" Minjae asks as the Frog hops across the floor.

"We're not in the Ezone anymore," Orla says to her sister.

"No kidding," Aela agrees.

"Yeah, this place has seen better days," Addy says as we unload from the Frog.

"Oh, juniors." Lucy shakes her head. "You're spoiled already."

Addy spins around and glares at Lucy, who just smiles.

When my feet hit the hangar floor, I can finally take a deep breath without feeling like I'm going to puke. The day we leave Alkalinia cannot come soon enough. Maybe Gedney knows when we're scheduled to depart. If we have to stay here all tour, I may not make it.

Better than fighting. Mira sends an image of me pinning down the Youli on their ship last tour.

Stop reading my mind! I snap, and instantly regret it.

Mira sends me some nasty energy and disappears to the other side of the hangar.

Great. Now Mira's mad at me. This day is going from bad to worse.

"We're the first ones here," Cole says once Steve departs. "What are we supposed to do?"

"Steve said the pod leaders are meeting with the admiral this morning and should be along shortly," Lucy says.

"Until then," Marco says, "let's test what these young ones have managed to learn without our help." He unzips the straps of his blast pack and guns for the ceiling. As he arcs down, he leans into a backflip and coasts along the floor, then lands right at Addy's side.

"Show-off," Lucy mumbles.

By the time Gedney and the other pod leaders arrive, the hangar is crowded with cadets. We're the only ones who have our gloves, so all the focus has been on blast pack training. Of course, that doesn't stop me from using my gloves to power my blast pack. Me and my manual grips do not mesh well. And I'm not about to embarrass myself in front of all the juniors.

Lucy waves Gedney over.

"Good morning," he says. "Ready to get to work?"

"Gedney, can we talk to you first?" Lucy and I walk with him to the corner of the hangar.

"We really need to see the admiral today," Lucy says. "It's important."

Gedney nods. "The admiral is planning on it. She'll be observing the training later this morning, and she wants to meet with you then."

"Can't we meet with her sooner?" Lucy asks.

Gedney's eyebrows point down. "Sooner? I just said she'll meet with you this morning."

"I know, it's just . . ." Lucy shifts into monologue mode and basically unloads every sketchy thing that has happened to us since we arrived on Alkalinia.

"I see." Gedney turns to me and says quietly, "Tell me more about these dreams, Jasper."

"That's just it," I say. "I don't think they're dreams. I'm pretty sure the Alks are running tests on us at night."

Gedney crosses his arms against his chest. "But you have no evidence of it?"

"Well, no, but . . ."

"Hello! Cadets! We must stick to our training schedule!" a voice booms from behind.

I spin around to find Maximilian Sheek at my back with his huge, unnaturally white teeth bared in a smile. Since when has Sheek cared about training? A dozen Alks hover behind him. Sheek tips his head in his favorite side-angle pose. Behind him, every last Alk does the same.

Creepy. They're, like, totally obsessed with Sheek.

"We'll get started momentarily, Max," Gedney says. "Could

you please remind the admiral that she has a briefing with my senior pod this morning?"

"I'm not your messenger boy, Gedney. And it's Sheek. Don't make me tell you again. As you're well aware, I'm the Director of Bounder Affairs, which means I'm in charge of pod leader assignments." He nods to his Alkalinian entourage and heads to the other side of the hangar, with them flying close behind.

"Was he threatening you?" Lucy asks Gedney as we walk back to the rest of our pod.

Gedney laughs. "Ignore him. He's just a peacock fanning his feathers. Now let's unfurl your gloves and teach those kids a thing or two."

Gedney waves everyone over. "It's crowded in here. This is going to be challenging."

"I've got an idea, Geds," Marco says. "We discovered a great place to train just down the hall. Should we head over?"

"Outside the hangar?" Gedney asks. There's no doubt he's aware that we're supposed to stay here, that the Alks actually think we're locked in.

"Yeah." Marco nods toward the stacked crates, acting super casual. "We discovered a way out a few days ago."

Gedney considers this. He looks around the hangar. Sheek is on the other side talking with Captain Han. "Fair enough. Pack up. Follow Romero. And hurry."

Marco leads the group behind the stack of crates and into the dark hall. As soon as we've all escaped the hangar, he activates his blast pack and zooms ahead. "Last one there eats BERF!"

Addy kicks off and is at Marco's heels before I manage to slip on my gloves.

When I make it to the VR gym, Cole is already standing by the controls. He's activated the VR and has it set to the jungle template. I swear I hear a monkey screech when I walk in.

"Whoa!" Minjae says. "What is this place? It's gorgeous!"

I explain to him about the VR tech and how they must use something similar for our quarters. Then I remember Minjae's art supplies and drafting table. "Yeah, I guess whoever developed this tech must be quite an artist."

"I'll say!" he responds. "The palette is so expansive, and the way they've recreated sound and movement is mesmerizing and totally immersive. Take that fern frond over there. You can both see and hear it rustle in the breeze. And it's completely natural!"

I stare at the giant leaf he's pointing at. I can't say I've spent a lot of time studying real leaves, but that one looks as close to real as any real one I've seen.

Gedney asks us to pair up, seniors with juniors, to work on building basic bounding ports. I spin around to look for Addy, but she's already zooming away into the jungle, chasing Marco. I guess we're not partners. No big deal.

It's really not a big deal. So why am I so annoyed?

Lucy and Mira stand with the twins. If there's anyone more irritated than me, it's Lucy. I can almost see smoke coming out of her ears.

There's a tap on my shoulder. When I turn around, Minjae asks, "Partners?"

I shrug. "Sure."

That leaves Cole and Desmond, and even though Cole whispers some complaints to me when Desmond collects his gloves from Gedney, I know he'll enjoy trying to one-up Des on Earth Force rules and regulations.

Minjae and I head out into the jungle until we find a quiet clearing. Once we have our gloves on, I ask him to show me what he knows. He taps in and starts to build a port.

"It's . . . different here, harder." He scrunches his faces in concentration.

"Relax," I say. "The more you try to force it, the more resistance you'll feel."

Minjae struggles a minute more, then drops the connection.

"Let me show you." I shake out my hands and jog in place, then I extend my arms by my sides. I close my eyes and feel the heartbeat of the galaxy pulsing through my veins. When I open my eyes, everything is in perfect focus; each detail is clear down to the tiniest blade of grass. And I can see now that it's virtual, because each blade of grass is too perfect—everything in here is too perfect. What makes us real is our imperfection.

Minjae's right, working the gloves in VR is challenging, but it's not impossible. I reach out and gather the atoms I need for my port. In seconds I have a large ball of light in front of me. I could drop the connection now. I *should* drop it, but what fun is that? I call up my recollection of the clearing I visited in this simulation last time with Marco, I focus my port, and—*BOOM!*—I bound.

I land softly and laugh to myself. Minjae's probably freaking out right about now.

Then I hear someone else laughing as well. Addy.

She's close. I tiptoe between the trees, making my way to where I hear Addy and Marco talking. I have no reason to sneak. But I am.

I crouch down and peer around a large fern. There beneath a low tree bursting with orange flowers, my sister sits with Marco. They're cross-legged on the ground, facing each other. I can't make out what Marco says, but Addy throws her head back and laughs. Then she leans forward and rests her hands on his knees. It's just for a second, but it almost makes me flee.

I stare at my shoes, and my cheeks grow warm. I shouldn't be here. When I look up, Marco lifts a hand to Addy's hair and brushes it back behind her ear.

Then I hear Gedney calling. Any second Addy and Marco will cross right where I'm crouched. They'll know I'm spying on them.

Is that what I'm doing? Spying?

I don't want to think about it. I lightly tread back to the clearing and then rush to the metal cube, where Gedney and the other cadets are gathered.

"What happened?" Minjae asks. "You bailed."

"Sorry," I say. "I couldn't resist the bound."

"Speaking of that, Gedney . . . ," Orla starts.

". . . when do we get to bound?" Aela finishes.

Gedney looks up from where he's inspecting the VR control panel with Cole and Desmond. "All in good time."

"What about hurry, hurry, hurry?" I ask.

Gedney laughs. "Speaking of hurrying, where are your other pod mates?"

"As if we know," Lucy says, rolling her eyes.

"Something you care to talk about, Miss Dugan?" Gedney asks.

"No." Lucy crosses her arms against her chest. "Why would there be?"

Marco and Addy finally make their way out of the jungle. When they reach our group, Lucy repositions herself near the door, like she can't get away fast enough.

"Do we get to bound now?" Addy asks.

Gedney laughs again. "Your pod mates just asked me the same question, Miss Adams. You kids need to understand that bounding is dangerous. Until you have a solid foundation in glove skills, you aren't ready. A single bounding mistake will scatter your atoms across time and space."

"What do you mean, '*time* and space'?" Minjae asks.

"I can't give you a good answer to that," Gedney says. "It's something I've been studying for years, and I've still only touched the tip of the iceberg. We know that the manipulation of matter involves both time and space, and when an error occurs, the matter doesn't just disappear. It is likely redirected into a rift—a limbo area, if you will—where time and space are different from what we know."

"A rift?" Aela and Orla ask at the same time.

"Enough about that now," Gedney says. "We need to get back on track. The junior cadets will train with me for the rest of the morning, but the seniors have a briefing with Admiral Eames."

"Can we stay in here?" Minjae asks. "This VR gym is awesome."

"I agree," Gedney says, scanning the tech panel. "This alien technology is very advanced."

"Is it Youli tech?" Addy asks.

At the mention of the word *Youli*, the other junior cadets flinch.

Gedney looks at my sister, then at me, then back at Addy. "Yes, I believe it is Youli tech. The Youli aren't the only race in the galaxy to have advanced virtual technology, but I'm fairly certain this is theirs."

"Why would the Alks have it?" Cole asks.

"I'm not sure why they have it," Gedney says. "My understanding is that the Youli have a trade embargo with the Alkalinians, so it would be surprising if they acquired it through direct commercial channels. Of course, the Alkalinians are known to acquire things in other ways."

"You mean they steal things?" Addy asks.

Gedney's eyes widen. "You are certainly direct, Miss Adams. I'll stand by my original statement: the Alkalinians are known to acquire things in other ways. It is quite curious, though. Quite curious, indeed. Now we need to get back to—"

"So the Alks and the Youli are enemies?" Addy interrupts.

Lucy throws up her hands. "If no one else is going to say something, I will." She turns to face Addy with her hands on her hips. "I think you're a bit slow on the uptake, Adeline. When Gedney says 'you are certainly direct,' what he means is you ask too many questions and you talk too much. So cut it out!"

Marco guffaws. "*Addy* talks too much? Are you kidding, Miss Chatterbox?"

Addy puts a hand out to silence Marco. She doesn't need

him fighting her battles. "Oh, I understand what Gedney means," she says to Lucy. "I also understand that we've been lied to by Earth Force our entire lives, and that doesn't even touch all the critical information that has been withheld, which is really just another name for lying. So I'm here now, and I'm not going to play that game anymore. I don't care if that makes you uncomfortable or mad or whatever. If Earth Force is asking me to fight their war, they're asking me to my face, and they're answering my questions."

When Addy falls silent, we slowly look to Lucy and then to Gedney, waiting to see what will happen next.

"Ummm . . . ," a quiet voice calls from the door.

Meggi stands there. Her eyes find mine, and her lips lift in an apologetic smile.

"The admiral will see you now," she says.

18

WE FOLLOW MEGGI BACK TO THE HANGAR.
We're lucky she saw us slip behind the crates. When she heard one of the admiral's guards say he was looking for our pod, she came to find us. If she hadn't, our secret exit wouldn't have stayed secret for long.

Meggi leads us across the hangar to a small room by the Frog tube. Inside, Admiral Eames sits at a low table with her top advisers.

"Cadets, come in," the admiral says. "Take a seat. We're in a room with low ceilings, which I think is good enough reason to dispense with formality." She dismisses Meggi with a word of thanks and turns her attention to the five of us.

"Officer Johnson informed me that you located the occludium tether," she says. "Well done. Who would like to brief me?"

We exchange glances. Marco and Lucy both nod at me. I take a deep breath. "Okay, sir, I . . . uh . . ." Her smile eases my nerves, and I take another deep breath. "What I mean to say is *we* located the occludium tether. It's connected to this building, the saucer, which we believe used to be an active spaceship. The tether is visible when you're coming over on the Frog . . . or . . . uh . . . I mean, the shuttle."

As I talk, the admiral's guards input what I say into their tablets.

"At the far end of the saucer is a generator room," I continue. "You can get there by following the runner lights. A narrow shaft connects in that room and leads to the ocean floor. There's a small bubble building at the end of the shaft that we believe houses the occludium tether. A silver glow around the structure verifies our hypothesis."

Cole smiles at me. He likes that I used the word *hypothesis*. What did he say? Observe, hypothesize, report. Checks on all three.

"Thank you, Mr. . . . Adams, isn't it?"

I can't believe she knows my name. "Yes, Admiral."

"I understand your sister is with us this tour."

Why is she saying that? Does she know Addy has been

telling the juniors about the Youli and other Earth Force secrets?

"That's right, Admiral. Addy is here for her first tour of duty."

Admiral Eames smiles. "She's lucky she has you as a role model." Then she nods to the rest of my pod mates. "Good work, cadets. I'll send a few of my officers over to check out the occludium tether tomorrow."

"Tomorrow?" Cole blurts out. "Why not today? Shouldn't we be ready to take the shield down?"

"I appreciate your concern, but we'll take it from here. I'm sure you're happy to get back to your training. Thank you for your service, cadets." She looks down at her tablet and swipes the screen like she's checking to see what's next on her agenda.

The guards on either side of the admiral stand. Her words are supposed to function as a dismissal.

Lucy throws me a panicked glance. "Wait!" she says. "Excuse me, Admiral, but we have some additional intelligence to report."

The admiral gestures for her guards to sit and nods at Lucy to continue.

"We think the Alks are up to something, Admiral. Jasper has had these really vivid dreams—"

"Dreams?" the admiral interjects.

"They're not dreams, exactly," I say. "I'm pretty sure some

of it's real. We think the Alks are running tests on us at night, and we plan to prove it."

"In your quarters?" she asks.

"They're VR, sir," Cole says. "Our rooms can easily morph into laboratories while we sleep."

"I'm familiar with the technology, cadet," she says, "but that is an outrageous allegation."

"With all due respect," Marco says, "the Alks are not really known as upright dudes."

Lucy glares at Marco. That was not the right thing to say.

"I'll remind you, Mr. Romero, that the Alkalinians are our allies."

This has gone way off track. We have to bring it back to the mission.

Tube. Connection, Mira says through her brain patch, sending me the same picture from the Frog.

Oh! So that's what Mira meant! We can get to the tether through the tube.

Mira's foot presses against mine beneath the table. *Tell her.*

"Admiral," I say. "There's a tube that's anchored to the ocean floor. It leads from the Alkalinian Seat all the way here, connecting to the saucer near the tether. I believe you could traverse between the structures without the need to travel by water. That might be necessary to take down the shield. If you would authorize us to investigate the tube, we could find an access point."

"Yes!" Marco interjects. "We saw some of those sneaky snakes down there this morning. We should be able to get into that tube, no problem!"

Sneaky snakes? Geez, Marco. You are not helping.

"Cadet!" the admiral says. "I've warned you once! You are not to disrespect the Alkalinians. Perhaps you don't understand how important this—"

"He didn't mean it, Admiral!" Lucy interrupts. "He just doesn't always think before he speaks." Lucy looks like she wants to keep talking and it's taking everything in her power to reign it in. She must have realized she cut off the admiral midsentence.

"Apparently, neither do you, cadet." The admiral levels a cool stare at all of us. "I've heard enough. I regret that Officer Johnson didn't provide more capable supervision of your pod here on Alkalinia. Obviously, you've grown far too comfortable with your independence. That stops now. You are not to conduct any further investigations—no looking for the tube, no nighttime science experiments in your quarters. I will station guards on the cadet hall. They will provide all the security you require. Understood?"

"Yes, sir," we say in unison.

"You'd do well to remember that Earth Force is a hierarchy," the admiral continues. "You follow orders that come down from above. Even if you don't agree with those orders, you need to follow them. Understood?"

"Yes, sir."

"I'm ordering you to fall in line with the rest of the Academy, and that includes complying with the Alkalinians' directives. I shouldn't need to say this again, but the Alkalinians are our allies. We wouldn't want to appear ungrateful for their immense hospitality in hosting the EarthBound Academy. Many things are riding on the success of our partnership."

She stands, and all of her guards jump to their feet. There is no question that the meeting is over.

As we prepare to leave, the admiral nods. "Cadets, again, thank you for your service to Earth Force."

"Are you sure no one followed us?" I ask as we track the lit runners away from the hangar. We want to debrief on our own after the nightmare of a briefing with Admiral Eames, and we may as well pay a visit to Serena in the process.

"That's the fifth time you've asked," Lucy says. "I've been watching our backs the whole way. Stop second-guessing me."

"I know, it's just that we don't want anyone else to know about Serena."

"How dumb do you think I am, Jasper Adams?"

"Oh! Can I answer that?" Marco pipes in.

Lucy whacks him in the arm.

Almost there. Last corner, Mira says.

"It's just up ahead," I say.

Mira stops and extends her arm, blocking our path.

"Shhh!" Lucy says. "I hear something."

We flatten ourselves against the wall. Sure enough, the whirring motors of flying thrones grow louder by the second.

Marco creeps ahead and peeks down the hall, then quickly recoils. "They're headed this way. Fly! Now!"

We take off in our blast packs and turn left at the next fork into a dark hallway.

Unlucky for us, we pick the only hallway with no doors. At the very end we finally reach a room. Marco twists the door handle, and we pour in after him.

Cole activates his tablet, and the light from the screen illuminates a few-meter radius. "Whoa. What is all this stuff?"

I turn on my tablet and shine it around me. The room is enormous, stretching back across the whole length of the hallway. Everywhere I look are piles of shiny objects in brilliant colors.

"Oh my God!" Lucy says. "These are jewels!" She illuminates her own tablet and props it up next to a pile of sparkling green gems. "I think these are emeralds!"

"Where'd they get all this stuff?" I ask, shining my tablet at a pile of clear crystals. "Are these—"

Diamonds, Mira completes my thought. She dips her long fingers into the stones and lifts up a handful of the rocks. They refract the light of my tablet and cast a rainbow glare on Mira's skin.

"Who keeps a stockpile of precious gems in an abandoned room?" Lucy asks.

"Who *has* a stockpile of precious gems?" Marco says. "This stuff has to be stolen!"

"We don't know that," Cole says. "Maybe they received these gems as compensation for their services."

"What services, Wiki? Stealing secrets and selling them on the black market? This settles it! We need to take matters into our own hands! We need to figure out what the Alks are up to!"

"No way," Cole says. "You heard what the admiral said. We have to follow her orders!"

"I heard her, all right," Marco says. "She said she'd post some guards. Really? *Guards?* You know as well as I do that guards will do exactly nothing to prevent the Alks from messing with us while we sleep. Are you ready to let that happen?"

"What choice do we have?" Lucy asks.

Marco leans his arm against the door. "We can make any choice we want as long as we don't get caught."

"Count me out," Cole says. "I'm not violating a direct order."

"Come on, you know Jasper was right back there. We need a safe passage between the Seat and the saucer. We have to find out how to get into that tube! You saw those Alks down there today. Maybe they were the same Alks we nearly ran into just now. We need to know what they're up to."

"Actually, no, we don't need to know that," Cole says. "The

admiral ordered us to respect the Alks, not snoop on them."

Marco takes a step toward Cole, but Lucy blocks him. "Let's take some time to think about it. As soon as we get out of this room, we're going to see Serena. She may be able to tell us why the Alks were here. Then it will be time to head back to the hangar. Okay?"

"Fine," Marco says. "But this isn't over."

"We'll talk about it later," I say, crossing to the door. I need some time to think things through, like Lucy said. I don't want to cross the admiral, but my gut tells me we need to do something. "I'm sure those Alks have passed by now. Let's go."

We don't encounter any other signs of the Alks on our way to the shrine. We crawl through the narrow opening and gather on the pillows in the middle of the room. Just like last time, once we settle in the center, the ceiling awakens and a majestic image of a planet comes into view. It rotates through multiple astral scenes and then zooms through the atmosphere to reveal old Alkalinia: a beautiful planet with purple rocks, deep crevices, glistening rivers leading to a turquoise sea. The mark of a modern and powerful civilization is carved into the surface.

I'm so entranced I hardly hear the heavy swish of Serena's thick body gliding into the room.

She rises from the stone when she reaches me. Her head waves in the air, and she hisses and clicks. She brings her mouth so close I can see my reflection in her silver fangs. Her tongue darts out and touches my nose. I hold my breath. She's not planning to attack me (I hope), but I don't know if I'll ever get used to a giant snake getting in my face.

"Cole!" I whisper. "The voice box!"

Cole digs in his blast pack and pulls out the box. He waves it in the air so Serena will see it. She pulls back from me and glides around until she reaches Cole. She hisses and dips her nose to the box.

"Go ahead," Cole speaks into the box. The box emits an odd clicking sound in translation.

Serena bows low over the box and hisses. Then she clicks. Then she hisses some more. As she speaks, her body shudders, and her tail waves in the shape of a giant S. Before I even hear the translation, I can tell she's in pain.

Mira touches my hand. *Despair.*

"My brothers and sisters were here today," the voice box translates. "I heard them in the halls. I smelled their pungent scent. Their voices carried to me news from beyond. Oh, young ones, my people were here. They were here, but yet they did not come. They paid no respect. They ignore me and turn their backs on their past. The Shrine of Remembrance has been forgotten."

Serena shakes her head and emits a sound—neither hiss nor click, it's more like a cry. It needs no translation. She's obviously devastated. She cries out again and then lashes the side of the shrine with her tail.

"Remember or repeat, young ones! Remember or repeat! We are doomed!" Her tail thumps against the wall so hard the ceiling panels shake.

"Touchy subject," Marco says.

Lucy flashes her palm at Cole. "Hand me the voice box."

"I'm so sorry, Serena," Lucy says once Cole passes it over. "Truly. All of us feel just awful that the Alks didn't visit you and remember and stuff. But maybe—I mean, did you ever stop and consider—they were possibly very busy on an important mission and didn't have time to stop. And, you see, that's why we're here. We're happy to watch the video, of course, but we also wanted to talk to you and see if you happened to know what the Alks were doing here today."

Serena coils in a circle and lays her head on top of her thick, scaled body. She blinks at Lucy and jerks her head back.

Lucy climbs off the cushions and over to Serena. She holds the voice box up to Serena's mouth.

Serena juts her head at Lucy's face with a loud hiss. Lucy rears back.

"I hear enough to know enough, young ones," Serena says. "The cycle of war and destruction continues. Remember or repeat!"

"That doesn't sound too good," Marco says.

"What exactly do you mean?" Lucy asks. "What were the Alks doing here at the saucer?"

Serena swings her head heavily as she clicks into the voice box. "They were securing their pipes and stockpiles. They were double-checking their shield. They do not remember. Remember or repeat!"

"Do you mean the occludium shield?" I ask. "Is that something unusual for them to do? Do you think something's about to happen?"

"Do you not understand, young ones? It is happening again. All will be lost. All will be destroyed. Devastation comes to those who do not remember. Remember or repeat! Why don't they come? Why don't they visit the shrine? They must remember!"

Cole taps my shoulder. "What does she mean, 'it is happening again'? And what does it have to do with the occludium shield?"

I shrug. I really have no idea what she's talking about. I'm actually starting to wonder if Serena might not be all there in her mind. Being alone like she is could probably drive anyone crazy.

Still, she's our best lead. We have to try to piece together what she's saying. It can't be that weird for them to send Alks over here to check the shield. What did she say? "Devastation comes to those who do not remember"? "Remember or repeat!" This place is called the Shrine of Remembrance. It shows how amazing Alkalinia was before their planet was destroyed and they were forced to relocate.

That's when it clicks. The Alks' planet, destroyed . . . in the last intragalactic war.

I grab the voice box from Lucy. "Serena, are you saying there's going to be a war?"

"I pray I am wrong, young ones. I must descend. I must return to my babies. All my babies will die. Tell them to come! They must remember!"

She slowly uncoils her heavy body and glides toward her hole, her eyes drooping in weary resignation.

Lucy takes the voice box back. "What babies?"

Serena emits a painful cry and continues into her hole.

Marco leans over Lucy and shouts into the voice box. "What stockpiles?"

Serena stops, but she makes no effort to return. I don't know if she's going to answer Marco's question.

"Wait! Give me the box!" Marco shouts at Lucy, grabbing it out of her hand and hurling himself over the cushions to where Serena waits.

"Please tell us," he says softly. "Stockpiles of what?"

He places the translator next to Serena's nose. She flicks her tongue and hisses.

"Venom."

"VENOM?" MARCO SAYS ONCE WE'VE CRAWLED
out of the shrine. "I mean, really? This place is lifted straight
out of my nightmares. Actually, I'm pretty sure this is a nightmare, and I'd like to wake up right about now."

"Like I've been saying," Lucy says, "you're afraid of snakes."

"I *hate* snakes. Having a dream about something you hate
as much as I hate snakes is called a nightmare, thank you very
much."

Lucy shrugs. "Potato, po-tah-to."

After Serena told us about the venom stockpiles, we pummeled her with questions. Apparently, venom is the Alks' currency. It's highly valued on the galaxy's black market. It can be

used as medicine, but it's more often used as a mood- and mind-altering drug, or even a weapon. And it drives a steep price. No wonder Seelok and his top aides drape themselves in jewels.

"We need to get back," Cole says. "Gedney will be wondering what happened to us."

"Not so fast," Marco says. "I, for one, am not signing up to die in this waterlogged snake den. That means the time to find a way to get to that tether from the Alkalinian Seat is now. You heard Serena—those Alks were over here examining their venom stockpiles and checking their occludium tether *today*. You tell me: Do you feel comfortable waiting until *tomorrow* for the admiral's guards to check on the tether?"

"That would be going against a direct order," Cole says.

"Better to go against a direct order and live than comply and die," Marco says.

And die. Marco's right. We could die, and it wouldn't just be us. The lives of all the cadets are at risk. *Addy's* life is at risk.

"I'm with Marco," I say. "We need to act now. We need to figure out where that tube connects. Plus, like we've been through before, Earth Force needs us. Even if we're caught, what are they really going to do to us?"

"You know what happened to Regis," Lucy says.

Marco throws up his hands. "You and the drama! They are not going to kick us out! We're their star Bounders! Their special forces unit!"

"Punishment is not the point," Cole says. "It's the principle!"

Addy's words from this morning echo in my mind. *We've been lied to by Earth Force our entire lives. . . . I'm not going to play that game anymore.*

"Earth Force can't stand on principle," I say, "not when most of what comes out of their mouths is lies."

Lucy looks from me to Cole. "I'm not sure what to do. Mira?"

Mira shakes her head and walks away from our group. *Too tired for words.*

My other pod mates look at me, expecting me to reach Mira.

Fine. I chase Mira down the hall. When I catch up, she stops. *Try*, I tell her. *We need everyone on board.* I gently take her hand, and we walk back together.

Mira sends me pictures. Our pod in the Ezone. Our pod at Gedney's lab. Our pod in the Youli vessel. Our pod on the craft destined for Alkalinia.

Then she tries to articulate what she's thinking, what she's feeling. *We're them, but we're us first. I trust us.*

Frustration radiates from her mind. *Go on*, I urge her.

Mira looks at me. Her deep-brown eyes are filled with tears. *I used to trust only myself. Now I trust us. All of us. Only us. We should do this together.*

The others look at me expectantly.

"Well? What'd she say?" Lucy asks.

"Um . . . it's kind of cryptic."

Mira smiles. A tear overflows and carves a path down her cheek.

"She trusts us," I continue.

"And?" Marco asks.

"And I think she's saying that we need to make the decision as a pod. We need to make the best decision with the information we have, regardless of what the admiral says. Because, at the end of the day, we're all we have."

"It's all about the pod," Marco says.

That was our slogan last tour. It was exactly right then, and it's exactly right now.

"I'm in," Lucy says quietly.

Mira steps beside Lucy.

I nod and look at Cole. "Well?"

Cole jerks his head from side to side and balls his hands into fists. The variables are not falling into place for him.

"Come on, Cole," I say. "Don't pull a Desmond."

Marco steps closer. His hands are balled into fists, too. "Don't hold this up, Dr. Do-Good! It won't be the first time you've gone against orders. Don't draw a line in the sand that doesn't exist."

"Please, Cole," Lucy says, taking Cole's hand. "Just help us find the tube. If we get caught, we'll just say we were exploring. The pod needs to stick together—you know, H2Os5."

Waters's Five. That's the name Cole came up for us back

on Gulaga for the Tundra Trials. Waters may not be around anymore, but reminding Cole of our pod nickname might be enough to push him into our corner.

Cole throws up his hands. "Fine. This one time. But don't expect me to like it."

Marco claps his hands and starts down the hall. "Great. Let's plan while we walk back."

I slap Cole on the back and take off after Marco. "For starters, we'll need an excuse to walk around the Alkalinian Seat without an escort. That's the only way we'll find the tube. And the tube is our ticket over to the other side if we have to take out the shield."

"I have an idea," Lucy says, skipping to the head of our group. "Two words: Maximilian Sheek."

Lucy's plan hinges on Sheek. She'll convince him to host a party for the Alkalinians in the Earth Force chambers back at the Seat. Sheek will give a long-winded speech about the history of Earth Force and how happy we are to forge the alliance with the Alks and all that nonsense. We'll position ourselves near the back and slip out unnoticed while everyone's distracted. (At least, that's the plan.)

Cole—who's still extremely disgruntled and particularly annoyed at Marco—thinks he can get us roughly to where the tube connects, based on our external observations from the Frog. I'm glad he's confident, because all I feel on this planet is claustrophobic and confused. I would never be able to navigate to the tube.

When we reach the hangar, Lucy immediately tracks down Sheek. We hang back, but I can tell by the way he's gesturing with his hands and laughing that he thinks Lucy's suggestion to throw a party is a great idea. As soon as she turns to walk back to our group, Sheek leaves the hangar and heads for the room where we met with Admiral Eames.

Gedney and the juniors are in the hangar practicing with their blast packs. When he sees us, he passes out some protein bars and tells us to eat, then fly. He doesn't even ask us where we've been. I don't know if that means he's giving us a longer leash as his senior pod or if it's a *Better for you if I don't know* situation. After all, he's safer in the dark. If we share with him what we're planning, he might feel even more torn than Cole. He might decide he needs to tell the admiral.

Of course, Addy gives me the third degree about where we've been as soon as I set foot in the hangar. I blow her off, but I know it's only temporary. She'll be back for info soon, and she'll be relentless.

By the time we're wrapping up to head back to the Alkalinian Seat, word has spread that Sheek is holding a reception in the Earth Force chambers, and it might even be filmed for future EFAN clips.

"Looks like your Sheek plan worked," I whisper to Lucy as we climb aboard the Frog.

"Did you ever really doubt me?" she asks.

"Does this mean we'll miss dinner?" Desmond asks. "I was looking forward to my egg salad sandwich with extra relish."

"That's what you picked?" I ask. "You could have anything in the galaxy, and you picked an egg salad sandwich?"

"Yes," he says, "with extra relish."

"It's true," Minjae says. "Don't stop by our room at dinnertime. It stinks."

Steve escorts us directly from the Frog to the room in the Seat that's set up as Earth Force chambers. Most officers and cadets are already here, and some of Seelok's top advisers buzz around on their thrones. Ridders and Han stand near the door talking with a couple of high-ranking Alks. Bad Breath is in the corner sulking. He's wearing his Earth Force uniform—Admiral Eames probably made him return his gold suit and jewels. So far there's no sign of Seelok, Sheek, or the admiral.

"What do we do?" Lucy asks.

"Hang by the door," Marco answers. "Once we're able to ditch, we'll head back to the siphon port and through those rear doors. The Alks always exit that way, so they must lead somewhere."

"Of course they lead *somewhere*," Cole says. He's still annoyed at Marco.

I shake my head, hoping Marco will just ignore Cole. "The rear doors are as good a start as any to find a route to the lower levels," I say, inserting myself between the two of them to cut down on the chance that they'll start arguing and draw unwanted attention to our pod.

Our junior cadets appear in the chambers and head in our direction. Addy slides in between me and Marco.

Moments later Sheek shows up with the admiral and her honor guard. An EFAN cameraman trails behind him. Apparently, Sheek travels with a personal camera crew.

There's still no sign of Seelok. He must want to make a grand entrance.

"Why are they filming?" I ask. "I thought the whole existence of the Alks was a secret."

"Someday it won't be," Lucy says. "And I, for one, want to make sure I'm on film." She steps in the direction of the camera.

"Drama Queen!" Marco whisper-shouts. "The plan!"

Lucy sighs and reluctantly returns to our group.

Finally Seelok appears at the door flanked by two Alks. He traded up in the throne department for this event. His flying chair is gold with shiny, iridescent trim like the inside of a clamshell. On his head he wears a woven net of sapphires.

"It sss-seemsss we have rea-ssson to sss-selebrate!" Seelok says. He waves his cyborg arm and the room shifts. The walls morph into mirrors that flash every color of the spectrum. The table in the center of the room disappears, and a dozen tall cocktail tables appear in its place. A bar in the corner has rows of fancy glasses and bottles.

The EFAN cameraman races around the room catching everything on camera. Then he zooms in on Seelok and films his every move. Seelok tips his head left, then right. He lifts his cyborg arm and twists it in a figure-eight wave to the crowd.

"Is it just me?" Lucy asks. "Or is he imitating Sheek?"

"Totally," Addy says, rolling her eyes.

Lucy smiles at my sister. I think it's the first moment of bonding they've had. Maybe they're destined to be friends after all.

Seelok glides to a position of honor next to the admiral. He hisses at the Alks in the room, and they all bow their heads.

"Thank you, Admiral," Seelok says, "for inviting usss to your chambersss for what I'm sss-sure will be an entertaining affair."

"The thanks belong to Captain Sheek," Admiral Eames says. "This reception was his idea. I'll turn things over to him."

Sheek crosses to the center of the room and smiles to the crowd. He gestures for the cameraman to pan around the room. Then, once the lens is focused on Sheek's face, he tips his head left and right, elongating his neck and widening his eyes for the camera.

Only once all the posing is done does he start to speak.

"Good afternoon. I am Maximilian Sheek."

The room swells with claps, clicks, and hisses.

"Are you kidding me?" Addy whispers.

"Thank you so much," Sheek continues. "Alkalinians, or let me say friends, the citizens of Earth are so grateful for your hospitality and kindness to extend your home to us for the EarthBound Academy cadets' third tour of duty. I know as Director of Bounder Affairs, I am incredibly glad that we've forged this powerful alliance. And may I just add that these changes you've made to the room are totally swank."

Again the room explodes with noise.

Sheek waves his hands. "With our planets united, the galaxy has no limits. Am I right?"

Everyone in the room screams and claps. Then a unified cheer rises up:

"Birthright, Bounders fight!
Birthright, Bounders fight!
Birthright, Bounders fight!"

Marco bumps my hip and nods at the exit. Lucy is already headed in that direction. I glance at Cole and Mira and nod, and we make our way toward the door. When we circle up in the hall, my whole pod is there.

MONICA TESLER

My whole pod and Addy.

"What are you doing?" I ask my sister.

"Looks like whatever you're about to do is a lot more fun than listening to Sheek. So I'm coming with you."

"It's not fun, it's dangerous," Lucy says. "Go back and listen like a good little junior cadet."

"What did you say?" Addy glares at Lucy. Whatever girl bonding they shared a moment ago just went up in smoke.

"Seriously, Addy," I say. "This isn't for you. Go back inside."

"I can't believe you're taking her side!" she says.

"Quiet!" Cole says. "We need to go!"

Marco takes off down the hall. He calls over his shoulder, "Let's go, Adeline! You can come with me!"

Addy grins and runs to catch Marco.

I stand there, completely unable to move. I don't want Addy coming with us, but why exactly? Am I protecting her? Am I annoyed that Marco told her to come along with him? I thought this was all about the pod. Our pod doesn't include Addy.

Lucy and Cole run to catch Marco. Lucy throws me a nasty look over her shoulder.

Mira takes my hand. *Let's go.*

Well, I guess Addy's coming with us.

Mira and I chase after the others. Just as Lucy predicted, there's not an Alk in sight. Probably most of them went to hear Sheek, but it's strange.

"You ever wonder why there aren't more Alks?" I ask. "Or if there are more, where?"

"We do keep seeing the same thirty guys over and over again," Marco says.

"Maybe they're on the lower levels," Lucy says.

"One more reason to be quick and quiet," Cole says, waving us forward.

We dash across the empty siphon port and through the rear doors used by the Alks, where we're dumped into a hub of crossing hallways. On the opposite wall there's a door with a keypad that looks like it might be an elevator.

Marco and I keep guard while Cole inspects the keypad. "I'm ninety percent sure it's a lift," Cole says, "and this looks pretty straightforward, as long as it doesn't set off any alarms." He presses a green button in the center, and the door slides open.

We crowd inside what we hope is an elevator. An interior control panel has buttons arranged in a vertical line and labeled in Alkalinian.

"Hmmm . . . I'm not sure what this is all about," Cole says, surveying the control panel.

"When in doubt, go with common sense," Addy says. She pushes the lowest button on the panel.

We all turn to stare at her. "Why'd you do that?" I ask.

She shrugs. "Odds are the lowest button will take us to the lowest floor."

"Sounds about right," Marco says as the elevator engages and starts to descend. He looks over at Addy, and they share a huge grin.

"Good thing that worked," Lucy says. "Or you would have brought this mission to a quick end."

"Good thing I pushed the button," Addy says, "or who knows how long we'd be waiting for someone to do something?"

Before Lucy or anyone else can respond, Addy grabs Cole and me by the forearms. "Remember when we planned to hack the lift in Americana East? You guys owe me a joyride!"

"I had my fair share of elevators last tour, thank you very much," I say, shaking free of Addy's grasp.

I glance at Mira, and she squeezes my hand. *Me, too,* she thinks.

I haven't even been able to adjust to our apartment building's lift system after what happened on the Gulagan space elevator last tour. Mira and I watched as the Youli broke the elevator shaft in two. The cab was propelled off the shaft and collided with the space dock. Everyone in the cab was killed. Mira and I barely made it off the dock alive.

The elevator stops, and the door slides back. Marco leans out, then waves the rest of us forward.

As we spill out of the elevator, Cole says, "By my estimates, we need to make it roughly five hundred meters north and two hundred meters west to reach the approximate location of the tube."

We take off down the hall. From the looks of it, this is where the Alkalinians sleep. Maybe. The rooms look more like hospital rooms than bedrooms. They're all white and devoid of any personal items. Each room has ten beds, and next to each bed is a metal stand with tubes connected to the floor. But since there's not a single Alk in any of them, I have to guess they're not hospital beds.

The hallway goes on. We pass lots of opportunities to turn off, but Cole stays the course.

"Will you remember how to get back?" I ask.

"We haven't made any turns, Ace," Marco says.

Then why do I feel so turned around?

Don't worry, Mira says.

Cole comes to an abrupt halt just before the next intersecting hallway. "I hear something up ahead."

"Let me do the honors." Marco pushes Cole aside and creeps to the end of the hall. He peers around the corner, then spins back to us. "He's right. There are Alks up there. But they don't look like the Alks upstairs. They look even more like snakes."

"Like Serena?" Lucy asks.

"Yeah, but not so big and old," Marco says.

Addy jogs ahead and peers around the corner.

I yank her back. "What do you think you're doing?"

"Seeing for myself, that's what."

"You're going to get us busted," Lucy says.

Addy rolls her eyes. "Those things look exactly like the other Alks. They just aren't sitting on flying thrones and don't have cyborg arms. They're like the ones who showed up on the scooters when we first arrived."

"Why do they have arms and the others don't?" Lucy asks.

"They have cyborg arms, remember?" Cole says. "Alks must amputate their natural limbs when they install the robotic ones. I'm guessing it's a status symbol."

"It doesn't matter what their arms look like," Marco says. "We have to get by them."

"Let me take a look." I sneak up to the corner and slowly lean forward.

Half a dozen Alks cruise on scooters like the escorts Addy mentioned. They're transporting something down a long, narrow hall. As one turns into a room near our end of the hall, I get a clear view of what he's carrying on the rear of his scooter. There's a tray loaded with small glass vials filled with yellow liquid.

Whoa. My stomach twists, and my heart jumps into my throat.

I've seen those before.

A vial. Yellow liquid. A syringe plunged deep into my neck.

I WHIRL BACK TO MY POD MATES. "THOSE
vials! I've seen them in my dreams!"

"Quiet!" Lucy whisper-shouts. "They'll hear us."

"Right." I try to steady my breath and lower my voice.
"Remember how I described the testing? The Alks have been
injecting us with whatever's in those vials."

"Are you sure?" Lucy asks.

I nod as a shiver rips through me. What on earth is going
on here? What are the Alks doing to us at night? Whatever
they're planning, it's no good. They've duped Admiral Eames.
And I have a growing suspicion that we're about to be blind-
sided in a big way.

"What are you talking about? What testing?" Addy asks.

"He'll explain later," Marco says. "We have to get by those Alks."

He's right. We have to stay on track, or this whole plan is a bust.

Just then the door next to us opens, and out scoots one of the Alks. He almost plows directly into Lucy, but he course-corrects around her.

"We . . . um . . . we . . . um . . . we . . . ," Cole stammers.

Marco elbows Cole. "Shut up, Wiki. He doesn't understand you."

The Alk turns and disappears down the hall where we spotted the others. On the back of his scooter is a tray of eggs.

"That was weird," Addy says. "Obviously he saw us. He just didn't seem to care."

No emotions, Mira says.

You're right. "Mira says the guy didn't give off any emotional vibes."

"Was he carrying eggs?" Lucy asks.

"We can talk later!" Marco says. "We've got to move! Cole, let's find an alternative route."

"Wait a second," Addy says. "We don't need another route. Those Alks don't care that we're down here. That guy didn't even notice. I say we just walk down the hall like we know what we're doing. Maybe we can even learn something about those vials in the process."

"You have a point," Marco says.

Lucy puts her hands on her hips. "You're not possibly saying you think that's a good idea."

"We can't get across that hall without them seeing us," Marco says. "We might as well act like we belong here. I bet that's the quickest way to the tunnel, too."

"Let's not stand around talking about it. Come on!" Addy turns the corner and heads up the hall.

Marco is right behind her.

"Jasper!" Lucy says. "You have got to control your sister!"

"Have you met Addy?" I ask. "That's not going to happen."

Lucy glares at me for another solid second and then storms around the corner.

Cole, Mira, and I follow Lucy. The hall is not so different from many of the ones we've been down before, although this one is a flurry of activity. Alks like the one we just saw are zooming up and down the hall on their low scooters. Most of them carry the tiny vials. One of the Alks zooms so close I could pluck a vial off his tray.

Just like Addy predicted, none of them seem to care about us. They're just doing their jobs. We hurry down the hall, following Marco and Addy. Marco looks over his shoulder. He points to a room at his side and then rushes on.

We reach the place where Marco pointed, and it's clear why. The room has transparent walls that let you look right in. A dozen Alks busy about inside, checking equipment and gauges. A huge vat sits in the middle. One of the Alks fills the vials from a tap on the bottom of the vat. He passes it to another Alk, who seals and labels the vial. A third swoops in to place the vials on a tray and carry them to another room in the rear. The doors to the back room slide open, and a cloud of chilled air puffs out. There are rows and rows of tiny vials extending as far back as I can see.

"What is this place?" Lucy asks.

"Not sure," I say. "But I have an awful feeling in my gut."

You know what's in those vials, Mira says.

I push her words from my mind. I need to focus on making it to the other end of this hall, then I can think.

"Over here!" Addy calls.

I cross the hall to where she stands looking into another room. In the center is an enormous, elevated box. The box is filled with gray speckled eggs. Lamps hang from the ceiling and glow orange above the eggs, probably keeping them warm.

Marco slides in between us. "Why eggs?"

I shrug. "Not sure, but I *am* sure I don't want to think about that right now."

Lucy slaps my shoulder. "Let's go!"

Marco and Addy dash ahead. I linger in front of the egg room. There's something we're missing.

In the next room four Alks lie on inclined exam tables. They all have cyborg arms, and they appear to be unconscious. Their robotic limbs are hooked up to elaborate machines that poke and prod and test reflexes.

"Good thing they're not awake," Cole says beside me. "I bet they wouldn't be too happy about us being down here."

"Why do you think they'd care?" I ask. "The other Alks don't even notice us."

"None of the others have cyborg arms. I think it's a symbol of Alkalinian hierarchy."

"And the higher up on the Alk food chain, the more likely you are to care about Bounders wandering around on their own?"

Cole shrugs. "It's just a theory."

Up ahead Marco and Addy reach the end and turn right. The rest of us are close behind.

"This way!" Cole says when we're all out of the Alk-filled hall. "I think we're almost there. He takes off in the lead. Three turns later we reach a dead end at two giant metal doors.

"If my estimations are correct," Cole says, "the tube should connect at this room."

"What are we waiting for?" Marco says. "Let's find out."

He grabs one of the door handles, and I grab the other. The doors are heavy, but they're not locked. We pull them back, hoping our good luck continues and that there is no one on the other side who *would* care about seeing a group of unsupervised Bounders down here.

"Bingo!" Addy says, leading us in.

Sure enough, the tube connection is directly in front of us, and so are walls of windows holding back the millions of tons of water. The queasy feeling I've been wrestling with all tour comes rushing back.

I bend over my knees, trying to suck oxygen into my lungs.

Can't get enough air!

Mira places her hand on my back. *Slow. Breathe.*

Her strength seeps into me. I close my eyes and take a deep breath. Then another. When I'm breathing normally again, I push myself up.

My other pod mates are standing next to the tube that heads out of the Alkalinian Seat and across the ocean floor to the saucer. I take another deep breath and walk over to them.

A pipe takes up most of the room in the tube. It comes right through the wall and continues on to a huge pump and storage cylinders.

Cole inspects the door that leads to the tube. "It's open now," he says, "but it looks like it could be sealed off."

"But what's that pipe for?" Lucy asks.

In front of the cylinders is a conveyer belt lined with vats like the one we saw in the Alk hall, the one used to fill the vials.

On the other side of the room, vats are stacked from floor to ceiling—at least two hundred of them—all labeled with Alkalinian characters.

Mira's words return to me. *You know what's in those vials.*

Everything we've been through in the last week comes rushing through my mind. Our quarters. My dreams. The vials. Serena and the forgotten shrine.

"Venom," I say.

All my pod mates stare at me, and for a moment no one speaks.

"What do you mean, 'venom'?" Addy asks. That's right, she doesn't even know about Serena.

"You really think all of this equipment, all of those vats, all of those vials, are for venom?" Lucy asks.

Marco shrugs. "What else could it be?"

"It must be," I say. "Serena told us it was their main currency on the galaxy's black market."

"Who's Serena?" Addy asks.

"Even Gedney said the Alks deal in illicit substances," Cole says.

"You really think they're injecting us with that?" Lucy says with a shudder.

"Maybe not all of us," I say. "Maybe just me. Or me and Mira. I'm not sure."

"*Hello?*" Addy says. "Can someone please clue me in?"

I take another deep breath and tell my sister about Serena and the shrine and my dreams and everything else that points to the disturbing conclusion that the Alks are bottling venom in what looks like a huge commercial operation.

Addy crosses her arms against her chest. "I can't believe you kept this from me. You promised no more secrets, Jasper!"

This again? "I'm not keeping secrets! I'm including you! When did I have a chance to tell you before now?"

Addy gets in my face. "How about yesterday in my quarters?"

"We had other things to talk about!"

"Yeah, like how I shouldn't be sharing so much with the other cadets! See? It's still all about secrets!"

Lucy shoves herself between us. "Only because you have such a big mouth!" she says to Addy.

"Quiet!" Cole says. "None of that matters! We need to finish what we came here for!"

For a moment no one moves. Then Lucy puts her hands on her hips and looks at Cole. Marco takes Addy's hand and walks her away from Lucy. Mira places her palm on my back.

Cole approaches the pipe and inspects the seal. "Where is the venom coming from? We've been over at the saucer multiple times, and the only Alks we've seen other than Serena are those guys who were performing maintenance."

"And Serena said that was out of the ordinary," Lucy says.

"There are lots of Alks down here," I say, "at least, a lot more than we've seen before today."

"True," Cole says, "but this looks like an output valve. That must mean the venom is coming from the saucer. Not to mention we saw no signs of venom extraction on our way over here."

"Venom extraction?" Marco says. "Wait a second, the venom is coming from the Alks?"

"Where else would it be coming from?" Cole asks.

Marco swings his hands to his head. "Those dudes are poisonous?"

I shrug. "I hadn't really thought of it like that, but I guess?"

"I *hate* snakes!" Marco says, sinking to a squat. "These Alks are so much worse than the Youli."

Cole claps his hands. "Hello! Over here! The tube, remember?"

We crowd around as Cole opens the door that leads to the tube. "The good news is there's definitely enough room in here for someone to cross. The Alks must have constructed the tube so they could maintain the pipe without going into the water."

"That means someone could make it to the saucer without

going by Frog," I say, peering into the tube. "If Earth Force needs to take out the tether, this is the best option."

"Maybe," Cole says. "We still don't know where the pipe connects at the saucer. Half of the place is falling apart. The tether might not be reachable, or at least easily reachable from the tube. That would be a disaster, especially under time pressure."

Marco steps into the tube. "Well then, we need to see where it goes!" He takes off jogging. Addy heads out after him.

"No!" I take a tentative step into the tube. It basically feels like stepping into the ocean. Water's on all sides, and I'm immediately disoriented. Up ahead the black sea creatures swim near the tube. One smashes the side with its heavy tail right where Marco and my sister stand.

"We have to get back!" I shout to them. "If we aren't there by the end of the reception, they'll definitely know something's up."

"Jasper's right!" Lucy calls. "We need to go!"

"Fine," Marco says, reluctantly retracing his steps out of the tube with my sister at his side, "but tomorrow we need to find where the tube connects at the saucer."

"And tonight we need to figure out what's really going on while we sleep," Lucy says.

"How are we going to do that?" Addy asks once she and Marco are out of the tube and the door is sealed behind them.

Lucy shoots an annoyed glance at Addy. "*We* aren't going to do anything, sweetie. *My* pod is going to find out what those Alks are doing with those vials."

"And I'm just supposed to go to bed and pretend I don't know anything about it?" Addy asks.

"Sounds about right," Lucy says with a patronizing smile.

We slide into the back of the Earth Force chambers moments before Seelok finishes talking. He must have decided to follow Sheek with a monologue of his own. He even does the side-to-side head tilt again for the EFAN cameraman when he finishes.

Once we're dismissed, most of the cadets race to their quarters. Two juniors from Ryan's pod ask Cole for *Evolution* pointers on the way. It sounds like they're checking in for a big night of gaming. The junior twins from Addy's pod— Orla and Aela—chat about what goodies will pop up in their candy buffet tonight, then they argue about which candy is best. If those two aren't completing each other's sentences, they're bickering.

When we reach our door, Addy grabs Marco and me by the arms. "Please let me help tonight." The words are for both of us, but she's looking at Marco.

"We can't." I shake off her arm. I don't know what's going on with her and Marco, but I don't like it. "The Alks are monitoring us. They'd know if you weren't in your quarters. I'll fill you in tomorrow."

"You just expect me to sleep, Jasper?"

I look around the hall. Most of the cadets are already in their quarters. "Keep your voice down! You can't tell anyone about this, Addy. I mean it!"

Again my sister looks to Marco.

"Listen to your bro," he whispers. "We need to keep a low profile, or we'll never best these Alks at their own game. There's a reason for secrecy. A good one."

"But how can I sleep if know they're injecting me with venom?"

"We've been sleeping here for more than a week, and we're fine," Marco says.

"Jasper, please," she says. "I want to help."

"Addy, the best thing you can do is act as if everything's fine. Not giving the Alks reason to be suspicious *is* helping."

"Hardly." She storms into her quarters without saying good night.

Marco shrugs and heads into our room. I lean against the wall and close my eyes. I need a break before debriefing with my pod about everything we learned today. Something tells me whatever comes next is going to be rough.

It's strange having Addy here with me. When we were little, we'd pretend we were in space on these awesome missions. We were so excited to begin our Bounder training.

Nothing turned out like I imagined. I can't keep Addy safe. I can't even keep her happy with me. Our pod is pulled at the seams, and it's not just because my sister is tagging along. Cole isn't comfortable operating outside the rules, and Marco seems to thrive there.

Where does that leave me?

Four officers stand at the end of the hall. They must be the guards Admiral Eames said she'd send to make sure the cadets are safe. Guards or not, nothing about Alkalinia seems safe right now. Even with all the stockpiles of jewels and riches on this planet, the most valuable commodity is right in this hall. All the trained Bounders in the galaxy are behind these doors.

Once we're settled in our quarters, Cole activates the SIMPLE. Lucy waves us over to the couch.

Marco flops down on the cushions. "Can't we have a break before we shift back into secret agent mode?"

"It's late," Lucy says, "and we need a plan for tonight. Once we have one, you can do whatever you want."

"I don't like it," Cole says. "Admiral Eames said not to do any investigating. We already defied her order once today. I told you I wouldn't do it again."

"Finding out what's happening in our own bedrooms hardly counts as investigating," Marco says.

"She specifically said 'no nighttime science experiments.'"

"You don't have to be involved," Lucy says.

"Plus, there won't be any experiments!" I say. "All we're going to do is observe! Observe, hypothesize, report. Those are your words, Cole! We'll observe tonight and talk tomorrow morning. If there's anything to report to the admiral, we'll do it! Okay?"

"You promise?" Cole asks.

I nod and discreetly cross my fingers behind my back. I'm not sure telling Admiral Eames is going to be the best idea, but we don't need to decide tonight.

"Fine," Cole says, "but keep me out of it."

"No problem," Lucy says. "Tell us again what you've been seeing at night, Jasper."

"Well, I'm not entirely sure what's real, but . . ." I tell them about how I'm lying on a bed in a bright, hospital-like room. Alks check gauges and monitors as they hiss and click to one another. They inject my neck with yellow fluid from the vials we saw earlier today. My eyes are open, and I can see, but I can't move, except that one time I tried to escape. And since they talk in Alkalinian, I can't understand anything the Alks say.

"Don't forget that I heard the alarm last night and saw bright lights under your doors!" Lucy interjects. She nods at me to continue.

"One night I felt like Mira was calling to me. I was sure it was a dream, but again I felt like I couldn't move. I struggled and finally managed to sit up, but when I did, I had the sensation that everything in the room shifted back into place."

"That's possible!" Cole said. "This is all VR. Remember how this room looked when we first came in? And how the VR gym at the abandoned habitat can shift?"

"Exactly." I explain how I could still hear Mira calling for me through the brain patch. I ran to her door and couldn't get in, but eventually the door unlocked and I found her safe in bed. Still, though, I couldn't shake the feeling that she'd been trying to reach me moments before.

"I'm not sure how we find out the truth," I say once I've shared the details of my might-not-be dreams.

"Well, for starters," Lucy says, "don't eat!"

As if on cue, the gears turn in the wall and out pops the nightly buffet. The smell of garlic bread races through the room and calls me to the table.

"What?" I can already taste the buttery bread in my mouth.

"We talked about this last night, Jasper," Lucy says. "There's something in the food knocking all of us out, and I'm betting it's venom. That's why we've been sleeping for fifteen hours every night. The first week we slept for *days* at a time."

"No one said anything about not eating," Marco says. He's

also eyeing the buffet. I think the chicken quesadillas might be calling his name.

"I think some of us should eat normally," Lucy says. "We don't want the Alks to know we're onto them. If the whole pod stopped eating and stayed up all night, I'm pretty sure they'd be clued in. Steve already knows that Jasper hasn't been feeling well, so hopefully it won't raise any suspicions."

"So what do you propose?" Cole asks.

"Everyone goes to sleep except me and Jasper," Lucy says. "Once the bright lights switch on in the bedrooms, we'll see what the Alks are really up to."

"How are you going to do that?" Marco asks. "I thought you said the doors are locked."

The patch. Mira sends me an image of us forming a mental link through our brain patches. It would let me see what she sees while she's in her quarters.

"That will never work," I say.

"Gee, thanks for your vote of confidence," Lucy says.

"I wasn't talking to you, I was talking to Mira."

Lucy rolls her eyes. "And?"

"And she suggested we link up so that I can spy on her while she sleeps. Basically, my brain could use her eyes. If the Alks are injecting venom or running tests on her in the bedroom, I would see it, even if I were sitting out here on the couch."

"Sounds like a pretty good idea to me," Marco says.

"Yeah, except it will never work."

It will.

"It won't."

It will.

"It won't!"

"Will you knock it off with the brain-talk!" Lucy says. "I'm with Mira. Give it a try. What's the worst thing that could happen? It doesn't work so we need a new plan? That's no worse than where we are right now."

We can practice.

Practice? That means one-on-one time with Mira. What would I rather do, spend time with Mira, or eat loads of garlic bread and pass out on my bed and be poked and prodded by Alks?

"Fine," I say. "But I'm starving."

"Make a plate for later," Lucy says. "You can eat after we spy."

21

AFTER A FORTY-FIVE-MINUTE BREAK—HALF
of which I spend torturing myself by watching Marco ingest a
whole quesadilla and two dozen buffalo wings, and the other
half I spend getting annihilated by Cole in the hand-to-hand
combat level in *Evolution*—Mira creeps into my brain and
sets off a burst of sparkly lights.

I fall out of my chair in alarm. "Don't do that!" I say to
Mira. "You scared me!"

Mira smiles. *Sorry. Practice?*

Fine. I follow her back to her room. Her bed is neatly
made, and I imagine this is what her room looks like back
on Earth, although I know it's not the same. My room here

is nothing like my room at home, even if it does kind of look like it. My room back home is peace, privacy, comfort, safety. My room here is . . . not.

Now that I have a hunch what the Alks are up to, I hate being in my room here. It looks like it's trying too hard, like the Alks threw in every ingredient they could think of to make a personal room, but there's absolutely nothing personal about it.

Mira sits by her pillow with her legs curled up beneath her. I sit on the other end with my feet firmly planted on the floor.

She closes her eyes, and her face has a certain stillness to it that I recognize as concentration. A second passes, and then I feel her inside my brain, reaching out like long fingers grasping for something. My instinct is to shut her out. It feels mega weird to share your brain with someone. Sure, Mira touches my brain a lot, but this is different. It's like she's trying to merge with me.

I stare at her face and force myself to stay open. I would try to help, but since I have no idea how she's going to accomplish this, I figure not interfering is the best option. It seems to take forever. I think back to the day Addy and I were in the basement of our apartment building, knee to knee. She begged me to tell her all my Earth Force secrets. How long ago was that? It feels like ages.

There was so much stuff in that dump—bins of old smartphones with cracked screens, and all those creepy dolls with the blinkless eyes and blood red lips.

Snap! A lasso loops around my brain and reins me in. Mira yanks me back to the moment.

Dolls? she asks.

I smile. *Forget it. Are we connected?*

Yes, practice?

This feels so strange. So intimate. Like she has a magnifying glass focused on my innermost secrets. *Okay.*

Close your eyes. Describe what I'm doing. Out loud.

I squeeze my eyes shut, and a picture appears in my mind. It comes in fuzzy and then starts to focus. It's me! I'm staring at myself from across the bed. I'm seeing things through Mira's eyes!

I look like a dork. My eyes are closed, and my palms are clasped awkwardly on my lap. I watch myself drop my hands to my sides. Okay, this is kind of creepy.

My brain jumps with a jolt of energy. That must be Mira's way of telling me to focus. She slowly stands, which feels like I'm standing. Then she bends to her trunk and pulls out her tablet. She slashes her finger to make letters: *J-A-S-P-E-R.*

"You just got your tablet and wrote my name."

Good. Try another.

This time she puts her hands on her head and spins around. The room whirls around me.

"Umm . . . you're doing some silly dance."

Ha! It wasn't so silly! Her sparkly energy says she's giggling inside.

I laugh. "It was totally silly!"

We play this game for a while. I get the hang of it, but I don't want to stop. I've never felt this connected with anyone before, not even with Addy.

One more, Mira says. She picks up her tablet again. On the screen she draws a heart.

Heat rises to my cheeks. What does that mean? Is that heart for me? Is that about us? Or is it just part of the game? What if she knows what I'm thinking? I don't want her to read my thoughts.

I open my eyes and sever our connection. I'm back in my body, staring at Mira across the room.

Mira looks like she's been struck. She spins away, tucking the tablet back into her trunk.

"I've got to go," I say. "I need to tell Lucy we worked out the plan."

Mira doesn't answer. She doesn't even look as I walk out of her room.

When her door closes behind me, I just stand there, unable to put one foot in front of the next. What just happened? Why did I break our connection? Everything was going so well, and I ruined it.

I'm such an idiot. That heart obviously didn't mean what I thought it might.

What I hoped it might.

Cole and Marco go to bed a bit early so they don't distract us. Not long after, Mira steps away from the piano and joins Lucy and me on the couch. She asks if I'm ready, and then she starts the probing like before. It doesn't take quite as long this time before she lassos my brain and secures the bond.

Keep ahold of me, she says in a way that makes me blush again. I really need to get that heart out of my head. Of course I need to keep the bond. She'll be sleeping, so maintaining the connection is my job.

"Good night," I say as Mira heads to her room.

"Good luck," Lucy says.

Mira smiles back at us before stepping inside and closing the door.

Lucy kicks her legs up on the coffee table. "So what should I do?"

"Well, for starters, don't let me fall asleep. And you might as well remind me every few minutes to check the bond with Mira. You know how easily I can space out."

"You? Space out? I never would have guessed."

"Ha! Ha! Ha!"

Lucy flips through a magazine and shows me pictures of the hottest trends in beachwear and the list of celebutantes debuting on EFAN next month.

"Oh! A quiz!" she says. "This will be fun!"

She shows me the magazine. In bold pink letters on top it reads, "How to Know If He Crushes on You."

Lucy crosses her legs beneath her and smooths the magazine page flat. "So I'll ask a question, and you answer. Got it?"

She doesn't give me a chance to respond before reading off the first question.

"'When your sweetie sees you sitting alone for lunch, does he (a) sit down next to you, (b) wave and walk on by, (c) ignore you, or (d) sit with your frenemy on the other side of the cafeteria?'"

"What's a frenemy?" I ask.

"Really? Oh, forget it," Lucy says, closing the magazine. "What's happening with the mind meld?"

"Not much. Mira is drifting to sleep."

Lucy leans back against the armrest and kicks her feet up on the couch. "What does it feel like? The brain patch, I mean."

"It's hard to explain. Have you ever known someone so well that they could tell what you were thinking before you even said it? It's like that times a million."

"I don't think I could handle that," she says. "I'm an actress. It's not like I'm totally fake or anything, but there is a certain person I show to the world. I wouldn't want someone to have total access to what's inside. It's too transparent. I'd feel too exposed."

"Yeah, I get that. Sometimes I feel exposed"—like an hour ago, when I was stupid enough to think Mira had drawn a heart for me—"but it's worth it. There's so much that doesn't get said because words can't really translate what you think. With Mira, I don't have to worry about that."

"Sounds romantic."

"Shut up. It's not like that."

"*Sure . . .*" Lucy waves her magazine like she's clearing the air of all serious topics. "Let's do another quiz! This one's called 'Which Summer Accessory Really Shows Your Personality.'"

"What's an accessory?"

"Are you kidding? Okay, just in case you're not, I'll give you some examples. The answers to the quiz include sunglasses, a clutch, stilettos, bangles, or a classic headband."

"What are bangles?"

Lucy tosses the magazine aside. "You're hopeless. Just focus on the brain link."

"There's not much to focus on right now. Either Mira is a really boring sleeper, or she's figured out how to block me from watching her dreams."

"You can do that?" Lucy asks, pulling the pink blanket over her feet.

"Mira can. I can't block anything. I'm like an open book, which really sucks."

"So Mira can read your mind and eavesdrop on your lovey-dovey feelings for her?"

I shake my head. "I'm not even going to answer that."

Lucy cozies up beside me. "Oh, come on! I'm bored. Tell me about your love life."

I shoot her a side glance. "You mean my nonexistent love life?"

"Fine. Don't tell me. It's not like everyone in the Academy hasn't known about you and Mira and your brain crush since first tour."

Why can I never escape this? Oh well. Lucy seems to know a lot about this stuff, and I don't see how talking to her about it could make the rumors worse than they already are.

"Do you really think Mira likes me? You know, in that way?" I regret the question as soon as the words leave my mouth.

Lucy pinches her eyebrows together. "Are you really that clueless? I thought you could read each other's minds and all. Of course she likes you, Jasper! She's almost as obvious as your sister."

Wait a second. What does this have to do with Addy?

"What are you talking about?" I ask.

Lucy rolls her eyes. "Please, how could you miss it? She

practically follows Marco around like a puppy dog."

She does?

"And that Sheek wannabe encourages her!" Lucy continues. "Asking her to come with us, calling her Adeline, bending low to whisper in her ear. He's already broken half the hearts in our class, I don't know why he has to move on to the juniors."

It's honestly like Lucy is speaking Alkalinian. I have no idea what she's talking about. Sure, I thought the whole *Adeline* thing was a little weird, but where'd she come up with all this other stuff?

"Are you even listening?" Lucy huffs.

She must have kept on talking, and I totally spaced. I try to figure out a response, but then Mira's eyes flick open, practically blinding the inside of my brain with the bright light of her bedroom.

I bolt up straight on the couch.

"Is it happening?" Lucy asks. "Are the Alks starting the testing?"

I nod and lift a hand, signaling her to be quiet.

Mira can see, but she can't move. Someone else is there. An Alk crosses in front of her sight line. He wheels a cart loaded with the vials we saw on the lower level, the vials we're almost certain contain venom. He fills a syringe with the yellow liquid and injects it into Mira's neck.

"This is no dream," I whisper to Lucy as I continue to describe what I see.

As the liquid penetrates Mira's bloodstream, her body feels even heavier. Her awareness is thick and slow. She's slipping out of the small grasp of consciousness she has.

We can't risk breaking the bond.

I'm not sure this will work, but I try to summon some energy and infuse it through our connection. It makes me feel twice as groggy, but it seems to boost Mira. Our collective grasp at consciousness holds strong.

There are more Alks there, Seelok among them. They're talking. The hisses and clicks are quick and excited. Something is happening.

In Mira's peripheral vision an Alk activates a screen. An image of a brain appears. It spins in a three-dimensional view so that the back of Mira's head is visible. The Alk clicks at Seelok, then points at the screen. His cyborg finger lands directly at the base of the neck, where a square mark is plainly visible. Seelok lets out a long, pleased hiss.

The Alk is pointing at Mira's brain patch.

The next morning we tell the others what happened.

Mira is curled in a ball on the couch. She's not too thrilled that the Alks were sticking her with venom and scanning her brain. I tell her not to freak out. After all, they're probably doing that to all of us; Mira's just the one we're able to spy on thanks to our brain patch.

"What do you think it means?" Cole asks.

"Lucy and I talked about that last night," I say. "They showed Seelok the patch, and he seemed pleased. It might have just been because something new was discovered, but it seemed like more than that. It seemed like they found what they were looking for."

"But how would they know about the brain patches?" Marco asks.

"That's the million-dollar question," Lucy says, "and why we need to spy again tonight."

Mira shakes her head. *Again? I don't know if I can.*

"No way," Cole says. "We know they're running tests. We need to tell Admiral Eames. You promised."

"But if we told the admiral, there's no way she'd let us try again," I say. "And there's a good shot we could really get to the bottom of things!"

"How?" Cole asks. "Unless you suddenly learn how to speak Alkalinian, you'll still have no idea what the Alks are talking about."

"I came up with an idea last night after Jasper went to sleep," Lucy says. "Cole, you can rig the voice box to work through Jasper's and Mira's brain patch! I'll be with Jasper, and I can listen to the translation. We'll know exactly what they're saying!"

"Oh sure," Marco says, "Cole will just whip up a major tech advancement in a day! Totally doable, DQ."

"Actually . . . ," Cole says slowly, his eyes brightening as he considers the idea. "It may not be that hard. Especially if I can use their gloves and jerry-rig one of our blast pack sensor straps to act as an interface, it just might work."

"I feel like keeping my atoms intact, thank you very much," I say. "We can't use our gloves in here."

"Sure you can," Cole says. "We won't be using them to manipulate matter, they'll just be passing information. Jasper will hear the Alks' words through his brain patch connection with Mira, and then his gloves will feed those words through the voice box for translation."

"You're sure that won't scramble us?" I glance at Mira. She doesn't look particularly worried.

"It's hard to explain, but I'm positive," Cole says.

"So you'll do it?" Lucy asks.

Cole shakes his head, wiping the excitement off of his face. "Absolutely not! Not without the admiral's authority."

"I figured you'd say that," Lucy says. "So I thought up an alternative. How about this morning at the saucer, we look for the tube connection. Then, after lunch, we'll ask Gedney to get us another briefing with the admiral. We'll own up to what we did—or at least, sort of; we have to think up some way to avoid talking about the brain patches.

MONICA TESLER

But anyway, we'll share what we discovered. That way, she'll have no choice but to take immediate action to stop the Alks. At the very least, she'll have to approve our plan to spy again tonight."

Cole keeps shaking his head. He balls his hands into fists. "Isn't that what we tried last time?"

"This time will be different," Lucy says.

"Come *on*, Wiki!" Marco says. "It's all about the pod!"

I shift closer to Cole on the couch. "You know something really bad is going on here, Cole. What we discovered last night proves it. Every single Bounder is at risk, including us, including my sister. If we hand the admiral all the information on a silver platter, she'll do something about it. She'll probably green-light another midnight spying mission. She'll probably let you reconfigure the voice box."

Cole is still shaking his head, but the shakes are getting slower. Finally his head stills, and he unfurls his fists. "We talk to the admiral this afternoon, no matter what?"

"No matter what," Lucy says.

Cole eyes the voice box. Lucy pulls out one of her gloves and waves it in front of his face. He really wants to build that interface.

"Fine," he says.

It's all about the pod. At least for now.

22

THE BREAKFAST SPREAD EMERGES FROM
the wall. I'm glad we all agree that our morning meal doesn't
contain any venom or other nasty Alk ingredients, because
I'm absolutely starved. Last night as Lucy and I chatted about
what I'd seen with the Alks in Mira's room, I choked down a
couple of wings and a hunk of garlic bread I'd set aside from
dinner, even though I didn't have an appetite. It's hard to eat
when you know your food is laced with venom. Even so, the
small amount I managed to swallow knocked me out. Lucy
and I woke up this morning on opposite ends of the couch,
wrestling over a pink fringed throw blanket.

We have only thirty minutes before the Frog leaves for the

abandoned saucer. Marco runs us through our plan. We'll practice for the first hour with the juniors, then we'll ask Gedney if we can practice bounding on our own. As soon as we get the go-ahead, we'll search for the tube connection. Then we'll join the other cadets and tell Gedney we need to speak with the admiral.

Once we arrive at the hangar, Gedney instructs us to run through blast pack maneuvers. He partners juniors with seniors, asking me to practice with Addy. I'm not thrilled. I know she'll give me the third degree. From the look on her face when Gedney calls out the pairs, she would have preferred a different partner, too.

We head to an empty corner of the hangar, and I kick off. She chases me along the wall and into a low dive. I cut the corner too close and end up on the floor with a soon-to-be bruise on my shoulder.

Addy touches down beside me. "You okay? You look awful."

"Obviously, that wasn't my finest move."

"That's not what I mean," she says. "Are you feeling okay?"

"Yeah, I just didn't get a ton of sleep last night."

"Because you were spying?"

"Not now, Addy."

"Why not? No one's listening."

"This place is packed with Alks and Earth Force officers. I'll fill you in later."

"What's the plan today?"

What am I supposed to say? If I tell her about our plan to look for the tube connection, she'll demand to come along. If I don't tell her, I'm keeping secrets.

I think back to this morning and what an effort it was to get everyone on the same page. It has to be all about the pod now. And only about the pod.

"Let's fly," I say to my sister. I push off fast, not waiting for her response, or more likely her lecture about ignoring her and keeping secrets.

After a while, Gedney calls us back for a group exercise. Then we get a snack break. I pocket half a dozen protein bars that Earth Force doles out, and eat a half dozen more. If I have to avoid Alk VR food, at least I won't starve.

Once I'm reasonably full, I round up my pod mates. "Ready?"

"I'm just thinking," Lucy says. "Should we tell Gedney? He's always been in our corner."

"No way," Marco says. "When it came time to stick with the admiral or join Waters on Gulaga, Gedney made his choice. So even if he seems to bend the rules for us, he's the admiral's man when it counts. We can't risk him selling us out."

"Are you saying *we're* like Waters?" Cole asks, his head starting to shake again. "Because what Waters did was definitely at odds with Earth Force. He was talking to the Youli behind the admiral's back!"

Geez. Why did Marco plant that seed? It could totally derail us.

Lucy glares at Marco, then brushes her hand down Cole's arm. "Oh, no, not at all, sweetie, we're nothing like Waters. Marco's just saying we need to stick with the plan."

Before Cole can change his mind, Lucy hurries us over to Gedney to ask about heading off on our own. Once Gedney finishes explaining to Orla and Aela how important it is not to switch gloves, he turns to talk to us.

"Gedney," Lucy says. "This room is so overcrowded, and our pod is . . . well . . . how do I put this delicately . . . a bit more advanced than the others. We'd like some space to stretch out and practice our bounding skills. Do you think we could go to the VR gym? We'll be back by lunch. Then we can practice with the juniors all afternoon, before it's time to head back on the Frogs."

Before Gedney has a chance to answer, Desmond tugs at his sleeve and starts firing questions about how blast packs fit into the occupational safety provisions of the Earth Force regulations. Behind Desmond, the twins are fighting again. This time they're hurling empty crates at each other. Gedney ducks as one narrowly misses his head.

"Please, Gedney, can we go?" Lucy asks.

Gedney waves his hand. "Be back like you said."

We don't wait around for him to change his mind, although I doubt he would. He has his hands full with the juniors.

We duck low and sprint down the lit hallway. When we make the first turn, we stop to regroup.

"Should we bound to the generator room?" I ask. "We're outside of the tether range."

"No," Marco says. "Let's walk."

"Why?" Cole asks.

Marco doesn't answer; he just keeps heading down the lit path.

"Seriously, why not bound?" I ask. "We don't have a ton of time, and I hate walking all hunched over!"

"We can't all bound, that's why," Marco mumbles.

"What do you mean—" I start. Then I hear footsteps in the hall behind us. "Someone's coming!" I'm about to search for a hiding spot when I hear my sister's voice.

"Wait up!" Addy calls. When she catches us, she slides in next to Marco and bumps him with her hip.

"What are you doing here, Addy?" I ask.

"Same as you," she says.

"You most certainly are not," Lucy says. "This is pod only."

"How did you know where we were going?" I ask.

"I told her," Marco says.

"You *what*?" Lucy says.

"She wanted to know what happened last night, so I told her. And I said she could come along today."

"It wasn't hard to sneak away," Addy says. "Gedney was a bit occupied with Desmond and the twins."

"I don't care if it was hard to sneak away or not," I say. "You weren't invited, and you're not coming."

"I told you *I* invited her," Marco says. "You don't have a say in what your sister chooses to do."

"Actually, he does," Lucy says, "and I do, too. This is a pod activity, Marco. If you wanted to include Addy, you should have asked us. And I, for one, would have said no."

"Of course you would say no," Addy says to Lucy, "because you've had it out for me since day one. I mean, God forbid anyone step on your toes as pod prima donna. Don't worry, I don't have any interest in taking over as Drama Queen."

"How dare you!" Lucy says, taking a step toward my sister.

Terrific. Now I'm caught in the middle between my pod mates and my sister. What am I supposed to do?

"No fights!" Cole says. "We have less than an hour. We need to go!"

Cole's words settle everyone down, probably because he's right. If we don't get going, this whole plan is a bust.

Addy's eyes drill into me. In fact, everyone is looking at me. Why is this my call?

I shake my head and let out a sigh. "You're here, Addy, so you might as well come along."

"What?" Lucy says.

Mira grabs Lucy's hand and gives it a tug. At first I think Lucy is going to hold her ground and argue, but then she spins around and runs up the hall with Mira.

Cole and I follow.

Addy and Marco take up the rear, whispering and laughing the whole way.

Once we reach the generator room, we follow the hallways on either side, trying every door we pass for a stairwell or some way to descend to the lower levels. All we find are locked doors and dead ends.

"How are we doing on time?" I ask Cole.

He checks his tablet. "Only thirty minutes left."

"I can't believe I'm suggesting this," Marco says, "but I know a way."

"Right," Lucy says. "You're filled with bright ideas today."

Marco ignores her and keeps talking. "Serena is always going on about descending, and coming from the depths, and stuff like that. I bet that hole she comes from leads down to the lower levels."

"Or maybe Serena meant that figuratively," I say. "Or, even more likely, maybe she's a little bit crazy."

"Serena?" Addy asks. "You mean that giant snake you told me about?"

"Are you actually suggesting we crawl through a snake hole to reach the lower levels?" I ask.

"Yes, Adeline," Marco says. "And Jasper, it's not any old snake hole. It's Serena's. So it's like a high-class, educated snake hole."

"I thought you were afraid of snakes," Lucy says.

"For the millionth time, I'm not afraid of snakes. I *hate* snakes, or at least most snakes. I don't hate Serena."

Cole takes off up the hallway.

"Where are *you* going?" Lucy calls after him.

"To the shrine," he says. "I haven't heard any other ideas, and we're just wasting time standing around talking about it."

We crawl through the narrow doorway into the Shrine of Remembrance. Just like the times before, once we're in, the domed ceiling flickers to life and fills with the image of old Alkalinia.

"What is this place?" Addy asks.

"It's their shrine," I say. "Serena's the guardian."

"Serena, the giant snake," Addy says. "Got it. But what about the pictures?" Up above, the image rotates around the planet and dives beneath the atmosphere, revealing the rocky shore and turquoise sea.

"That's Alkalinia," Marco says. "Or, I should say, it used to be Alkalinia. According to Serena, their planet was destroyed in an intragalactic war."

"What planet are we on if it's not Alkalinia?" Addy asks.

"I'm pretty sure the Alks are squatters here," I say.

"We need to move," Cole says. "We're short on time. And the longer we linger in the shrine, the more likely the sensor will alert Serena to visitors. I'd rather not run into her in the hole."

"Good thinking, Wiki," Marco says. "Plus, if I wait any longer, I might chicken out."

We crawl to the corner of the shrine and find the hole. Lucy peers inside, then waves her hand, indicating for me to head in.

"Ladies first." I smile at Lucy and nod at the dark hole.

"I insist," Lucy says.

"For goodness' sake," Cole says, "get out of the way." He fires up his tablet to cast some light and creeps into the hole.

I head in after Cole. It's slow going because Cole has to hold his tablet while he crawls. Not to mention, the hole is narrow. It was definitely not meant for humans. We ease forward. The hole bends down, hopefully leading us to the lower levels of the habitat.

"This is bringing back some really awful memories," Lucy says behind me.

"Trash worm?" Marco calls out.

"What's a trash worm?" Addy asks.

Marco distracts us with a dramatic retelling of our journey through the trash tunnel on Gulaga. At the time it wasn't funny at all, but as he explains what happened to Addy, we're all cracking up. I'm laughing so hard I can barely keep crawling. I mean, whoever heard of using a worm for trash removal?

"So you had to climb a mountain of trash?" Addy asks.

"It was the only way through the tunnel!" Marco replies.

"And this worm almost ate you?" Addy asks.

"Technically, it did eat us," Cole says. "Mira and I were *inside* the worm. We're lucky we didn't drown in its digestive juices."

"That's disgusting," she says.

"Actually, it was heroic," Lucy says, "a word you clearly don't understand, because your idea of an adventure is tagging along with your big brother."

"That's a bit harsh," I say. I'm not really sure why Lucy has it out for Addy.

Marco ignores Lucy's attempt to sidetrack things. "The funniest part is that we totally reeked. No one in Gulaga would get within a five-meter radius of us once we left the tunnel because we smelled so bad. We couldn't figure out what the problem was. We'd been in that gross tunnel for so long we thought things smelled pretty good once we got out."

That was so funny. The Gulagans thought it all made sense once we told them Neeka was our junior ambassador. I guess getting trapped in the trash tunnel wasn't that big a stretch when it came to Neeka. She was kind of trouble prone, after all.

"Then we got sent to these Gulagan baths where these huge Tunnelers pummeled our backs with karate chops," I tell Addy.

"And then we found the Nest," Lucy adds.

"You know, it's kind of strange," I say. "Our quarters here are awesome. They have everything we could possibly dream of wanting. But they're not nearly as cool as the Nest or even the pod room at the space station."

"That's because they're not real," Marco says.

"Quiet!" Cole says. "I hear something."

The sound of swishing and hissing swells from up ahead.

"Whatever that is," I say, "it's definitely real."

"Maybe it's Serena," Lucy says.

"That's an awful lot of noise for Serena," I say.

"I thought this place was abandoned," Lucy says. "If it's not Serena, who's here?"

"Just keep going," Marco says.

The tunnel grows colder and damper as we crawl. With every meter we cover, winding farther down the hole, the swishing grows louder. It sounds like live fish slapping against the side of a boat, and that doesn't include all the hissing. It's

　　　　MONICA TESLER

way too much noise for one snake. I'm not looking forward to finding the source of that sound, particularly not while I'm crawling on my hands and knees through a dark tunnel without any room to turn around.

Fortunately, the hole starts to widen, and we soon find ourselves in a large room with a low roof and a cold stone floor like the shrine. Serena is coiled in the corner.

We pile into the room and look at one another.

Lucy steps forward. "Hi, Serena!"

When the words leave Lucy's lips, Serena rises up and rears back like she's about to strike. Her tongue flicks. Then the tension slowly leaves her body. She lays her head on the floor and glides in our direction, unwinding as she goes.

Cole activates the voice box and sets it on the ground. Serena positions her head above it and hisses. "Young ones? Why are you here?"

Lucy kneels in front of the voice box. "We're looking for something, and we needed to get to the lower levels. So we thought we'd ask you for help."

That's not exactly our plan, but it's probably a pretty good answer right about now.

Serena makes her way to a screen on the other side of the room. It shows a camera view of the shrine. She waves her little arms over a sensor and checks something on the screen. Then she returns to the voice box.

"I didn't know you were coming." She must be wondering why the sensor didn't alert her.

The swishing noise is louder than ever. It sounds like it's coming from the other side of the room. Part of me really wants to know what's making all that noise. Another part says that I definitely don't want to know.

"Can you help us?" Lucy asks.

Serena rises up and flicks her tongue. She glides by each of us, until her black marble eyes focus on Addy. "Who is the new one?"

My sister swallows and presses her shoulders back. "I'm Addy."

"She's my sister," I say.

Serena smiles, or at least it's pretty close to a smile for a snake. "Sister? How nice. Family is so important. Come and meet my babies."

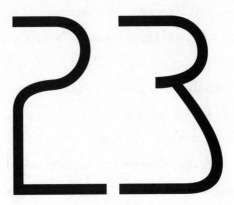

SERENA SLIDES ACROSS THE FLOOR TO
the other side of the room. I can't tell what's over there. It
looks like the room drops off. A hundred meters away there's
another wall. But what's between here and there?

We follow Serena, who glides to the very edge. The swishing swells like it might swallow us with its deafening hum.

I step next to Serena and look down. A humongous pit
opens in front of us.

The floor below is an iridescent ebony with flecks of green
and yellow. And it appears to be moving.

Wait . . . that's no floor. Those are *snakes*.

I blink and try to focus, but it's hard to process what I'm

seeing. The floor is covered with thousands of small, writh-ing, hissing snakes.

"Oh my God!" Lucy says. "Are those—"

"They're snakes," Marco whispers. He grabs on to Addy. "I hate snakes."

Serena hisses into the voice box. "I don't know what snakes are, but these are my babies."

"You're their mother?" Addy asks.

"Yes. Come. They'd love to meet you." A ramp descends from the side of the room into the pit. Serena glides over and leads us down.

I can't believe how many snakes are down there. Serena has fifty times as many babies as Alks we've seen the entire time we've been here.

"We're really going to do this?" Marco asks.

"I thought you weren't afraid of snakes," Lucy taunts.

"Ignore her," Addy says. "I've got you." She takes his hand and coaxes him toward the ramp.

As we travel deeper into the pit, I see that each baby snake is anchored in place by a small loop around its head. A cord comes up from the floor and circles the little snake's neck like a collar. The end of the cord fits inside the snake's mouth.

"Why are they tied up?" Lucy asks.

"I'm all for that," Marco says.

When we reach the floor, Serena raises her head and looks

out across the pit. The little snakes seem to get excited. Their bodies shimmy faster. Their little necks pull against the collars like puppies against leashes.

Serena waves to us with her tiny arms.

We gather around, and Cole presents the voice box. Serena proudly hisses into the box. "These are my children. They're busy now. It's milking time. But they're very glad to see you. They so rarely get visitors."

I look out across the sea of snakes. Thousands of them are hooked up with the small collars. The cords attach to tiny tubes in the floor that stretch the length of the pit. I trace their path to the far end. They feed into a large cylinder topped with a pumping mechanism that is rhythmically driving up and down.

The tubes connect the snakes to the pump.

"Serena," I ask. "What do you mean, 'it's milking time'?"

"My babies are giving their venom."

"Oh my God!" Marco flattens himself against the far wall of the pit. "They're poisonous? I've got to get out of here!"

Wait a second . . . these baby snakes are venomous?

"This is great!" Cole says.

"It is?" Lucy's pressed up against the wall like Marco, as far from the snake pit as possible, which unfortunately is not that far.

"Yes! It means we must be near the other side of the tube!"

Cole lowers his mouth to the voice box. "Serena, we're looking for the venom tube that runs along the seabed. Does it connect over here?"

Just then a loud beep signals the shutdown of the pump. The collars disengage from the little snakes, and they're no longer restricted. Dozens of them rush toward us.

Lucy screams and jumps behind me. Marco's mouth hangs open, and his face glistens with sweat. Addy steps in front of him. What do we do? Will they bite us? Should we run up the ramp?

Serena slides her long body out to greet her babies. They glide around her, lifting their tiny heads to rub against hers, darting their tongues at her thick black skin. She glances back at us and waves her head.

Behind her, the snakes part, leaving a narrow path.

"I think she wants us to follow her," Cole says.

"No way," Marco says.

"Come on," I say. "It may be the only way to the venom tube."

Marco looks at Addy. She puts her arm around his back and guides him forward.

We follow Serena into the pit. The tiny snakes roil around us, leaving us a small path but dashing and diving between our legs. Their skin feels smooth and muscular, like Serena's. They must know we're friends, because none of them show any hostility.

MONICA TESLER

But nothing can erase the reality that we're wading through a den of snakes. I don't know if Marco will survive this. He's practically hyperventilating. The only thing that seems to anchor him is my sister's hand, which he's now clutching so hard his knuckles are white.

"If one of us has to come back here," Marco says. "I nominate you, Ace. Or Wiki."

"I'll do it," Addy says.

"Nah," Marco says. "Jasper was right. I shouldn't have invited you. This is way too dangerous."

Addy lifts their clutched hands. "A simple thank-you would have sufficed. Oh, look! I think that one likes you." A small snake is curling its way up Marco's leg.

"Get him off me!" Marco shouts.

Addy calmly plucks the snake off of Marco's pants, gives its small head a pat, and tosses it into the writhing pile of its brothers and sisters.

We finally reach the other side and clamber up onto the low wall that holds back the baby snakes.

Serena grabs a tiny snake with her small hands and lifts it up. She nods at Cole for the voice box. "Meet Seelia. She's one of my youngest."

The tiny snake shakes her tail and hisses. Serena brushes her tongue across Seelia's nose, then gently sets her down among the others. Seelia darts into the horde of snakes, instantly unrecognizable in the mass of thousands.

"Umm . . . ," Marco starts, "can we move a bit farther away from the snakes?"

Serena slips up beside us. Her babies cry out in a fit of hisses and clicks. She hisses back in a soothing tone, probably assuring them that she'll be back later, as she leads us to a door and then out of the snake pit.

"So let me get this straight," Marco says into the voice box once the door closes behind us. "All of those snakes are your children?"

"Yes," Serena says, "I am their mother."

"What happens when they get bigger?" he asks.

"Once their venom dries out, they are taken. You should know better than I. You have been to the other side. I have not."

Other side? As in the other side of the tube? Because we definitely have not run into a band of teenage snakes just hanging out. I have no clue what happens to her kids once they outgrow the milking farm.

"Does she mean that her babies go to live at the Alkalinian Seat?" I ask the others. "That they grow up to be Alks?"

"Of course that's what she means," Lucy says. "These snakes are baby Alks. Serena's their mother, so she must be an Alk, too."

"But she's so long!" Cole says. "She doesn't look like the other Alks."

"Sure she does," Addy says. "She's just older, and wiser, and hasn't been surgically enhanced with a cyborg arm. And there's something else you seem oblivious to."

Lucy rolls her eyes. "Please, grace us with your insight, Adeline."

Addy ignores Lucy's sarcasm. "Serena is the only adult female Alk I've seen."

All of our eyes—even Lucy's—go wide. Addy's absolutely right. How come I haven't noticed that before?

"That's so strange," Marco says. "It's clear that Steve and Seelok and most of his close advisers are male, but I haven't even noticed the gender of the other Alks."

"Yeah, it's like it doesn't exist," Lucy says, "at least with all those scooter dudes we saw yesterday in the lower levels."

No emotions. No identity. Nothing, Mira thinks.

"Mira feels like they don't even have an identity," I say. "Is that what happens to the baby snakes when they're brought to the Alkalinian Seat?"

"What about what's happening here?" Addy says to us. She grabs the voice box. "Do you know what the Alkalinians do with all the venom your babies produce?" she asks Serena. "Are you okay with that?"

"I'm not sure I understand," Serena says. "The children stay with me while they produce venom, then they are taken. I miss them, but that is what happens."

"It's not like Seelok is going to ask Serena's permission," I say under my breath.

"Well, I'm not okay with that," Addy says. "It sounds like forced child labor, not to mention what it is they're laboring over."

"What I want to know is what happens to all these baby snakes," Marco says. "There are thousands of them, and we've seen barely a hundred Alks on the other side, and that's including the scooter dudes."

Addy's about to say something when Cole puts up his hand. "Stop! Don't get any more sidetracked! We're on a tight timeline, remember?" He takes the voice box back from Addy. "Serena, there's a pipe that carries the venom from this side to the other. Can you show us where it is?"

"And while you're at it," Marco shouts into the voice box, "we need a different way back upstairs. I am not crossing that sea of snakes again."

Serena nods. She seems sad, not that I know what a sad snake looks like. One thing is for sure—she misses her babies, and it sounds like it's only a matter of time before the ones in the pit are taken from her, too. That's enough to make anyone sad.

Serena leads us through a small doorway and down a narrow hall that borders a machinery room. My guess is those machines process the venom for transmission through the tube and over to the Alkalinian Seat to be loaded into the vats we saw yesterday.

Across from the machinery room is a door guarded by a security panel covered with Alkalinian symbols.

Serena lifts up and presses the code with her short, stubby hand. "I've seen the guards come through here before," she says into the voice box. "Good for you that I have an eye for detail and remember the code. Though I've not been myself, I believe you'll find what you're looking for inside—the pipe and an alternative route to the upper floors."

The door buzzes open, and we head through. Serena stays behind. She hisses and bows her head.

We thank Serena and let the door swing closed behind us, sealing us out of the snake pit.

The room we're in mirrors the room on the other side of the tube except that it's missing the wall of windows looking out at the ocean (no complaints there). There are more large vats connected to a second pump, which in turn is connected to a pipe. The pipe bisects the room and exits through the wall, presumably into the tube. A sealed door hides the tube from view.

I jerk on the door handle. The door is heavy, but it opens, thankfully. Except now that I can see down the length of the tube, I can also see the water surrounding the tube on all sides. My stomach sinks.

"It's unlocked," Lucy says. "That's good news."

"What about from the water side?" Marco asks. "If Earth Force needs to take down the tether, they'll be coming from the Alkalinian Seat. It doesn't matter how easy the door is to open from here if it's locked outside. Go ahead, Jasper. Check it out."

Somehow the fact that I was first to check the door from this side means I volunteered to check the door from the water side. I'm about to protest, but instead I shrug. I just waded through a pit of snakes. How bad can two seconds in the tube be?

I pull the door all the way open and step inside. The door barely closes behind me before the claustrophobia sets in. Water surrounds me, and I gulp for air, half feeling like I'm already drowning. I turn around and stare down the tube. I can see all the way to the Alkalinian Seat. Off to my right, through the glass and fifty meters of open ocean, the bubble holding the occludium tether glows silver. Its shaft extends up to the generator room above.

I take a few steps farther into the tube. One of the black sea creatures swims nearby. As if the creature senses me, it spins around with a swing of its tail and glides closer. It fixes its black marble eyes on me, then it lashes the plastic side with its ebony tale. The whole tube trembles.

I jump back. Get me out of here!

I scramble to the door and confirm that it's sealed. Then I look for a way to open it.

The sea creature doubles back for another pass.

Thump!

The venom pipe shakes, and the tube echoes with the sound of the creature's collision. I glance behind me. More sea creatures race in my direction, baring their silver fangs.

A lever is mounted to the right of the door. In a panic I grab it with both hands and pull. The door clicks and swings open, and I rush through, then slam the door closed behind me.

"You okay?" Lucy asks.

"I guess," I say. "Those nasty sea creatures are out there. At least we know we can open the door from the outside. Someone could definitely cross through the tube."

Cole hurries over from the side of the room. "I found stairs. We need to go. We've already been gone too long."

Luckily, the stairs dump us out in an old systems center down the hall from the generator room. Even though the computers look like they haven't been used in years, the door is locked—which is why we couldn't get in here before. We're able to unlock it manually from the inside. We hurry into the hall and start heading to the hangar.

"I want to see the occludium tether!" Addy says when we tell her what's in the generator room.

"There's no time," Cole says.

Addy ignores him and heads in.

"Lovely," Lucy says.

"I'll get her," I say. "You guys go back. Tell Gedney we had to have a brother-sister talk."

"About what?" Cole says.

Lucy grabs Cole's arm and starts down the hall, with Mira right behind them.

"Don't worry. I'll handle it," I call after them.

Marco makes for the generator room, but I block him. "I'm not kidding, Marco. I need to talk to Addy. Alone."

Marco throws his hands up and takes a step back. "Good luck," he says, then turns and chases after the others.

I walk in and find Addy by the windows, gazing down at the venom pipe and the shaft that leads to the bubble on the ocean floor, where the occludium tether is housed.

"Would you have to climb all the way down there to deactivate the tether?" she asks.

"We think there's probably a remote shutoff somewhere up here. But without an Alkalinian to show us, we'd probably need to descend the shaft. According to Gedney, there's a manual shutdown at the anchor spot."

"How does Gedney know?"

"Earth Force traded the occludium to the Alkalinians. They had to provide their tether specs in order for us to give them the correct concentration."

Addy turns to face me. "We gave the Alks occludium? You mean, we wouldn't need to do any of this if we hadn't traded with them in the first place?"

"Something like that."

She shakes her head and turns back to the window. "Earth Force will never cease to baffle me."

"About that," I start, not entirely sure where to begin or even what I'm going to say. "Earth Force may do some baffling things, and we may not agree with all of them, but they're still calling the shots. I feel like you don't always remember that."

"Excuse me?"

"It's just . . . I think you should be careful, that's all."

Addy crosses her arms against her chest. "Is this another lecture?"

"No. I'm just looking out for you. You kind of give the impression that you think you can do whatever you want, and it might land you in trouble."

She laughs. "Says the guy who just violated a direct order from the admiral not to investigate and then crawled through a snake hole to find the entry to a venom pipe that I'm pretty sure the Alks want to keep top secret. Who thinks they can do whatever they want, Jasper?"

She kind of has me there. "I get that it might seem hypocritical, Addy, but most of the juniors are falling in line a bit more than you."

"Ahh . . . I get it. This boils down to the same thing that has Lucy all tied up in knots."

"What would that be?"

Addy smiles. "You're jealous."

"Jealous? Of you?"

"That's right. You're mad that I hang out with your friends, that I can insert myself into your pod whenever I want. It took you a long time to form these relationships, and you don't think it's fair that I get to piggyback on that. I kind of get that, J. But isn't that exactly what a big brother is for?"

This conversation has seriously derailed. "No. That's not it at all."

"Oh, isn't it? You don't care that Marco and I are palling around? 'Cause Lucy sure does."

Is that what's been bothering Lucy? "Forget it, Addy. If you don't want my advice, fine."

"That's just it, Jasper. I didn't ask for your advice. And I definitely don't need it."

She spins around and marches out of the generator room. I hope she's heading back to training, but I'm definitely not going to ask. I'm done trying to talk with Addy, at least for now.

I turn around and gaze out the window. Some of the sea creatures still swim around the venom pipe. They swoop low as they glide by the tube, then swing wide and circle around for another pass. They're scary, but there's something familiar about them. Their long bodies, their tiny arms, their beady black eyes. They almost look like Serena. Maybe this planet is in the same system as the original Alkalinia, and the life forms share descendants.

All I know is I have no desire to be up close and personal with those huge sea creatures ever again.

As I walk back to the hangar, I steel myself for a talk with the admiral. She's not going to be happy that we took matters into our own hands, particularly after she ordered us not to, as Addy so pleasantly reminded me. Even so, our pod accomplished a lot on our own. We have new intelligence on the late-night testing, we located the occludium tether and a route across to it, and we even found the nucleus of the Alkalinian venom operation.

Now we'll hand the information over to Earth Force and get back to the business of following orders.

WHEN I ARRIVE AT THE LOADING BAY,
everything is in chaos. Cadets crisscross the hangar in their
blast packs, dive-bombing one another with protein bars
and carob-coated fruit balls and other Earth Force stan-
dards that the officers carted over for lunch. On the ground,
cadets chuck crates with their gloves. Everyone is screaming
and cheering. Meggi is running around trying to wave the
fliers to the floor. The twins target her with empty fruit ball
boxes. Meggi jumps out of the way at the last second and
lands on her hands and knees. She rolls onto her back and
launches a crate at Orla, knocking her to the floor. Aela
dashes to check on her sister.

My pod mates run over when they spot me. I can tell from their faces that something's happened, and it's not just the pandemonium in the hangar. Are we in trouble? Did the admiral already discover that we violated her orders?

"We're too late," Lucy says. "Admiral Eames, Sheek, Gedney, all the Earth Force officers, they're gone."

"What do you mean, 'gone'?" I ask, shouting over all the noise. From across the hangar Addy sprints to join us.

"Did you tell him?" she asks, catching her breath.

"Tell me what?" I demand. Whatever this is can't be good.

Marco leans close. "Apparently, Seelok showed up and invited all the officers to a special reception of his own. A *dinner* reception. They left twenty minutes ago to get ready."

A dinner reception . . . all the Earth Force officers in one place . . . eating Alkalinian food . . . "Do you think the Alks are up to something?"

"Well, we know what they put in their food," Lucy says. "And we know they're planning something. We're just not sure what it is yet."

"Do you think they're trying to take the officers out, at least temporarily?" I ask.

"It's a distinct possibility," Cole says matter-of-factly.

"Can we stop them?" I ask. "Maybe we can find Gedney before the reception starts."

"Good idea," Lucy says. "We'll shake Steve when we get back to the Seat and somehow warn the officers."

"That won't work," Cole says. "As soon as we try anything, the Alks will know their plans are at risk and act accordingly. The officers could be in even more danger."

"We can't do nothing! We need to mobilize!" Addy shakes her arms impatiently. I suspect it's not the first time she's suggested this. "Let's round up the cadets and find out where the Alks are holding the reception. We'll storm the place!"

"No," Cole says. "The Alks have the advantage. They're armed. We're outnumbered. The tether is up. We can't even get everyone off this planet without their help. We shouldn't raise an alarm until we know what's happening and can formulate an effective military strategy."

"Not to mention the chance that *nothing* is happening," Lucy says. "Nothing bad, anyway. Maybe the Alks are actually throwing a super fun dinner party for the officers!"

"*Alks* and *super fun* don't go together," Marco says. "I say we take out the tether now!"

"Or maybe our pod should bound to the space station," Lucy says. "We're outside the tether range. We could ask some of the officers there what to do."

"No," Cole says. "Any of those options would raise a red alert and put every Earth Force officer and cadet in jeopardy.

The Frogs will be here any minute. If we're not on board, they'll know. We'll be conceding victory before the battle even begins."

"I agree with Cole," I say. "We need more information. I hate to say it, but the best option is to head back to our quarters like nothing is wrong. Cole can rig the voice box. Tonight I'll connect with Mira, and we'll spy on the testing again, this time with translation. Once we have concrete information about the testing, we can plan our strategy."

I look at Cole. I'm not sure whether he'll be on board with the late-night spying. We promised we were done defying orders.

Cole nods. "It's the only reasonable option. Until we have confirmation of the officers' safety, we have to assume they're out of commission."

Addy throws up her arms. "I can't believe this! The Alks could be taking out every Earth Force officer on this planet, and we'll be sitting in our quarters playing video games."

"If they wanted us dead, we'd already be dead," I say. "Think about it. There's more to this than we understand yet."

Addy scrunches up her face. "I suppose you're right, but what about me? What should *I* do tonight?"

"Act normal," I say, "but this time don't eat the food."

My sister opens her mouth like she's going to protest, but

instead she marches to the other side of the hangar. She's not happy about being left out. Again.

Please, Addy, don't cause trouble. Not tonight.

Steve and his Alk pals have a hard time rounding up the cadets to return to the Alkalinian Seat. We don't help. We just sit on some crates and eat fruit balls. It's actually mildly entertaining, and would be extremely entertaining if we weren't preoccupied with what might be happening to Gedney and all the Earth Force officers.

By the time we make it back to our quarters, I'm exhausted. After all, I barely slept last night. And now I'm signed up for another round of spying. The day we arrived, we thought we'd hit the jackpot—all-you-can-eat buffets of our favorite foods, endless levels of *Evolution*, and private bedrooms. Little did we know that our food was laced with venom and we were test subjects while we slept.

As soon as the door to our quarters closes behind us, Cole waves us over to the couch and activates the SIMPLE. He wants to get to work on the voice box. I bring him one of my bounding gloves and a sensor strap from my blast pack. He assures me that using the glove to operate the sensor strap for this purpose won't trigger the Alks' scrambler. While he takes apart the box to rig the interface, I head over to the piano, where Mira is playing.

I sit down next to her on the bench.

MONICA TESLER

Mira smiles. *Play together?*

I left my clarinet at the space station.

Play together? she repeats. An image of the piano passes from her mind to mine.

I shake my head. *I don't know how.*

Mira shares a memory with me: the bridge in Gulagaven when we escaped from Regis, Randall, and Hakim. She helped me fly my blast pack by showing me mental pictures of where to place my fingers on the manual straps.

You want me to play piano that way?

She smiles again.

Um . . . I'll try.

She helps me place my hands in the correct positions on the keys. Then she reaches up and gently brushes my eyelids closed. Her fingers are cold, but soft as butterfly wings. She's so close. I feel her breath against my cheek. She smells like rose shampoo.

I take a deep breath, which comes out in a stutter. My heart slaps against my ribs.

My heart. All I can think about is the heart Mira drew yesterday. I try to force the image away because I know the odds are pretty high that Mira's reading my mind right now. A jumbled mess of sparkles and nerves jumps from Mira's mind to mine, confirming my hunch. I almost open my eyes to break our connection, but then a picture follows. My third finger tapping three times on a key.

I mimic the movements. *Tap. Tap. Tap.*

Good.

She speeds up the sequence: *3-3-3, 3-2-1-2-3-4.*

I tap the pattern. Shockingly, it sounds like a song I've heard before.

Mira keeps feeding me notes, and I keep banging them out. The song isn't too complicated, so after a bit I get the hang of it.

Keep going on your own, she says.

I keep tapping out the pattern. Next to me, Mira places her hands on the keys. When I reach the beginning of the pattern, she joins the song. Soon we're playing a jazzy duet.

I open my eyes. Mira is watching me and smiling. Her body rocks back and forth to the rhythm.

"I think I've heard this song before," I say.

"Heart and Soul."

Wait . . . what? What does that mean? What is she saying? Is she thinking about the heart, too?

More sparkling laughter. *The song is called "Heart and Soul," silly.*

Oh. I laugh, too, because even though I feel like a complete dork, it's funny. And I'm spending time with Mira, which is awesome.

I don't know how long we play, but eventually the food emerges from the wall, and Mira's hands fall silent on the keys.

You need to eat, I tell her. Because in an hour she needs to be asleep, and I need to be watching.

One more round? she asks.

I play the pattern through a final time, and Mira crosses her hands in front of me, working her fingers up the keyboard in a grand finale. I place my hand on her left shoulder, so when she straightens, my arm's around her. She tips her head to mine. Blond wisps of hair tickle my cheek. If only time could move a little slower, we could sit together, just like this, for a while longer.

Lucy and I huddle on the couch again. All of our pod mates are in bed. Mira was the only one who ate much. She didn't have a choice. We can't risk that the Alks don't perform the testing because her venom levels are too low or they suspect something's amiss because she didn't eat. This is our one shot for information. If the Alks get suspicious about the rest of us (and Addy next door) for our sudden loss of appetite, we'll have to figure out how to handle that later.

What used to be awesome felt like torture. Tonight's buffet featured spaghetti and chocolate chip cookies again. Why did they have to serve my favorite meal on a night I couldn't eat? I nibbled on the Earth Force protein bars I swiped today at break time. They tasted like old cardboard compared with the Alk spread across the room. All I could do was smell the sweet aroma of melting chocolate and swallow down the saliva that kept pooling in my mouth.

"Still got the connection?" Lucy asks now.

"You've asked me that at least a dozen times," I tell her. "Yes, Mira and I are still connected."

"Good," Lucy says. She's quiet for a moment (not common for Lucy), then she says softly, "I wish Waters were here. I bet we'd never be in this mess if he were."

"Maybe, maybe not." I've been thinking about Waters. I don't like to admit it, but I really wish he were here, too.

"Do you think he's right about the Youli? That they're not as bad as Earth Force wants us to believe?"

I shrug. I'd like to believe that Waters is at least partially right, that the Youli aren't all bad, that peace is a possibility, but then I remember the glare of their spaceship as it cut beneath the space elevator and snapped the shaft in two like a twig. "I'm not sure. All I know is that Waters made his choice, and it didn't include watching out for us."

"I guess so," Lucy says, "but don't you think he's still watching out for us, maybe just in a different way?"

"If so, he has a strange way of showing it—as in, not showing it at all."

A knock at the door makes Lucy and me jump. Our eyes go wide. Who would be at our door at this hour?

"Still got the connection?" she asks.

The knocking gets louder.

I nod. "Who do you think that is?"

"Maybe it's Steve. What should I say?"

"Tell him I'm not feeling well and that you're taking care of me."

Lucy nods and rushes to the door as the knocking continues. She pulls back the door. "You can't just—"

Addy bursts into our room and races to the couch. "What's happening?"

"What are you doing here?" I ask.

"Are you kidding? I wasn't going to just stay in my quarters and pretend nothing was going on. Are you okay? Has the testing started?"

Lucy stands in front of us, fuming. "Out! Now! This doesn't involve you!"

"Of course it involves me! It involves all the Bounders! When are you going to get that through your pretty ribboned skull?"

Lucy doesn't answer. Instead she looks at me. As in, this is my problem, and I need to solve it.

I shake my head. "I'm barely hanging on to this brain connection with Mira. Figure it out."

"Fine." Lucy turns to Addy. "You want to be involved? He's all yours." She storms to her room and slams the door.

Addy curls her feet beneath her on the couch. "That was entertaining."

"Not really." I close my eyes and check the connection. "How'd you even get out of your quarters?"

"Marco told me how you've been rigging the doorjamb at night so your lock doesn't engage."

Of course he did. "Look, Addy, I don't have the energy to say this nicely, so I'm just going to say it plainly: you're causing problems with my pod."

"Are you sure? Because as far as I can tell, the only person who has a problem with me is Lucy. The other issues in your pod have nothing to do with me."

"What on earth are you talking about? What other issues?"

"Obviously, you don't all share the same opinions about Earth Force."

"Oh, that's just Cole. He's obsessed with rules, but he always comes around."

"Are you sure that's all it is? Because there's going to come a day when it matters."

"Yes, I'm sure. Stop acting like you're talking to your Bounders' rights group." Before she can respond, I put up my hand. "Not now, Addy. I need to focus on the connection. It looks like Lucy isn't coming back, so I'm going to need your help."

I explain to her about the brain link with Mira and the special interface Cole rigged. I tell her how she has to keep me focused as I report back what I'm seeing through Mira's eyes and as the Alkalinians' comments are run through the translator.

MONICA TESLER

Addy asks questions and inspects the interface. It feels good to be working together, and especially not to be arguing. Once she understands what to expect, we settle back on the couch and wait.

"You know, I'm kind of jealous, too," Addy says. "You and I are so close, Jasper, so connected. It's strange to see you like that with someone else."

I had no idea she was jealous of Mira. "We'll always be connected, Ads."

"I know, it's just a lot of change happening at once." She snuggles under a blanket on the couch. "Can you believe it was only a couple of weeks ago that we sat together in that dingy basement?"

I smile, remembering the creepy dolls and dusty headphones. That's where I spilled all my Earth Force secrets. "Is the Academy what you expected?"

"Yes . . . no . . . sort of. I'm more angry than ever at all the Earth Force lies. That hasn't changed. But you know what I love, Jasper? The freedom. I finally feel like I can make a difference in my future and the futures of so many others in the process."

Freedom? Really? I don't feel a bit free under the strict Earth Force regime. It's weird we can share something but have such different experiences. Still, I know I need to open my mind and try to relate to Addy's perspective. In a funny way, she kind of reminds me of Barrick back on Gulaga. Even though he was an outcast, he seemed more comfortable, more free, than almost anyone I've met.

"I know I've been a pest," Addy says, "but I'm happy to be here with you, Jasper."

"Me, too, Ads."

There's a flicker in my brain, and then bright lights shine behind my eyes. I signal to my sister.

"Mira?" she asks.

I nod.

Addy places the translator on my lap. I wrap my single gloved hand around the sensor grip. Cole threaded my other glove through the voice box and connected it to the end of the strap to act as an interface. We practiced once before he went to bed, and it seemed to work (and didn't activate the scrambler, thank goodness). Now we'll know for sure.

"What are you seeing?" Addy whispers.

"Nothing yet."

Mira's eyes are open, but I'm pretty sure she's unconscious. Like yesterday, our connection lets me see with Mira's eyes. All of the VR in her room has been deactivated. She's on her bed, which now looks like a plain metal cot. The walls and ceiling are orange. Bright lights beam down from above.

I hear voices in the background.

"Someone's coming," I tell Addy.

An Alk appears next to Mira. In his cyborg arm he holds

a syringe filled with venom. He lowers his flying throne so it's level with Mira's neck and injects the yellow liquid. Even though I can't see the injection, since it's outside of Mira's range of vision, I can feel it. It's like I'm the one getting a shot. I tip forward. My limbs feel like lead.

Addy grabs my shoulders and holds me back against the couch. "You've got this, Jasper," she whispers. "Hold the connection."

The Alk situates a small dome around Mira's head, then activates the screen beside her bed. Just like yesterday, a scan of her brain appears on the screen. The Alk adjusts the dome and repositions the scanner projection. Now Mira's spine and brain stem are featured. The Youli brain patch is plainly visible in the center of the image. The Alk manipulates the projection and zooms in on the patch.

Next the Alk wheels a metal cart alongside Mira's bed. An assortment of tools is spread out on top. He selects a small metal poker with a head as thin and as sharp as a needle. Then he disappears from my sight.

A sharp pain pierces my neck and races down my spine. I scream and grab for Addy with my free hand.

Addy squeezes my palm. "Are you okay?"

The pain comes again, longer this time.

I tense and hold my breath.

"What's happening?" she says.

I slowly exhale and brace for more pain. I have to focus. I have to maintain the connection.

I force myself to look at the brain scan. The next time the pain comes, I see the poker appear on the scanner. He's piercing her skin and jabbing at the Youli patch. Because of our connection, each jab feels like it's jutting into my brain, too.

Sweat pours down my forehead as the jabbing continues. Addy has her arms around me. I bend over, fighting against the pain. Addy rubs my back. I focus on the rhythmic motion of her hand and my intimate connection with Mira. Those are the only things getting me through this.

The Alk opts for a different tool. This one has a tiny looped wire at the end. He tests it against his scaly skin. A spark jumps from the wire. He angles it toward Mira's neck. The current blasts through my body. I rear back and scream.

"That's enough!" Addy says. "You have to disconnect."

I gulp for breath and almost sever the connection, but then I hear something.

"I think someone's coming." My words come out in a gasp for air.

The Alk sets down the loop tool and steers his throne back from the cot. Finally I have a reprieve from the pain, but the aftershock reverberates all the way to my fingers and toes. This is one time a bit of venom wouldn't be so bad. At least it would numb this pain.

The hissing and clicking of other Alkalinians grows louder. As soon as they're in range, the voice box should be able to translate.

Seelok flies into my view, flanked by two of his main advisers. He studies the brain scan, zooming the image in and out. Then he turns to the Alk at his side and hisses.

This is the moment of truth. I squeeze the hand grip as tight as I can. Please let this work!

The voice box translates: "Is everything ready?"

It works! I pump my free fist in the air. Addy bounces on the couch.

His adviser replies: "Yes. As soon as they confirmed, we implemented the protocol. They will bound to the perimeter, and our shuttles will tow them into the hangar."

Addy stops bouncing. I focus on Seelok. Who is going to bound to the perimeter?

"And your guards are in place?" Seelok asks.

"They will be. Once all is confirmed, we should be able to dispose of the Earthlings quickly, as the venom will still be in their systems. We made sure of that this afternoon."

I sneak a peek at Addy. She presses her hands to her mouth.

"You're sure you've identified which ones need to be preserved?" This question Seelok directs to the Alk who was jabbing at Mira's brain.

"This is definitely one of them." He picks up the poker and

moves in front of the scanner. "As you can see, there are Youli cells implanted in her brain stem."

The Alk jabs Mira's skin, and the pain runs through my body. I push past it. I can't lose the connection.

"Are there others?" Seelok asks.

"Yes, a boy," the Alk says. "We were unable to perform final verification, but all early testing showed an affirmative result."

"He's talking about you!" Addy whispers.

"Why wasn't verification possible?" Seelok asks.

Another Alk zooms into view. It's Steve. "We suspect he fell asleep in the common room playing a game many of the subjects mentioned during the intake survey. It was an unforeseen consequence."

He thinks I stayed up late playing *Evolution*!

"Where is he now?" Seelok asks.

"Both children are in their quarters," Steve says. "As soon as we're given the go-ahead, we'll secure the two of them for transfer."

"Excellent," Seelok says. "The Youli should arrive within the hour."

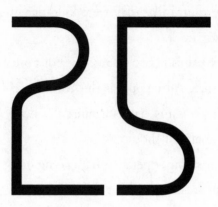

SEELOK AND HIS ADVISERS EXIT THE
room, with Steve close behind them. The Alk conducting
the testing checks his notes, turns off the scanner, and then
wheels his medical cart out of view. Moments later the VR
activates in the room. Mira sleeps peacefully on a soft bed
with a teal comforter and clean white sheets.

For a second I do nothing. What if they come back? What
if there's more to hear?

"Are they gone?" Addy whispers.

Her words jar me. I cast aside the voice box and spring to
my feet. "We've got to do something!"

"Do you think they were serious? Are the Youli really coming here?"

"Did they sound like they were kidding?" I ask, rubbing the back of my neck.

"No, but what did they mean they'd dispose of us?"

"I'm not sure. All I know is the Youli are coming for me and Mira." I press my hands against my head. "We need a plan to stop them!" I shout.

Lucy's door swings open. "What's going on?"

"The Youli are coming, that's what!"

Addy quickly fills her in on what happened, while I pace back and forth in front of the couch.

"Cole was right!" Lucy cries. "We should have told the admiral when we had the chance. If we hadn't waited, we wouldn't be in this mess."

"You don't know that," Addy says. "Things could be worse. We might not have been able to use the translator, and no one would know the Youli are coming."

"But—"

"It doesn't matter now, Lucy!" I shout. "We need to wake the others! Get Marco and Cole! Alert as many cadets as you can and get them to help you. We're certainly no match for the Youli asleep."

"Marco and Cole, maybe. But the other cadets ate. They're out cold. I'm not sure I can wake them up."

"Addy can help you figure it out! And use the SIMPLE to call the space station. Have them send the quantum fleet. Tell them to bound directly to the Alkalinian Seat coordinates in forty minutes to evacuate. I'm going to deactivate the occludium tether."

"I'm coming with you!" Addy shouts.

"No. You're staying here and helping Lucy!"

"You can't go alone!"

"I'm not. Mira's coming with me. I can't risk her being taken by the Youli."

The only problem is I have to wake Mira up. With all that venom in her system, it won't be easy.

I stand at Mira's door and focus all my energy on two words: *Wake up!*

I sense her stirring. I try again. *Wake up!*

And again.

Wake up!

Wake up!

Wake up!

I pound on her door and keep screaming with my brain. I have to wake her!

I ram the door with my shoulder and pound some more. I rear back again and bash against it with all my weight.

The door swings open and I stumble forward, knocking a very wobbly Mira to her knees.

She's awake. Thank goodness.

"We need to go!" I tell her. "The Youli are coming! We have to deactivate the occludium tether!"

The Youli . . . ? Mira slurs, or at least the brain-talk version of slur. She's out of it.

"Yes, the Youli! You have to focus, Mira. I need you with me. Grab your gloves and meet me at the door. We need to go now!"

I run to my room and grab my blast pack, then I dash back to the couch and grab the voice box. I stuff my free glove into my pack, then I pull my other glove, which Cole rigged to the voice box, but nothing budges. I inspect the box and try again, but I can't figure out how to free my glove.

"Addy!"

Addy leaves Marco's door and runs to the couch. "What? We're trying to wake the others!"

"Help me. I can't get my glove free."

Addy looks at the voice box and tugs at my glove. No luck. "I don't want it to rip. It would be useless."

"What if I need to bound?"

Addy spins me around and unzips my blast pack. She shoves the voice box inside with the glove and sensor grip still attached. "We may need the voice box, too. Let's go!"

"No, Addy! You stay here. You need to help Lucy rally the others."

My sister bites her lip. She wants to fight me.

Please, Addy, there's no time.

She nods. "Fine. Hurry up! If you don't have that shield down, there won't be a rescue!"

I give her a quick hug and dart to the door.

"Good luck, Jasper!" Lucy shouts behind me.

Mira is slumped against the door, fast asleep. I run to her side and drape her arm across my back. "Wake up, Mira!" I shout as I haul open the door.

When that doesn't work, I reach for her brain. *Wake up!*

Mira's head jerks. *Jasper?*

Walk!

I half carry her out of our quarters and into the hall. We take a few steps, and I stumble, sending us both to our knees.

Mira isn't light. Add her weight to my inherent klutziness, and this just isn't going to work.

Wake up! I shout again as I struggle to pull her to standing.

She shifts her balance onto her own feet, and we continue down the hall. She walks okay for a few seconds, and then she starts to slump again. This isn't working. Maybe I should have left her with Lucy and Addy. Maybe I should take her back.

No. Seelok said the Youli are coming for us. I can't leave her asleep in the quarters. What if something goes wrong? She'd be right there waiting for the Youli to whisk her away!

How do I reach her? How do I really wake her up?

Maybe . . . music.

I try to remember the notes of the song we played together this afternoon, "Heart and Soul." I tap my fingers against my leg and hum the melody in my mind: *3-3-3, 3-2-1-2-3-4.*

Mira! You're on! We're playing a duet!

Again I tap out the melody and hum along in my mind.

At first Mira doesn't react, but when I start the third round, a basic bass harmony rises up to join the music. And when it does, Mira stands up straighter and carries most of her weight as we rush down the hall.

I speed up the song and coax her faster once we turn the corner into the hallway that leads to the siphon port. We have to make it across the bay and to the elevator without anyone spotting us.

When we reach the bay doors, I leave Mira leaning against the wall and creep forward to scan for Alks. About a dozen Alks are down at the other end of the bay readying the Frogs. They're rigging them with cables, probably preparing to tow the Youli vessels through the water and inside the occludium shield.

The Alks all ride on the low scooters, like the ones we've seen assisting Seelok and his aides. They look the same as the Alks we spotted on the lower levels carting the vials of venom. Those guys didn't seem to notice us. They definitely didn't care what we were doing.

MONICA TESLER

We have to get across the bay. We have no choice but to make a run for it and hope these Alks don't notice us or aren't interested, like the ones in the venom labs.

I head back to Mira. She's sitting down with her back against the wall. The good news is her eyes are open.

What's happening? she asks when I bend down to help her up.

How much do you remember?

The sensation of complete blankness comes back from Mira. That must mean she doesn't remember anything.

"I'll fill you in soon," I say. "But for now you'll have to trust me. We need to run across the siphon port quickly and quietly. Can you do that?"

Mira nods. She pushes with her feet as I pull her hands, and soon she's standing. We walk to the door, and I peer around the edge. All of the Alks are still busy with the Frogs.

"Ready?" I grab Mira's hand. "Go!"

I run into the bay, pulling Mira behind me. She drags and shuffles her feet much louder than I'd like. I keep my eyes fixed on the rear doors. Almost there.

We make it across without attracting attention. I steer us through the hallway to the elevator and press the button.

What's happening? Mira asks again as I steer her into the elevator.

"Hold on." I wait for the door to slide shut. When I turn to Mira to tell her what's happening, her eyes are closed.

"Mira?"

Her eyelids flutter.

"Hey! Stay with me!" I squeeze her arm and hope she's listening. "The Youli are coming!"

At that, Mira's eyelids fly open. Her shock radiates from her brain to mine.

Now that Mira's clearly awake, I may as well clue her in on everything. "The Alks plan to dispose of all the cadets and Earth Force officers except us. I don't know exactly what that means, but it can't be good. The Youli want you and me alive. They know about us, probably from what happened back on Gulaga and then on their ship at the intragalactic summit. The Alks found our brain patches. They're planning to hand us over to the Youli."

The Youli are coming here?

Yes, I tell her. *I'm pretty sure they're coming for us.*

It takes Mira a moment to process what I'm saying, then she sends me an image of the occludium tether.

"That's the plan. Lucy and Addy are waking the cadets and calling the space station for backup. You and I have to get the occludium shield down."

The elevator door slides open. I sprint out, expecting Mira to be right beside me, especially now that I've shared what's going on. Instead she's slumped in the elevator. The venom's just too much for her.

I run back, slide my shoulder under her arm, and help her out. She practically collapses on top of me.

Wake up! I shout through our neural connection.

She stumbles forward and tries to straighten, but I'm still supporting at least half of her weight. If this is how it is, so be it. At least she's semiconscious. I head off down the hall with Mira at my side.

Then I grind to a stop as a horrible realization washes over me. I have no clue how to get to the venom tube.

"Mira, you remember the way, right?"

I look over. Her head hangs loosely between her shoulders, and her eyes are closed.

Mira, please! You have to help me!

I'm sure I've made a wrong turn. It shouldn't have taken us this long to reach the venom tube.

Her head tips up. *What's happening?*

The Youli, remember?

She nods and tries to focus.

"How do we get to the tube?"

Mira looks around. *Where's the elevator?*

Great. She doesn't even know we're on the lowest level. It looks like this is up to me. I steer us down another hall, which looks curiously similar to the hall I turned us down two minutes ago. This is a nightmare. If we don't make it to the tube, across to the saucer, and down the shaft to the occludium tether, our ships can't bound in. If they try, their atoms will be lost, which is even worse. And bounding outside the tether is no use. The bounding ships have no propulsion technology. Unless the aeronauts get out and swim through the contaminated water to reach the Alkalinian Seat, they have no way of making it past the tether.

The next hallway we come to is protected by double doors. That's definitely not the way we came the first time, but maybe it will help us cut over to the tube. I pull, half expecting the doors to be locked, but they swing back easily. I lead Mira into the hall.

As soon as we're inside, I realize the hall is VR-equipped like our quarters. Everything is covered in the squishy orange material and has the vague smell of rotten fruit. I spy a door at the far end of the hall and take a few steps toward it, then a computerized voice announces something in Alkalinian.

My stomach twists. This was a mistake. We need to get to the other side of this hall as quickly as we can.

A chime sounds, and then two laser beams activate from the ceiling, targeting Mira and me. They wave around us until they seem to latch on to our skulls.

They've found us! We've got to move! I quicken my pace down the VR hall, pulling Mira behind me. The lasers move in sync with our steps.

Then a second chime sounds, and the lasers snap off.

Another step, and we're no longer on Alkalinia. I'm on the air rail in Americana East, waiting for my stop. Across the aisle, Will Stevens and some guys from the grade above me are laughing. They're laughing at me. The doors open. It's my stop. I try to stand, but my feet are anchored to the floor.

"B-wad!" they shout.

I shake my head. This isn't real. It's the VR simulation. Those lasers must have been scanners. But what is this VR tech? It's like it searched my brain for an awful memory.

"Wasn't that your stop, B-wad?" Will asks. His buddies slap him five and collapse on the bench laughing. Out the window, the buildings of Americana East fly by.

This isn't real. I'm not on the air rail. I'm on Alkalinia.

But Mira is no longer by my side.

26

MIRA!

This isn't real, Jasper! Your feet aren't really plastered to the floor.

I force my legs to move and race down the length of the train car, which inexplicably morphs into a bridge. Before I can process where I am, Regis runs at me and dives for my legs. I collapse to my knees and peer over the edge into the abyss below.

My breath catches in my throat. This is virtual. It isn't really happening. Just push them out of your mind.

I squeeze my eyes shut and stand, willing myself not to see Regis when I blink them open.

I don't. I'm not in Gulagaven anymore. I'm outside on the

frozen tundra of Gulaga. It's cold, and the light is fading. If I don't get inside fast, I'll freeze to death. The ground beneath me shifts and sways, and a slimy tendril loops around my leg and pulls me to the ground.

I struggle to get up. I've got to run. I dash across the tundra, heading for the cliff. Something isn't right. I've been here before, but I wasn't alone. I was with Mira. Regis stole her glove. We got caught out after curfew and nearly froze to death. We were rescued by Barrick and the rebels.

But we're not on the tundra. We're in the VR hall on Alkalinia.

Mira!

Mira!

"Mira!" I shout. "Mira, where are you?" I shake my head, trying to stop my brain from thinking I'm running across a field of slimers.

The light shifts from night to day, and the slimers grow into high grass. Up ahead a large, lithe cat limbers toward a river. In the distance a herd of beasts that look like woolly mammoths graze.

This is the Paleo Planet, which means—

A boulder flies through the sky and crashes on the ground in front of me.

I dodge a second rock, which grazes my shoulder and smashes behind me.

Mira! Answer me!

The ground trembles, and a low rumble sounds in the distance. A cloud of dust rises at the horizon. It whirls and swells in my direction. I can make out shapes in the dust cloud: a million charging wildeboars.

I spin and sprint in the opposite direction. The wildeboars close in from behind, but I skid to a stop. Ten meters ahead is a Youli. He extends his palm and reaches for my atoms.

"No! You're not real! None of this is real!"

Think, Jasper! You've got to stop the VR program!

I squeeze my eyes shut. We're not on the Paleo Planet, I tell myself. We're in the VR hallway. We are still limited by the dimensions of the room. As long as I keep my eyes closed and keep telling myself that this is VR, I should be able to find the wall.

I stretch out my arms in front and walk forward. The pounding of the wildeboars' hooves grows so loud I can barely hear myself think. My body braces for impact.

This isn't real. This isn't real. This isn't real.

A few more steps. This hallway wasn't that wide. Just keep going.

My left hand squishes into something. It must be the wall. I keep my eyes closed and follow the wall, hand over hand. I eventually reach the corner and palm over a few more paces. There's a break in the material. Please let that be the door. I find the handle and push back the swinging door.

As soon as I do, the program stops. The orange walls return. In the middle of the hall Mira sits on the ground, curled in a ball.

I drop my blast pack to prop the door open and run to Mira's side. Her hair is pulled out of its elastic. A shudder rips through her. She bends her head to her knees and gently rocks.

Even without the VR, I see her in the sensory gym at the space station. Regis just humiliated her in front of all the cadets. I stood up to him in front of everybody. That was one of the first times in my life that I was truly brave.

I place my hand on Mira's shoulder, and she flinches.

"Mira," I whisper, "we really need to go."

She doesn't respond. Another shudder rips through her.

I don't think she had the same VR experience as me, but whatever it was, it must have been awful.

Mira. I lift her hand and lace our fingers together. *The Youli are coming. Everyone's counting on us. We need to deactivate the occludium tether.*

She turns her head, and her brown eyes find mine. They're filled with despair but also something else: determination.

She lets me help her up. We retrieve my pack and leave the VR hall. I decide to walk as far as I can without turning.

Hopefully we can reach the far end of the Seat, trace the windows to the corner, and double back to reach the tube connection.

Soon we pass rooms like the ones we saw before with empty beds. Sure enough, they're sleeping quarters. This time all the beds are filled with Alks—the scooter Alks, who don't have cyborg arms. The Alks are hooked up to tubes that connect to small metal tables next to their beds. Could it be that they're pumped with venom? Or some other substance that makes them compliant and unfeeling? That could explain a lot about their odd, indifferent behavior.

There's no time to think about it. We make our way to the far wall and turn left. When we reach the corner, we turn left again and backtrack to the venom tube. It certainly wasn't the quickest route, but at least we made it.

The hall is quiet. None of the Alks we saw yesterday are around. They must be sleeping like the others, which is a good thing. Even though they didn't bother us, we don't need to take any chances. Secrecy is our only advantage, the only chance that this mission is a success.

We pass the rows of labeled vats filled with venom and head for the tube. I pull back the door. I can see all the way across the open ocean, from the Alkalinian Seat to the saucer. All we have to do is cross it and take down the tether.

I stand at the foot of the tube with a groggy Mira by my

side. When we first spotted the tube over a week ago, we had no idea what it was for, no clue that the thick yellow goop that flows through the pipe is one of the most valuable substances on the galactic black market: Alkalinian venom, milked from thousands of baby Alks on the other side of this tube.

The tube's clear plastic walls hold back the open ocean. Who knows how many metric tons of water threaten to crush that tube and everything in it? But I can't think about that now. I have to do this.

Let's go. I squeeze Mira's hand and take a tentative step into the tube. Her hand slips from my grasp.

"Hey!" I turn to Mira. Her eyes are closed.

Great. She's nearly asleep on her feet again. She recovered from the VR nightmare only to slip back into venom-induced narcolepsy.

I shake her arm. "Mira! Wake up!"

Her eyes blink into focus, and she nods.

"We're at the venom tube. We need to move! Quickly!"

I tug Mira through the door and into the tube, then take off running. The door clangs shut, and the noise reverberates through the tube. The vibrations send a ripple through the water beyond.

So much water. Way too much water. I take a deep breath and focus on placing one foot in front of the next.

Just keep moving, Jasper. Everyone's counting on you.

Mira struggles to keep my pace. She shakes free of my hand, and when I glance back, she's fallen behind.

"Hurry, Mira!" The tube echoes with my shouts, and I shudder. It's brain-talk from now on.

I should stop for her, but I can't. One of us needs to make it to the end of this tube.

And I can't handle the water. It's pressing me down, collapsing my lungs, making it impossible to breathe.

Must. Not. Hyperventilate.

I block out the water as best I can and push on.

The plastic walls of the tube are clear, but the reflection from the venom gives them a sickly yellow cast, like looking through a filter. I can't believe the Alks have been poisoning us with this stuff. According to Serena, in small quantities the venom causes sleep, muscle fatigue, even temporary paralysis. In larger doses it can kill within seconds. Mixed with other ingredients it can be a powerful medicine. To the Alkalinians, it's currency.

But it comes at an awful price. It comes at the lives of Serena's children, because something obviously happens to them after they've served their purpose. I don't know if the Alks kill them or if they die off, but I know they're not moving from writhing snake pit to minithrones. Clearly, that's not the future for those tiny snakes we saw earlier today. It seems like the only Alks Seelok leaves alive are his entourage and the scooter workers.

Up ahead one of those nasty sea creatures glides through the water, heading straight for the tube. Its black, iridescent skin reflects the yellowish light. Its tail curves through the water, propelling it closer every second. I try not to look.

Thump! It whacks the tube.

The creature crests the tube and doubles back. In a terrible instant its black eyes lock with mine. I can't break its gaze. It opens its mouth to reveal enormous, glistening silver fangs.

I shake my head and run.

Thump! It glides above me.

Thump! Thump! Two more sea creatures circle the tube.

I'm only halfway across. I've got to pick up the pace. Behind me, Mira has fallen even farther back.

Mira! Let's go!

She glances up and pushes forward, but her movements are floppy. She weaves from the venom pipe to the edge of the tube and back again.

Maybe it was a mistake to bring her.

No! If she'd stayed in the room, she would have been there for the taking once the Youli arrive.

The Youli . . . I sprint even faster. Up ahead more of the sea creatures dive and spin around the venom tube, lashing the plastic with their muscular tails. Mira and I must be attracting them.

Thump! Thump! Thump!

The tube shakes with the thunderous force of the impacts. I hope those creatures don't damage the tube. If this thing cracks while we're in it, that will be the end of us.

I glance behind me. Mira is barely walking. She balances her weight against the venom pipe.

More creatures swim to the tube, diving and swirling and lashing their tails.

Then the water swirls with a strong current, and the tube rocks on its foundation. I'm thrown against the plastic barrier and onto my knees.

What's happening? Did the tube dislodge from the seafloor?

The sea creatures glide away and swim together toward the saucer, clearing the view outside the tube. I project their course to see what's caught their attention. A large silver sphere bobs in the water just beyond the occludium tether.

Gripping the venom pipe, I pull myself up and stare at the sphere, trying to understand what I'm seeing. It's familiar but out of place.

Oh my God. That's a Youli ship!

Mira! The Youli! Run!

I race for the end of the tube and disengage the latch. The door swings open. I drop my pack and brace the tube door, then I dash inside. Once Mira gets here, we'll run up the stairs to the generator room.

Or even faster, we'll bound there. We'll be outside of the tether range.

I return to my pack and pull out the voice box with my stuck glove. As I wait for Mira, I inspect the box and try to free my glove.

A hiss from behind makes me jump. I brace and spin, ready to force my way through whatever Alkalinian threat awaits.

Serena slides in front of me and hisses into the voice box.

"What are you doing here? Where are your friends?"

I keep trying to free my glove. "I can't talk, Serena. I'm in a real rush."

Serena lifts her head and gazes through the doors into the venom tube. "What are those creatures?"

I glance back. The black sea creatures have returned to the tube. They twirl and spin and whack against the thick walls. The water swells and shakes the foundation. Another Youli vessel must have bounded in.

Mira is still a hundred meters from the end of the tube, and she's not moving fast. It will take too long for her to cross. I have to get the tether down now. I need to do it alone.

I reach out with my mind. *Mira, I'm going to deactivate the tether. Wait for me!*

Jumbled emotions come back from Mira. I can tell she's about to protest. But then there's the sense of resignation. The Youli are here. We're out of options.

Serena slips past me into the tube.

I can't get my glove free, and I can't waste any more time trying. I lift the voice box to my mouth and turn it to full volume. "Hey, Serena! Keep Mira safe, okay?"

I don't wait for an answer. Plus, Serena is already deep into the tube. I shove the voice box with my trapped glove back into my pack and take off running.

I race up the stairs to the systems center and down the hall to the generator room, then dash across to the hatch that connects to the narrow shaft that descends to the occludium tether.

From the nearby windows I have a better view of what's happening, and it's not good. Six Youli vessels wait just beyond the tether range.

Make that seven.

The arrival of the seventh ship sends a strong current rippling through the water. The shaft sways and pulls against the anchored bubble holding the occludium tether.

Please hold. Please. Just a few minutes longer.

Meanwhile, Mira has covered a lot of distance in the venom tube. Serena has nearly reached her. All around them the black sea creatures swarm.

From the Alkalinian Seat, a Frog pops out of the loading tube, with another close behind. They scuttle toward the Youli vessels with their tow cables ready to rig.

I don't have much time. I have to take down that tether and trust that Lucy and Addy have called for Earth Force backup.

I disengage the hatch and prepare to descend the shaft.

Wait . . . there's motion at the other end of the venom tube. Someone else is in there and moving fast.

Is that an Alk? Is he coming for Mira?

No, that's no Alk.

That's Addy.

"ADDY!" I SCREAM, THEN INSTANTLY REGRET
it. There could be an Alk anywhere, and if there's one close
by, he'll know I'm here.

I silently will her to go back. What is she doing? Why does
she always need to be a hero?

There's someone else in the tube, maybe twenty meters
behind Addy. That has to be Marco. He's fast, but she's faster.
He never quite got his speed back after breaking his leg on
the Paleo Planet.

I can't afford to worry about them now. I have to focus. I
have to take the tether down. If I don't, everyone will likely
die—Addy, Mira, Marco, Lucy, Cole, Gedney, everyone.

I pull open the hatch and take a shaky step into the shaft. It's the only way to reach the bubble structure that's anchored to the ocean floor a hundred meters below. The occludium tether is housed in the bubble.

You can do this, Jasper.

I press the door to the shaft closed, then shut a second, redundant door that should keep the shaft sealed off from the water in case it disconnects—not something I want to think about right now.

I take a deep breath. This is possibly the last place in the world I want to be. Claustrophobia crowds my brain and darkens the edges of my peripheral vision.

Inside the narrow shaft there are plastic rungs leading all the way to the seafloor like a ladder. Mounted handrails run parallel. I grab hold of the rails and start the descent.

The shaft sways in the current. I wobble with each step like I'm crossing a link bridge at a playground.

I try to keep my eyes glued to the rungs, but it's hard. Addy, Marco, and Mira are in the venom tube. Youli ships are two hundred meters away. Soon they'll be inside the perimeter and gunning for the Bounders.

Unless . . . could the Alks have done something to the cadets already?

I hope Cole and Lucy are okay.

The shaft rocks hard, and I am thrown to my knees and

skid several meters down. Finally I wedge my foot between two rungs and stop.

What on earth caused that current?

Outside the perimeter three Earth Force ships have bounded in.

They weren't supposed to be here yet! They were supposed to wait until the shield was down and bound inside the Seat! How are they going to reach the cadets?

Immediately the Earth Force ships fire upon the Frogs and the Youli vessels. They implement the popcorn strategy Earth Force used at the intragalactic summit—bounding in and out to fixed points, all beyond the tether. The same distraction tactic allowed our pod to plant the degradation patch on the Youli vessel.

Oh, I get it! This must be an advance team. I bet Cole masterminded that strategy. The rescue team will bound in once the shield's deactivated.

And getting that shield deactivated is up to me.

Let's go, Jasper!

I pull myself up and continue descending.

Even though we started a firefight, the Youli have a strong advantage. Half of their ships are fending off Earth Force, but the other half are already inside the shield, being towed by Frogs. In minutes they'll reach the Alkalinian Seat, where most of the cadets and officers are fast asleep.

A flash of light blinds me, and I crash down as the shaft pulls against the saucer. I scramble to my knees as lights flash in every direction. Earth Force is firing at the Youli, and the Youli are firing back. And what lies between the Earth Force ships and the Youli vessels being towed to the Seat? This shaft.

Jasper!

The word rings in my skull.

Jasper!

Mira?

Mira's emotions run at me: first panic, then relief, then panic again.

I'm okay, I tell her. *Almost at the tether! Keep Addy safe!*

For a moment my brain hums with a surge of energy. Mira must be trying to send me a brain boost, but it's not very powerful. She's probably still weak from the venom.

I try to spot her in the venom tube, but it's swarmed with the sea creatures. I can't see inside the tube at all. I don't know if my sister is okay. I can't tell if Marco has reached her. I have no idea if Mira is even in the tube anymore.

I need to keep moving. More flashes. More shots. The shaft flips around like a jump rope. This isn't working. I sit down on the rungs, point my feet toward the tether, and scoot on my butt the rest of the way down.

A light beam from one of the Frogs sweeps across the water. It zeros in on me like a spotlight.

I have to get to that tether.

Diving forward, I tumble head over feet.

Laser lights flash around me. The shaft bends and pulls against the saucer seal.

I roll again, bringing me halfway to the seafloor.

I have to make it to the bubble. The Youli wouldn't dare fire at me there. They could explode the whole Alkalinian Seat if they ignited the occludium.

Over at the venom tube, the sea creatures crowd in numbers I've never seen. What are they doing? Is Addy still in there?

Bam! The shaft jerks sideways. I'm thrown into the railing, then my body slams down on the rungs. I plummet to the bottom headfirst.

Thud! My vision winks out when I hit the floor of the bubble. I blink and try to lift my head. The edges of my vision go black.

Jasper!

Mira's voice sounds distant and echoes in my mind, like she's calling me across a canyon.

Jasper! Get up!

My brain surges with an influx of energy to my patch. Mira must have zapped me again. It's not much, but it's enough to get me going. I struggle to my feet, the room spinning. Or maybe I'm spinning? No, it must be the water. It's swirling around me, rushing against the anchored bubble where I'm standing, dragging the shaft through the current.

The shaft.

It whips above me like a wind sock, waving back and forth through the current in wide arcs.

It's no longer connected to the saucer.

I'm no longer connected to the saucer.

Thank God for the redundant door.

My mind reels. A flashback overtakes me. I'm at the space station, staring at the image of a disconnected, malfunctioning chute flinging Ryan back and forth through space.

Just like then, I need to act. I need to shift into autopilot and do what needs to be done. I shake my head to knock my vision into focus, then pull myself up and scan the machinery in front of me. What did Cole say? Look for an off switch.

The bubble shakes as more lights flash. Black shapes fly past, headed for the venom tube.

Jasper, the shield!

Mira's words fill my brain with razor-sharp focus. I home in on the controls in front of me. I locate the manual override, three bright-red buttons and a heavy gold lever.

Here goes. I press the buttons. The screen on the machine panel lights up with Alkalinian script. I can't read it, but I'm hoping it's telling me the shield is about to come down. I push on the lever. It doesn't move. I don't have time to mess around. I grip the lever with both hands and jump, forcing it down with my body weight.

A flicker of silver fills my sight, then a loud noise like a sonic boom ripples outward, and I'm thrown backward against the bubble.

Please let that have worked. Please let the shield be down.

I should be able to tell for sure with my gloves. They should be able to detect the presence of an occludium shield. I grab my pack and pull out a single glove.

Then I remember. I dump my pack and out tumbles the voice box, with my other glove woven through, attached to the sensor grip. Stuck.

I try to free my glove, prying at the voice box, pulling at the sensor, but it's no use. It's absolutely and completely stuck.

I lean back against the bubble wall, mind racing as I search for a solution.

I'm alone at the bottom of the ocean in the middle of a laser battle with the Youli. They know I'm down here. The shaft is detached. I can't use my gloves.

There's no getting out of this.

I can't keep Addy safe like I promised my parents. I can't even get to her. Some brother I've turned out to be. I would stay in this bubble with Regis for an entire tour of duty if it meant I could save my sister.

Strong currents swell against the bubble and whip the

shaft. The bubble groans as the shaft strains against it. There's no redundant door down here in the bubble like there is up top at the saucer. There's not even a seal. That shaft won't stay attached for long. Once it breaks from the bubble, the water will rush in. I'll drown, if I'm not instantly killed by the contaminated water.

That's it. I'm not going to make it.

Is the shield down? Did I at least accomplish that? If I die here at the bottom of the contaminated sea, will my death mean something?

Dad's words from the day I set out on my third tour reach me: *Your mom and I don't say it enough, Jasper, but we're proud of you. . . . I'm sure Earth Force is honored to have you in their ranks.* Maybe, Dad. If I knocked out the occludium shield, maybe you're right. But I can't reach Addy. I'm so sorry.

Debris rains down on the bubble from the saucer above. I'm knocked sideways, and I land behind the tether equipment. Something must have been hit. When I open my eyes, I think I'm seeing double. Then I realize the glorious truth. There are twice as many ships in view because Earth Force has sent reinforcements. There are three more vessels inside the perimeter. That has to mean the shield is down.

Let's hope it also means that some of the Earth Force ships landed directly inside the siphon port. The Bounder rescue should be under way.

I crawl to where the shaft connects to the bubble and look for a way to seal myself in. It's useless. I can't get back to save my friends. I can't even save myself.

Mira! I strain to reach her with my brain. I've never been the best at brain-talk when I can't see her. *Mira, my glove is stuck! I'm trapped! I don't think I'll make it! Please help Addy!*

I sense Mira's brain, and I can tell she's trying to reach me, but it comes back to me all jumbled.

Something . . . not sure . . . Serena . . . Her thoughts are filled with images of the black sea creatures and Serena shrieking inside the tube.

I climb up and press my hands against the bubble glass. The venom tube is shaking. The creatures are knocking it off its foundation.

Where's Addy? I shout in my brain.

Then I'm screaming out loud: "Addy! No! Addy!"

The mob of sea creatures shake the tube. They dislodge it from the seafloor. Then the tube is lifting, and the sea creatures part as they rip the tube in two.

"No! Addy!"

Yellow venom pours out of the wound in a fountain, and from the middle of the tube Serena rises up into the ocean. The sea creatures swarm her until she's shielded from view.

"No!" I pound my fists against the glass.

Anyone in that tube is surely dead.

368   MONICA TESLER

The shaft whips against the bubble as the aftershock from the tube break ripples through the water. The seam starts to rip. I see it in slow motion, the water trickling in, then starting to gush.

I'm surely dead.

Then a power seizes my neck, like I'm being strangled. My atoms freeze. I can't move.

What on earth . . . ?

I'm ripped from the bubble and hurled through space.

I'm bounding.

But I don't know how.

Or where.

28

MY HIP STRIKES THE COLD, HARD GROUND. I throw out my hands to stop my head from crashing next. I suck in a deep breath, relieved that water isn't rushing into my lungs.

I push up onto my knees. I have no idea where I am. Everything is dimly lit, and what I can see is gray and formless.

"Addy!" I have to find my sister.

Jasper?

I spin around. A few meters behind me, Mira is pushing herself to her feet.

I stand up and run to her, pulling her into a hug. Her clothes are damp, and she smells sweet, like cotton candy.

"Have you seen Addy? Is she okay?"

She made it out with Marco.

You're sure? I ask.

Mira sends me an image. It's Marco and Addy running for the end of the venom tube and slamming the seal door.

Something inside my chest unclenches. "Thank goodness. Why are you wet? Is that seawater?"

She shakes her head. *Venom.*

"Oh my God. Are you hurt?"

Mira shakes her head.

The last thing I remember, the seal was breaking on the bubble and the venom tube was tearing apart. Those black sea creatures were everywhere. "What happened to the venom tube?"

Serena.

I remember Mira trying to tell me something about Serena when I was in the bubble, but I still don't understand.

Serena, she thinks again. Then she sends an image of the throngs of black sea creatures.

She's connected to them in some way?

A wave of sadness passes through Mira. *Her children.*

Whoa. It's like Mira just gave me the missing piece to the puzzle. That's why those sea creatures looked so familiar. They're Serena's children. When they're no longer needed in the venom pit, they're cast out to the contaminated sea. And apparently, some of them survive—and grow a lot bigger and scarier, probably thanks to the contamination.

Did Serena know? I ask.

Not until today.

Serena told us she'd never been in the venom tube, that she'd never even been beyond the door she unlocked for us. So today was a reunion—a horrible, heartbreaking reunion. And the venom tube broke along with it.

Mira leans her head against me. I circle her cold, wet shoulders with my arm.

Now that I know Addy is safe, I finally take in my surroundings. There's nothing familiar about this place. No saucer. No Alkalinian Seat. No venom tube. Not even any water. Everything is dull and dark. Wherever we are, I've never been here before.

"Where are we, Mira? How did we get here?"

I brought us here.

How?

I'm not sure. When I bounded, I grabbed you.

But where are we? I look around again. There's nothing. No buildings, no plants, no people. There's not even any color.

I don't know, Mira says.

"We need to get back!" I say. "They need our help with the evacuation!"

I'll try. Mira closes her eyes and reaches out with her mind to build a port. Then she opens her eyes and shakes her head.

"What is it?" I ask.

Nothing. See? She closes her eyes and reaches for me with her mind. Once she makes the connection, I can see what she sees, feel what she feels.

Mira opens her mind to build a port, but where there is always connection and order and rightness, there is nothing. Her mind is as empty as the barren world around us.

I open my eyes. Mira's eyes are still squeezed shut. Her hands are out in front of her, but her gloves don't glow. Then her eyes find mine, filled with panic.

I shrug. "Take a break. Maybe we're just tired."

We try again in a few minutes. Ten tries later and still no success. Something is blocking her ability to bound.

"Let's look around. Maybe the block is location specific. Hopefully, we just have to get out of range, and you'll be able to tap in."

I take Mira's hand, and we set out. The ground is squishy, like a giant sponge that soaked up every ounce of color from this place. My shoes sink with each step. After we've been walking for five minutes and have seen absolutely nothing, I stop. I hold my breath as she tries to tap in. Nope. Her gloves still don't work.

My heart's been pounding in my chest ever since I heard Seelok speak of the Youli. How much time has passed since then? Thirty minutes? An hour? More?

Now my heart pounds for a different reason. Something about this place is all wrong, and it's not just that Mira's gloves don't work.

Something catches my shoe, and I trip.

I crouch down. A pile of bones lies at my feet.

Mira kneels beside me. She grips my arm. Fear radiates from her mind.

We have to get out of here. I stand and cup my hands around my mouth. "Hello?"

Nothing. Not a sound. Not even an echo.

"Hello?" I try again.

I drop my hand to my side and Mira grabs it.

Once more I call out. "Hello? Is anyone out there?"

My heart beats so loud I feel my pulse in my ears.

Then, ever so faint, there's the sound of a human voice.

"Hello?" I call again. "Over here!"

The sound grows louder. Someone is shouting back. Mira squeezes my hand. Then the sound of footsteps rings in our direction. A second later a man runs out of the semidarkness.

"Oh, thank the heavens above," he says as he charges toward us. "You've finally come. I told them it was just a matter of time. Wait a second . . . how old are you?"

Four others approach. There's a total of three men and two women. All of them are wearing old-fashioned Earth Force uniforms.

"Kids?" one of the women says. "We've been stranded all this time, and they send kids for us? What's going on?"

I take a step back. "Who are you?"

And when they tell us their names, my blood chills. They're names I know. They're names I've read in textbooks and heard in web stories since I was a little kid.

The aeronauts from the Incident at Bounding Base 51. The aeronauts who were lost almost fourteen years ago.

Mira's anxiety comes raging back. Her grip on my hand is making my fingers numb.

"You've been here all this time?" I ask.

"Yes," one of them says. "It feels like an eternity."

Another shakes her head. "Don't mind him. He's just used to the red-carpet treatment. The worst part of this was not being able to take a shower for two days."

What? None of this makes any sense. They've been missing for more than a decade. Unless . . . Gedney once said something about space and time being interrelated.

"This may sound like a strange question," I say, "but . . . how long have you been here?"

They look at one another. The one who made the shower comment shrugs. "We've had no way of tracking time, but I estimate it's been just over forty-eight hours."

The rift, Mira thinks.

She's right. We've landed in the rift with no way out.

I squeeze Mira's hand. At least we're together.

"Is that right?" the woman asks. "It's been about two days since the failed bound?"

I glance at Mira, then I take a deep breath. "Umm . . . no. It's been about fourteen years."

Two of the men start laughing, but the sound of their laughs is quickly swallowed by the dark void of the rift. The seconds stretch out, and as they do, it's clear that the lost aeronauts are beginning to realize that somehow what I said is true.

"You're certain?" one of the men who laughed asks.

I nod.

"My parents . . . ?" the woman in the back gasps.

The man next to her sinks to his knees. "My children!"

"How do we get out of here?" the man who found us asks.

Mira's fear bristles in my brain.

"I'm not sure," I say. "We need to figure that out."

We need to figure it out fast. Because as every minute ticks by in here, we lose days in our world.

Acknowledgments

In many ways, writing is a team sport. My name is on the cover, but many others deserve credit for *The Forgotten Shrine* making it to the bookshelf.

My incredible editor, Sarah McCabe, boarded the bounding ship and piloted us forward. The series has greatly benefited from her editorial eye, and I'm so grateful to have the chance to work with her. The Bounders have a fabulous home at Simon & Schuster/Aladdin. I'm thankful that my books are in the hands of such a stellar group of publishing professionals.

Two early champions of the Bounders series will always have my deepest gratitude: my agent, David Dunton; and my first editor, Michael Strother.

I'm fortunate to have a wonderfully supportive network of author friends. My dream is to rent a huge house on a lake where all of us can hang out in person for a whole week. Let's make that happen, okay?

This year I've had the pleasure and privilege of interacting with many young book lovers and Bounders fans. They've shared fan art, story ideas, and lots of enthusiasm about the series. These are my favorite author moments! Thank you!

I'm lucky and grateful for the supportive community in which I live and write—from my children's schools to my local booksellers, to my extended family and wide network of friends. I have tremendous support, and for that, I'm truly blessed.

The heart of that community is in my own home with Jamey, Nathan, and Gabriel. You are the real deal. All of you.

Jamey, thanks for letting the boys go first. This one is for you.